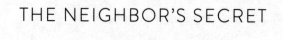

THE NEIGHBOR'S SECRET

Also by L. Alison Heller

The Love Wars
The Never Never Sisters

The

NEIGHBOR'S
SECRET

L. Alison Heller

FLATIRON
BOOKS
NEW YORK

THE NEIGHBOR'S SECRET. Copyright © 2021 by L. Alison Heller. All rights reserved. Printed in the United States of America. For information, address Flatiron Books, 120 Broadway, New York, NY 10271.

www.flatironbooks.com

Designed by Donna Sinisgalli Noetzel

Library of Congress Cataloging-in-Publication Data

Names: Heller, L. Alison, author.
Title: The neighbor's secret / L. Alison Heller.
Description: First Edition. | New York : Flatiron Books, 2021.
Identifiers: LCCN 2021025632 | ISBN 9781250205810 (hardcover) | ISBN 9781250205827 (ebook)
Subjects: GSAFD: Mystery fiction.
Classification: LCC PS3608.E453 N45 2021 | DDC 813/.6—dc23
LC record available at https://lccn.loc.gov/2021025632

Our books may be purchased in bulk for promotional, educational, or business use. Please contact your local bookseller or the Macmillan Corporate and Premium Sales Department at 1-800-221-7945, extension 5442, or by email at MacmillanSpecialMarkets@macmillan.com.

First Edition: 2021

10 9 8 7 6 5 4 3 2 1

This one is for all the caregivers

and also for Z, for whom I'd do (almost) anything

Curses, like chickens, come home to roost.

—SUSANNA MOODIE

THE NEIGHBOR'S SECRET

I saw the two of them leave the party.

They were five minutes apart, but they each slipped through the back gate and into the woods the same way—quick as foxes, like they didn't want to be seen.

I could think of no appropriate reason for them to sneak off together, but I told myself it was none of my business.

Since they found the body, I've been replaying what I saw. What happened between them, out where no one could hear?

I think it was murder.

ONE YEAR EARLIER

To: "The Best Book Club in the World"
From: proudmamabooklover3@hmail.com

Hello Cottonwood Book Club!

If you haven't picked up your copy of LOLITA it's time to get crack-
ing. . . . Our first meeting of the year is September 4th at Harriet
Nessel's house, 7:30 sharp! Are you as excited as I am???
    We're baaaaaack!

Xoxo,
Janine

P.S. Themed snacks only, please!

CHAPTER ONE

t all started that brilliantly sunny Thursday morning, with Janine and her gossip.

As the familiar green minivan cruised around the bend in the road, Annie considered flattening herself against the Jensens' hedges. She truly appreciated Janine and everything that she did for the neighborhood, but sometimes, especially first thing in the morning, the woman could be a lot.

Like how now, Janine had pulled over to the side of the road with a screech, zipped down her window, leaned out her head, and excitedly flapped her hands in front of her face, like she'd taken a bite of a scalding-hot breakfast sandwich.

Gossip, Annie suspected, as she tugged the dog's leash to coax her over to Janine's car. Or worse, bragging.

Janine's daughter Katie was always *achieving* things, which was wonderful. In theory, Annie rooted for Katie—for all children—to succeed, but something about Janine's presentation always caused a flash of panic within Annie: *Should Hank and Laurel be composing oboe concertos? Why haven't they written cookbooks for charity?*

Annie would have to remind herself that Laurel's grades were excellent, that Hank was a joy, that both were curious and kind people, and that people who bragged about their children were usually overcompensating for something.

"Did you hear about the vandal?" Janine asked. Her face was

pink with excitement and there was a halo of frizz around her blond ringlets.

"The what?"

"Read your texts, Annie. Someone spray-painted the street sign on Canyon Road, right by your house. It now says SLOW CHILDREN PEE."

Annie swallowed her laugh and matched Janine's frown. Janine leaned further out of her car window.

"The Gleasons claim he also yanked the windshield wipers off their son's van, although honestly that thing is in such bad shape, I'm not entirely convinced it even *had* wipers before. Anyway. You fixed your conflict for tonight?"

There had been minor drama when Sandstone K-8 had scheduled its annual blood drive on the same night as the September book club meeting. Because the eighth graders handed out juice to the donors, Laurel's attendance was mandatory.

"Mike's rearranged his schedule to take the kids," Annie said. *Not like anyone will be eating at the restaurant anyway,* he'd said glumly.

Janine gave a satisfied nod. "Until tonight then." She blew an aggressive kiss in Annie's direction. "Mwah!"

As she zoomed off, Janine's voice trailed out the open window, "Remember to park in your garage, Annie!"

Annie and Mike had the only one-car garage in all of Cottonwood Estates: someone was always going to have to park outside.

As she continued uphill, Annie tried to retrieve the vague feeling of contentment she'd been enjoying before Janine appeared. Her daily walks were meditative and, if Annie was honest, less for the dog than for her.

She'd started the habit almost fourteen years before, when Laurel was a newborn. At first, the four-mile loop around her neighborhood had taken Annie hours to complete. Her entire existence had felt wispy and unfamiliar back then, and some days the sound of her sneakers slapping on concrete seemed the sole proof that Annie was real.

(*Sole* proof! Back then she wouldn't have had the brain power to catch the pun.)

What had she been thinking about before Janine's announcement?

Not that.

Janine, Janine, the Cottonwood Queen, May I recommend a little less caffeine? Annie wished she could take credit for the couplet, but Deb Gallegos had come up with it a few years back at a barbecue. Janine had laughed harder than anyone.

The neighborhood would probably be up in arms about the graffiti; it took effort to maintain the safe, deceptively low-key feeling that Cottonwood Estates cultivated, and occasionally, people cracked under the pressure of doing so. Last Memorial Day weekend, all hell had broken loose after the McNeils' friends parked their RV on the street for three days. There had been months of angry memos and name-calling until an emergency meeting amended the neighborhood bylaws to ensure such a blight would never again stain the pristine lawns of Cottonwood Estates, at least for no more than twenty-four consecutive hours.

Annie, who had grown up in a very different kind of neighborhood—on the *wrong* side of Highway Five—recognized that her neighbors could be a little precious.

They were good, generous people, but most of them didn't understand that there were far worse things in life than a little graffiti.

Annie did.

Lena Meeker did, too.

Annie had almost reached Lena Meeker's house at the top of the hill. She still—even now—held her breath when she walked by, like a child going past a graveyard.

The first time Annie had been inside was for a swim-team dinner when she was around fifteen, only a few years older than

Laurel now. The Meekers had hosted even though their daughter, Rachel, was young and relatively new to the team, because that was the kind of thing they did.

A teammate's father had driven a group of them over and after he'd pulled into the driveway, he had squinted and tilted his head against the windshield.

"Is this a resort?" he'd asked.

The house was sprawling elegance, wood and glass, with oversized windows to capture the view. Inside, Annie had leaned her forehead to the glass and looked west. No other houses were visible, just the shimmering wave of aspen leaves on the hills, the snowcapped purple Rockies behind them.

Better than a postcard, Annie had thought.

Now, she walked quickly past the low garden fence separating Lena's yard from the road. The giant cottonwood tree in the back corner of her lot was the development's namesake, and every spring, it snowed down fluffy cotton seeds on the neighborhood below.

A few months after they'd moved in, Mike and Annie had, one mild spring afternoon, unfolded aluminum beach chairs in their small backyard. While Laurel napped inside, they'd brought out mugs of lemonade and rested their feet in the grass. For a brief moment, everything finally felt normal.

But then the wind picked up and cottonwood tufts—so many, too many to count—showered down on them with the intensity of a summer squall. Annie had known exactly where they'd come from, and she'd been unable to stop sobbing.

It had taken time and therapy and antidepressants for Annie to pull herself back from the brink and begin to function. But she had. In the past thirteen years, Annie had gotten her master's, they'd had Hank, she'd gotten a dream job at Sandstone.

Lena Meeker had all but disappeared.

On the night of the swim-team dinner all of those years before, Lena Meeker had seemed to Annie as delicate as a summer breeze.

Annie had asked where the bathroom was and Mrs. Meeker had put a light hand on Annie's shoulder and pointed down the hall. *There you go, dear.* Her touch had been so gentle, the air around her so sweet, that Annie wanted to sink into it all like a feather bed.

Annie remembered staring at the back of Rachel Meeker's small head, the mass of dark curly hair coaxed into an elaborate braid—probably Mrs. Meeker's careful work—and feeling a strong current of jealousy, even though Rachel was just a little kid.

A group of them had gone upstairs, peeked in a room that had to be Rachel's: canopied bed, personalized art, a giant giraffe stuffed animal whose neck stretched almost to the ceiling.

Life's unfairness hit Annie like a slap that night. *She* wanted a mother who'd braid her hair and a beautiful room with a ridiculous stuffed giraffe. Rachel Meeker probably didn't even appreciate any of it.

Annie now winced with shame at the memory.

Lena Meeker had lost so much—

Annie's front teeth scraped her bottom lip. For distraction, she glanced at the copper mailbox and came face-to-face with its large round goofy eyes, oblong nose.

Not eyes—goodness, were those?—testicles.

A giant smiling penis had been graffitied along the entire side of Lena's mailbox. Annie could practically hear a dopey teenager still guffawing somewhere in the valley below.

Annie grew irate thinking of Lena Meeker innocently checking her mail, seeing the damage and feeling that stunned *but-why-me* victim's shame. The woman had been through enough. Someone should warn her.

How many times had Annie pictured knocking on Lena's door? *You won't remember me, but . . .*

(The fantasy was always brief: Annie had never been able to decide what she'd say next.)

For the rest of her life, Annie will remember how she'd dragged the confused dog up those three wide stone steps to stand at Lena

Meeker's front door. She felt the morning sun on her back, a buzz of nervous adrenaline in her stomach. She was vaguely aware of how tightly she gripped the leash with her left hand, how the rough nylon abraded her palm.

Annie balled up her right fist and knocked.

CHAPTER TWO

t wasn't that the knock frightened Lena, although it was startling.

She had been deep into chapter 7 of *Beyond the Fields* (just
wonderful!). Odile, escaped from the concentration camps, was
hiding up in a tree in a Bavarian forest, salivating at the smell of
cheese and bread from the German family's picnic a few feet below her. Trying to stop herself from fainting from hunger, Odile
shifted slightly in the tree and accidentally rustled its branches.
The family's little girl looked up and—

Had Lena perhaps imagined the knock?

Nope, there it was again. Three impatient raps.

Tommy, her UPS man, rang instead of knocked and it was too
early for packages anyway. Rudy the landscaper wasn't due until
eleven, which reminded Lena, she had to collect fresh mint leaves
and get his tea brewing soon.

Another two knocks, insistent, harsh: *I know you're in there!* An
aggressive Gestapo knock.

Lena always wondered while reading Holocaust novels, which
she did with some frequency: When the Nazis were rounding up
people from the ghettos, did anyone just not answer?

Presumably breaking down a door would be nothing for the
SS—they were capable of much worse—but did anyone in the
ghetto successfully grab that small window of time to escape?

Lena would bet they didn't. When faced with true evil, your

mind tricked you into minimizing it. *Work with it,* it commanded, *just go along.*

At least, Lena's mind commanded that; maybe other people had more admirable instincts.

A third series of knocks pounded on Lena's door. In her mind, Rachel shook her head in alarm.

Don't answer it.

The version of Rachel who lived in Lena's mind was constantly judging Lena's bad choices. It hadn't always been that way between them, but unfortunately, before the night everything changed, Rachel had been going through an obnoxious stage. Lena had, back then, openly complained about how Rachel treated her, which she now regretted. Hearing the stories, Lena's best friend Melanie had compared sixteen-year-old Rachel to a demanding hotel guest.

Lena decided to ignore the door, and turn back to Odile.

Had the little girl picnicking with her family heard the crack of the tree branch? Odile looked down and the little girl looked up into the foliage and yes, met Odile's eye.

She had been caught.

Lena gasped—aloud—just as the bell rang twice in quick succession, sharp and accusatory.

This was why everyone answered when the Gestapo knocked: it was futile to do otherwise. The authorities never gave up. Lena had read with rapt attention about one fugitive who responded to the knocks of federal agents by darting into a back room, trying to hide under the bed.

Not an effective strategy, as it turned out.

She placed her finger in the middle of the book to hold her place, and carried it with her down the front hall.

When she opened the door, she tried to place the small woman on the other side of the door, who was immediately familiar. She stared at Lena from under the brim of a dark baseball hat, her lips pursed tightly in a not-quite-smile.

It was the Fierce Walker, the slight woman who thrust herself around the neighborhood loop at a breakneck pace in rain, shine, or snow, pumping her little arms and dragging behind her that muscular ugly taupe dog, who now stood next to her on Lena's front step.

The dog had yellow eyes, which slanted as it regarded Lena with a sharp-toothed pant. Not a Nazi dog, Lena was pretty sure— they only used German shepherds—but hardly cuddly.

The Fierce Walker worked to maintain a brittle smile, because what else would Lena inspire?

Lena and Tim had picked the Cottonwood Estates neighborhood all those years before because of the natural beauty and the community—the bridge clubs, the cocktail hours, the tennis tournaments, the poker nights. Everyone in each other's business was wonderful for social creatures like the Meekers!

But there was a dark side to having everyone in each other's business that Lena hadn't foreseen. For starters, the judgment. Even if Lena never heard it, she could *feel* it drift uphill with the wind: *Poor, lonely Lena, rattling around in that big house.*

The Fierce Walker had obviously heard the whispers of the wind. She chewed on her bottom lip and Lena could see, beneath the woman's dark glasses, the darting movement of her eyes, from Lena to the ground and back to Lena.

To put her at ease, Lena waved her right hand in a friendly way. It was a regretfully awkward movement, given that Lena was still holding the book, the pages of which flapped ridiculously.

But it seemed to work: Fierce Walker inhaled and then sighed like a woman in love.

"That. Book," she said, and clutched her heart.

Lena leaned closer, despite herself. "I just got to the part where Odile is in the tree."

"With the family below her? I was *dying.*"

"Tell me it turns out okay."

"I'm not going to spoil it for you. You'd never forgive me."

The Fierce Walker frowned suddenly, like she'd received a silent reprimand from an unseen handler to remain on task. She pushed back her shoulders and jutted out her jaw.

"I'm Annie Perley and I live down the hill on Pinon Road," she said.

"Lena Meeker," Lena said even though Annie knew this, of course she did. Poor Lena Meeker. A cautionary tale. Tell your children.

Annie removed her sunglasses and folded them onto the collar of her shirt, revealing a cluster of tiny tattoos—an elephant, a star, a butterfly—on her inner wrist. She was younger than Lena had imagined, and freshly pretty, with smooth, pale skin and delicate features.

Lena smiled: she'd always appreciated beauty, and Annie had the comforting attractiveness of a stock photo model. But waves of intensity evaporated off her, and for a dizzying moment, Lena worried that Annie would start the sympathy stutter, *So sorry, thoughts and prayers and I can't even imagine.*

"I've seen you trekking around the neighborhood," Lena said to cut this off at the head. "And marvel at your willpower. I wish I had the drive in regards to exercise, but alas I never have. I have all the momentum to start any kind of fad, but it's the follow-through that stumps me. The consistency. Too many bad habits, too ingrained, I guess. Do you do the entire loop every day?"

Lena was aware she was babbling, but the angsty look in Annie's eyes was gone, so it had been worth it.

Annie nodded. "As pathetic as it sounds, exercise keeps me sane. And it helps Yellow."

When she patted the dog's head, Lena surmised that he/she/it was Yellow, even though it was more of a muddy greige.

"We got her when my son Hank was learning his colors," Annie explained. She shot a wry look at Lena. "Or not."

Lena managed a passable casual laugh. This wasn't going horribly, not at all, or maybe it was?

Annie Perley paused and reddened slightly. Another correction from the off-site handler. There was something unsavory to discuss, Lena sensed. Presumably, the Fierce Walker had not knocked on the door to talk about Lena's book selections and lack of commitment to exercise.

"Can I help you with something, Annie?" Lena said.

"No, no, I'm just here because. Well"—Annie Perley mashed her lips together for a moment, summoning courage to deliver unwelcome news—"there's a penis on your mailbox."

It sounded physically impossible, but Lena found herself following Annie across the driveway. There was something so resolute and *directed* about her.

At the mailbox, Annie raised her eyebrows grimly. *Voilà.*

Thick lines of aerosol black paint covered Lena's custom copper mailbox. "I think it's a face?" Lena said. "With a really long nose?"

Annie shook her head and tapped her fingernail against the copper. There was a decisive ping.

"Only one hole," she said.

"Oh." Lena frowned. As far as uninvited penises went, it had a disarmingly cheerful innocence. "It's kind of friendly-looking."

"It's those big round puppy eyes," Annie said with a sigh, as though the penis was just being manipulative and couldn't be trusted.

Other properties had been hit, too. Lena, Annie explained— again with that intense eye contact—should not take it personally. Lena was about to respond that of course she didn't take it personally, but then she realized that she did. The universe had taken a while to deliver a mailbox penis to Lena, but now that it had, her only question was: Why the delay?

"I can help you try to get it off," Annie offered. She smacked her forehead as the double meaning hit her. "Sorry. I just meant— what I'm trying to say is I can help you *remove* it."

Annie's laugh was a wave of nervous high-pitched giggles and her cheeks reddened to a lovely deep pink. Years ago, Lena, who had been quite social (mind-bogglingly social! flitting around, hosting parties, fiddling, fiddling, fiddling while Rome burned) would have identified this warm magnet pull toward Annie Perley and thought: *new friend.*

She would have invited Annie to her next party, deposited her in a conversation with someone fun and lively, offered a gougère just out of the oven, fragrant and steaming.

Everyone had always gone crazy for Lena's gougères and she had become increasingly nutty about getting them perfect. You're missing the party, Tim would accuse.

And what had Gary Neary joked that night? *The gorgeous gougères.* Lena had giggled like it was high comedy, just like Annie Perley was doing now.

This was the problem with meeting new people: they dredged up old recollections, even when they didn't mean to. Lena had never been able to conclusively destroy the unwelcome memories, but her occasional therapist Dr. Friendly had taught her a visualization process—flatten the memory like a trash compactor would, note its diminishment, move on.

She thought desperately of five minutes in the future when Annie would be gone and Lena could curl up on her couch with Odile.

But Annie, flushed and still hopelessly giggling at the wordplay, didn't appear to be going anywhere. She clutched Lena's arm and wiped her eyes and bent over and her sunglasses clattered down from the front of her shirt to the lawn, which only intensified Annie's laughter.

Lena regarded the penis's goofy face. It *was* funny. And so was Annie, doubled over with laughter, grasping helplessly onto the grass for her sunglasses. If Annie's chortles were fizzy champagne, Lena's were a vintage car engine sputtering a bit before roaring to life.

A voice floated up from somewhere deep within Lena. "Would you like to come in for coffee, Annie?"

Annie wiped her eyes with the back of her wrists. The invitation hovered between them like a balloon that Lena wished she could pop.

She'd been too forward, hadn't she? Lena was so out of practice, but the way Annie gravely studied Lena's house behind them—as if Lena had proposed becoming roommates instead of a warm beverage—wasn't right either.

"I'm due at the school by ten thirty," Annie said. "But for a little while, why not?"

Lena thought that Annie sounded disappointed in her own response, as if she had at her fingertips a million reasons why not, but had for some reason been powerless to use them.

CHAPTER THREE

"This is total crap," Paul said.

Jen's mouth had been open in formation of an apology to Principal Dutton, to Harper, to the entire school community for what Abe had done.

She shut it. Apparently, they were taking a different approach.

Paul sat next to her at the small conference table in Dutton's office. A craggy blue vein pulsed at his temple. Across from them, Dutton blinked his watery gray eyes. White flakes covered the shoulders of his navy sport coat and Jen felt an automatic stab of embarrassment for him.

No! Dutton was the enemy. A curse on him: dandruff in perpetuity.

"Without any real witnesses, how do we even know that Abe stabbed this kid," Paul said. "You just said the teacher—"

"Mr. Marley," Jen said quietly.

"Mr. Marley." Paul spat out the name, which Mr. Marley deserved. Another enemy, he was lazy and tired and, according to Abe, completely oblivious of the cruel middle school shenanigans occurring on the daily under his watch. Art period was like *Lord of the Flies* at peak pig-killing hour. "*Mr. Marley* admitted he didn't see any of it, so we're relying on the word of that girl, who is essentially Harper French's henchman—"

"Veronica," Jen added.

She always got a jealous thrill when Paul went on the attack in these Abe meetings. Jen either dissolved in tears, which was of no help to Abe, or slipped into Girl Friday mode, like now, helpfully supplying the details.

At two in the morning, however, Jen would jolt awake with righteous anger and imagine doing a series of roundhouse kicks straight to Dutton's solar plexus until he begged for mercy.

(No wonder Abe had stabbed someone. So much repressed anger in his DNA.)

"Veronica and Harper have been taunting Abe for *months*," Paul said, "so don't give me this bullshit about your zero-tolerance policy."

Jen folded her arms over her chest. *Yeah: what he said.*

There was a reason Paul had climbed so high up the corporate ladder: the man knew how to brawl, facts be damned.

Dutton was no match. He was pasty and crumbly, and his gaze skipped and dipped across the room.

"You seem to be stuck on the issue of *if* the stabbing happened," Dutton said.

Jen had misjudged. His voice was not crumbly at all. It was firm and calm.

"Abe admitted it. His report was nearly identical to Harper's: they were both at the art-supply table and Harper took the beads that Abe was reaching for—well, Abe says he already had them in hand, but even taking him at his word, I think we can all agree that stabbing a classmate with an X-Acto knife is hardly an acceptable reaction."

He looked between Jen and Paul with gentle disappointment. "And I'm sure you're not suggesting that Foothill's zero-tolerance policy—which your entire family signed—is inapplicable to a stabbing?"

Paul's left shoulder jerked in a half shrug.

Last fall, when the three of them had sat around this same table and talked, harmoniously, about the importance of safe spaces, Jen and Paul had been thrilled to hear about the zero-tolerance policy.

(Why had she been thrilled? Although many emotions had coursed through Jen this morning, shock was not one.)

Right now, she felt above emotion, weightless and drifty and almost bored by Dutton's enumeration of Abe's struggles during his short tenure at Foothills: running out of class, his lack of social engagement, ditto academic engagement, such a shame for a boy who tested so high, not to mention the destruction of the trash can in the boys' bathroom last spring.

Any of those, and certainly the trash can incident, Dutton pointed out, would have been enough to trigger the zero-tolerance policy.

Jen's floating feeling intensified into a case of the spins. She gripped Paul's knee and he placed his hand over hers, which helped to ground her for a moment.

If she shut off a part of her brain and listened to Dutton, it did seem logical that stabbing a child with an X-Acto knife would be grounds for expulsion, didn't it?

Yes!

No!

Jen had lost the ability to judge.

What was this dizziness? Was Jen having a stroke? And if she were, would the school rescind Abe's expulsion? Jen pictured Dutton standing over her, grave-faced and apologizing.

A stroke might be worth it if it shut up Dutton, who was still going: Abe's lack of affect, the volatile moods. The quicksilver friendships (such *poetry,* Dutton!). We don't know, Dutton was saying, what will set Abe off and his reactions to things are so—he paused to access the right word.

Violent, Jen thought, but Dutton settled on *out-of-proportion.*

Abe was growing into the type of person Dr. Scofield had warned her about.

(Dr. Scofield? Where had that come from?)

Jen and Paul had spent an hour tops with the man, nearly a decade before. They'd cycled through so many experts that year:

neuropsychologists and developmental pediatricians and therapists. Every single one had slapped on a different diagnosis.

Scofield had been the worst. He had been a child himself, barely out of grad school, with slicked-back hair and sockless loafers and no bedside manner. Jen had spent half of the meeting mesmerized by the thick caterpillar hairs around his ankles. Something (masochism?) had made Jen keep his business card, though, place it in the top drawer of her bureau, slipped within the socks.

She'd purged so many papers before they'd moved from California last year but not Scofield's card, *so don't go playing all coy, Jen, about why the name "Scofield" might pop into your head after Abe has stabbed a classmate.*

Not just any classmate, perfect little Harper French, who had once left a Popsicle on Jen's white chenille couch. It had melted, orange and sticky, into the middle of a cushion, and Jen had pretended she didn't care. "It's just a *thing,* sweetie," she'd said with a laugh. "An object. My fault for buying white."

There was a knock on the door. Mr. Marley appeared, as low-energy as ever, in one of his ubiquitous homemade tie-dyed shirts.

"Abe has cleaned out his locker," he said. "Not much in there."

Abe stood hunch-shouldered right outside the doorway, clutching the almost-empty cardboard box. He looked pale and uncertain and ah, yes, here came the prick of tears.

So much for seventh grade. If Jen ever got a do-over in life, she might pick that moment with the Popsicle and the couch, and scream obscenities at Harper French until her voice was raw.

She was aware people would disapprove of this: you weren't supposed to hold a grudge against a child. But it was basic animal instinct: when a Canada goose sensed a threat to her gosling, she attacked.

Jen stood up, did not apologize for the indelicate screech of her chair scraping the linoleum. She walked over to Abe and put her arm protectively around his shoulder, which felt bony and delicate.

"We're leaving," she said.

No one dared say one word as she, Abe, and Paul brushed past Dutton and Mr. Marley. They strode out of the office and down the hall, heads held high. For a moment, as they walked out of the front doors into the cloudless sunny day, Jen tasted triumph.

Jen and Paul had arrived separately and even their brief logistical conversation in the parking lot—*I'll take Abe, meet you at home*—didn't puncture the mood.

She and Abe walked to the car in silence, arms linked. She peeled out of the visitors' spot like a renegade. *Hasta la vista, suckers!* To make Abe smile, she punched the gas and careened too quickly down the road from the school.

It was when Jen braked for the stop sign that the reality of Abe's expulsion hit.

What on earth now?

Homeschooling, she supposed.

Given Paul's travel schedule, the logistics would fall on Jen. When they'd moved from California, she had not minded giving up her teaching job. Jen had dropped so many balls in the process of juggling Abe's needs with her schedule, and she'd always felt like she was neglecting someone or something.

But that didn't mean she was ending her career. A few months ago, Jen had received a small grant from the Mellon Kramer Fund to research a book on ethology, the study of animal behavior under natural conditions.

With a little focus and attention, the project could be incredibly fulfilling, and Jen had been relying on the uninterrupted hours when Abe was at school.

And now?

"Well," Abe said. "That was an eventful morning."

With the morning light streaming behind him through the car window, he looked like an angel.

Jen and Paul were each rather ordinary-looking, but somehow Jen's round features and Paul's sharp angles had come together to create in Abe one physically stunning person. Even when he was an infant, Jen had marveled at those rosebud lips, that symmetrical bone structure, those sharp-edged cheekbones—who knew a baby could even *have* cheekbones—her son was a *beauty*! The world's secret doors would open, people would warm to him, want to give him the benefit of the doubt.

Almost immediately after came the worries: But life comes so easily for the beautiful; what if he never develops inner strength or grit? And will beauty make him more vulnerable to pedophiles?

New parents were the most clueless people in the whole wide world.

Abe's stunning looks had turned out to be the least remarkable thing about him. And if Jen had believed beauty mattered before, now she knew better. It was the unseen stuff: character, adaptability, resolve, the ability to connect with others. You were born with those buffers. Or you weren't and even the most patient and committed parent (Jen was not) couldn't teach them.

Jen knew exactly why she'd kept Scofield's card. He had colonized her brain with five little words, planted a Big Red Flag right there in her amygdala.

Abe had turned toward the window and Jen watched his profile, the line of his chiseled jaw under his warm amber skin. He'd refused a summer haircut and his long swoopy bangs made him look like a pop star.

Jen wished there was a way to know for certain what he was thinking.

"Even if Harper was being awful," she said, "hurting her—violence—is never the answer."

Abe nodded.

"It could have been really, really bad, Abe."

Abe's dark eyes showed consternation and he raked his fingers through those boy-band bangs.

What had concerned Scofield, the "Big Red Flag," hadn't been the hamster's injuries. Kids were clumsy and impulsive, he said, they made mistakes. It was that after he'd hurt the rodent, Abe had showed *a startling lack of remorse.*

And that had been only a rodent.

"You could have permanently damaged Harper's arm," Jen said. Her voice was wobbly as she realized the truth of this. "Severed a nerve or an artery."

Abe's leg jiggled up and down until Jen placed a flattened palm on his knee. He turned back to face her.

"Harper French," he said finally, his voice certain, "pretty much got what she deserved."

And then Abe gave Jen the tiniest of tiny smiles, so minuscule that she could almost pretend to have missed it.

CHAPTER FOUR

"The internet tells us"—Annie glanced at her phone screen—
"that it's nearly impossible to remove paint from copper."

"How helpful," Lena said from the kitchen.

Based on all of the clattering and opened cabinets, Annie suspected something complicated was in the works.

She was perched tentatively on Lena's giant, cream-colored L-shaped sofa. The house still screamed wealth: Annie's palms rested on soft suede cushions. Dramatic veins zigged and zagged through the marble kitchen. The art on the walls was colorful and bold and unexpected, like it belonged in a museum.

Behind Annie was a floor-to-ceiling bookcase, done in a gorgeous light-grained wood. On almost every shelf, planted among the book spines was at least one framed photograph of Rachel Meeker. Annie desperately wanted to turn around and gawk at them. Instead, she forced herself off the couch and walked over to the windows to check on Yellow, who'd been quarantined on Lena's lawn.

Yellow sniffed Lena's rosebushes in a familiar way that made Annie silently plead with the dog to not soil them, or the grass, which was lush and entirely free from brown patches. Even now, in late summer, Lena probably had the funds to water the entire thing all night, every night.

She looked out to the north, where Highway Five snaked through the valley like a concrete river. Annie remembered how years before, at the swim-team party, some of the kids had attempted to identify the roofs of their houses in the valley below.

"Paint thinner might work," Lena said as she popped up from behind one of the kitchen islands. "I don't think I have any, though."

"I'll check our garage," Annie said. "Are you sure I can't help you out back there?"

"Almost done." Lena was using kitchen shears to snip mint leaves off their stems. She smiled politely. "You said you're due at the school?"

"Sandstone K-8. I work three and a half days a week as a counselor, you know, socio-emotional stuff or disciplinary problems. If there's a trauma in the family—"

It was horrible timing, but Annie couldn't stop herself from just then glancing at a photo of Rachel. The girl's large serious dark eyes were like a beacon, poor thing, and oh my goodness, had Lena caught Annie staring?

"What a great book selection," Annie said quickly.

"I used to have a separate library upstairs," Lena said, "but I was always grabbing books to read in here and stacking them all around and I finally realized, why not just make a library wall?"

Annie suppressed a smile. Why not indeed?

Ah, to be budget-free. *You know how the four of us are always jockeying for a turn in the shower,* she could blithely ask Mike, *why not just add another bathroom?*

Based on the familiar titles on the shelves, Lena's tastes, like Annie's, leaned toward historical fiction. Annie didn't know the particulars of Lena's days—she was toned and her skin glowed—so obviously she hadn't gone full-on Miss Havisham, but according to Harriet Nessel, who had lived in Cottonwood Estates forever, Lena had been very in-the-mix before the accident.

That part, at least, wasn't Annie's fault. People were going to react to tragedy however they reacted.

Annie snuck another peek at Rachel Meeker, who looked right

through her. If Annie moved across the room, those round accusing eyes would probably follow wherever she went.

"I think you're my reading soul mate," Annie said.

"I don't know what I'd do without books," Lena said. Her voice, quiet and a little sad, made something pulse quickly in Annie's heart.

"Readers are the best people," Annie said. "Think about it: our hobby is putting ourselves in someone else's shoes."

"I suppose."

"My friend Deb always says that book clubs are the gold standard of humanity—whoa." Annie clapped her hands together as Lena set down the tray on the coffee table. "How lovely is this?"

Lena had served a platter of tiny round tea cakes, decorated with the sprigs of mint. Two porcelain cups on saucers sat next to a creamer and a precious little sugar bowl with miniature silver tongs for the lumps.

All this fuss for a neighbor announcing your mailbox had been graffitied? And who had tea cakes just sitting around like this? Rachel's devastated eyes agreed with Annie that yes, it was exactly as sad and lonely as it seemed.

Go on, Rachel said, *you owe us.*

"Lena," Annie said brightly as Lena sat down and elegantly crossed one leg over the other. "Speaking of how wonderful readers are, do you know about Cottonwood's book club?"

Lena uncrossed her legs, leaned slightly backward. "I've seen the emails."

"There's a meeting tonight. You should come—"

"No," Lena said simply. "I don't think book club is for me."

Lena caught Annie's glance at Rachel's photo. Her brow knit together for a split second.

"You want to know something funny?" Annie said quickly. "I was on Rachel's swim team and came to a team dinner here. You're how I learned about this neighborhood."

"What a coincidence." Lena managed a tight Mona Lisa smile

that caused Annie's insides to feel as pressurized as a shaken soda can. "Isn't life funny?"

Annie took a small bite of a tea cake. It had an almond flavor, which had never been her favorite, but she forced herself to chew and swallow. The pieces tumbled down her throat like a rockslide.

"Yes," she said. "It is."

From the craft room window, Lena watched Annie walk-run down the hill with the homely dog, a jaunty bounce in their steps.

I was on Rachel's swim team.

She'd said it so casually.

A tiny little tremor of a phrase that caused a tsunami of memories: the *should I quit swim team* phases when Lena had pushed Rachel through, the obsessed years when Rachel had been so consumed that Lena wondered if quitting might have been healthier, how Lena's fingers had been constantly on fire with the prickly mint of muscle balm for Rachel's left persnickety shoulder or the sting of oranges sliced for meets, how Rachel's suits would commandeer the mudroom sink, drifting and submerged like octopi.

The night Tim died, summer practices had just started up again.

Rachel came home late for the Meekers' party, dripped water on the kitchen floor, idly reached out a damp hand to snatch a cube of cheese from the board, as if she had all the time in the world.

"Are you working the party," Lena had snapped, "or watering it?"

Back then, Lena had been worried that Rachel was turning out spoiled, with an underdeveloped sense of personal responsibility. They had been fighting for weeks about whether Rachel, who had just turned sixteen, deserved a brand-new car. The decision felt life-or-death, like Lena was waging a battle for Rachel's very soul.

What was that elementary school corrective for when the children got bossy?

Worry about your own soul, Lena.

Lena would now give anything in the world to erase that

imperious comment—*are you working the party or watering it*—
and replace it with anything Rachel's heart desired.

Rachel had returned the cheese cube to the tray, gone upstairs,
emerged not long after in that white flowered dress that she would
never wear again, her hair slicked into a messy wet braid.

Maybe Lena's barb had rolled off Rachel's back. Or maybe
she had decided to save it up as ammunition for some future argument about the car that never got to happen. She had silently
finished setting up the food table without complaint, and then—

Lena forced herself to flatten the memory like it was an empty
cardboard box.

She certainly didn't want to think about what happened after
that.

CHAPTER FIVE

t was Abe who remembered.

"Don't you have book club tonight?" he asked Jen in a half shout. His headphones were on.

"I'll skip."

"What?"

Jen tapped her ear and he pushed off the right earpiece.

"I'll stay home with you guys," she said.

In the hours since the expulsion, the three of them had been cocooned in the den. Paul worked, Jen pretended to, and Abe had played a loud and violent game of Foxhole, his favorite multi-player video game.

All games of Foxhole were loud and violent, but they were also, Jen and Paul told themselves, extremely interactive and thus not a total wash. Going forward, could Foxhole count as PE?

"I'm fine," Abe said. "Holla123 says being homeschooled is actually kind of fun."

"Go to book club," Paul said to Jen.

"Yeah, go," Abe said, "it's your one thing, Mom."

Jen trotted out her book club membership when she wanted to appear normal. Jen's mother fretting aloud (again) about how Jen didn't have a support system since the move? *I've met some lovely women at book club, Mom!*

Paul breezing in from a business trip with stories of the outside world and pausing to ask gently if Jen talked to anyone, anyone at all while he was gone, about something other than Abe?

Book club! Everything's fine, nothing to see here.

The actual club discussions were fine if a little stale, ditto the reading selections, which were, truth be told, a little on the commercial side for Jen's tastes, but it was worth her while to attend. Someone in the group had found out that Jen had a Ph.D. and the way they all now looked to Jen for opinions and subtexts?

She pretended not to need the attention, but she soaked it up, a desperate parading peacock.

At one of last year's meetings, she'd gotten loose-tongued tipsy, and tried to come clean to Harriet Nessel. My degree is in organizational psychology, Jen had lectured, not literature.

"I know," Harriet said. "You study animals now."

"I study the people who study the animals," Jen had admitted. "It couldn't be farther from popular fiction."

"I guess that depends on your thoughts about the animal/human divide," Harriet said drolly. "Has so-called civilization removed us as much as we like to think? Food for thought, dear, food for thought."

Point: Harriet.

(Harriet had probably been tipsy, too. The drinks at book club were always shockingly strong.)

Jen realized that she probably missed teaching more than she had admitted to herself, and even if it wasn't the cure-all she pretended it was, for the time being, the Cottonwood Book Club was the closest she was going to get to an exchange of ideas.

Abe and Paul were right. She should go. Jen rushed upstairs to grab a sweater and put on earrings, because the other women always looked so put-together and even though Jen pretended she didn't care, obviously she did on some deep level—and then, as she stood in front of her bureau, Jen's hand extended like some horror movie claw to reach into the sock drawer, palm Dr. Scofield's business card, and slip it into the back pocket of her jeans.

By the time Jen got to Harriet Nessel's house, a long line of cars extended far down the street. She pulled behind a dark SUV. Its door opened and Priya Jensen, one of the club's core members, stepped out, tall and gorgeous as ever. She tossed her silky black hair over her shoulder, waved at Jen, and went inside.

If Priya or any of the others knew that book club was Jen's "one thing," they would probably stage an intervention, albeit one with themed finger sandwiches and a gift bag stuffed with lavender-scented hand lotions and candles.

Priya and the rest of the book club group regulars—manic Janine Neff and Deb Gallegos, who did the elaborate drinks, and Annie Perley, who reminded Jen of a plucky kid sister from a situation comedy—were constantly planning Fun Events: cocktails and tailgates and ski weekends. All of their kids seemed to be friends and most attended Sandstone K-8, the local public school.

Before their move, Jen had flown out to visit schools on Abe's behalf. At Sandstone, she had been struck first by the blindingly aggressive level of activity: everyone—teachers and students—seemed to be kicking balls, or singing and dancing, or hurrying through the halls while talking and laughing. They were shiny-haired, white-toothed, zipped up in brightly colored fleece jackets.

Jen had walked out before the tour began.

Foothills Charter School was out-of-district, which had been inconvenient at the time, but was now a blessing. The women of book club wouldn't have heard any gossip about Abe's expulsion.

After Jen's first book club meeting, Janine made it a point to invite Jen to a barbecue, so Abe could meet the other kiddos his age. While Jen had felt a bizarre pride that she'd faked normalcy convincingly enough to be asked, she had ultimately declined. Abe had no place at a barbecue in this neighborhood.

Jen wasn't embarrassed by Abe, but she knew that he invited judgment. The slouch, the slightly forced smile, the intense and stony stare. He was *that kid*.

But Abe was so much more than that kid!

When people put him in a box or alienated him or she saw that inevitable flicker of derision across their faces, Jen burned like a devil doused with holy water.

Jen wasn't one of *those* moms, the kind who insisted her child was perfect, but there was so much hypocrisy. Everyone preached tolerance to difference, but nobody practiced it.

She was stalling.

Jen took Scofield's card from her jeans pocket and held it between her thumb and forefinger. He'd bet big on himself and sprung for the expensive card stock: the thing didn't even buckle.

This shouldn't surprise. Scofield was all about image, with that slicked-back gelled hair and that pungent cologne, probably to mask the odor from those bare feet shoved into loafers. He was immature and brusque and mansplainy and hadn't let Jen get a word in.

Jen knew now that it was flat-out *wrong* to label a child as young as Abe. They could probably find several respected doctors who would agree it had been malpractice.

Someone must have sued Scofield by now, or maybe his license had been revoked. But even if he was still practicing, Scofield certainly wouldn't remember Abe.

And here was Jen, carrying his card from state to state, like some sort of groupie. She considered calling him every time she read the newspapers after a horrific mass assault. The assailants were very frequently a young man, teens or early twenties, isolated and in pain. Inevitably, there had been signs from childhood that he hadn't fit in, and Jen could not stop herself from reading those signs as a road map, a point of comparison to Abe.

Jen reminded herself that she, not Scofield, was the world's foremost expert on Abe.

She would agree with anyone that Abe's disposition wasn't particularly sunny, but Abe wasn't cruel. And as far as the hamster story went, Jen reassured herself that Abe had always been fine with their cat—if not affectionate, then at least neutral.

He wasn't like those young men in the news, Abe just needed to learn how to cope a little better, but—

What if he never did?

What did people say about the young man who had taken hostages in the supermarket and the other who had brought assault weapons to the fraternities he had been rejected from?

They had been loners, too.

Forgotten shadows in the back of the class, most likely. At root, desperate to connect.

When Jen read about these lost souls, she felt for them as much as the victims (which was warped: empathy shouldn't extend where they'd gone). Mostly, though, she felt for their poor parents. What warning signs, what chances to intervene had they missed?

Two other women walked past Jen's car, *Lolita* copies in hand, but she couldn't let herself go inside until she called Scofield.

Call him. Nothing else has worked.

It rang. Once and then again. When the message switched to voicemail, there was his voice—still so young!—and a beep.

"Dr. Scofield, hello. My name is Jen Chun-Pagano and you saw my son about seven years ago. Long enough ago that you probably don't remember us."

Jen gave her number, cut herself off, hung up.

Just a rule-out, she told herself. Just to confirm that Scofield was as unhelpful as she and Paul remembered him to be.

The women were already circled around Harriet Nessel's living room when Jen creaked open the screen door. Thirty heads turned to stare.

"Jen, sweetie," Janine said, "grab yourself a glass of Lolita Lemondrop from the kitchen and come on back."

"Yes, please," Jen said, a little too desperately, and the women laughed. The desperate need for alcohol was a running joke with this group.

When she returned to the living room, giant mason jar in hand,

Jen settled into an empty spot on the piano bench next to An-nie Perley, who pointed at the Lolita Lemondrop and mouthed, *Lethal*.

Jen smiled, nodded, took a gingery sip. It was delicious, actu-ally, with a warm heat that lingered in the back of her throat.

Janine was explaining excitedly that they would start with in-troductions! Everyone had to say their favorite book or genre and then something fun and unexpected about herself!

"For instance," she said. "I'm *Janine*!" She stabbed her index finger into her chest with surprising torque. "And my favorite book is *The Giving Tree*! My something unexpected is that I have a tattoo"—she winked exaggeratedly—"but I'm *not* telling you ladies where."

Through the years, Jen had developed a little game where she imagined how other people might handle raising Abe. The women of book club—there had been a man in the group last year, but he was notably absent tonight, scared off, perhaps, by last spring's startlingly passionate discussion of that menopause book—had such canned and untested beliefs about "parenting," namely that any and all behavioral issues should yield to Respectful Discussion and/or Diminished Screen Time and/or Organic Diets.

Janine was a bragger, especially about her daughter Katie. Would she be putting a spin on whatever material Abe gave her?

He's not quite Lizzie Borden yet, but the ER doctor said his blade skills were very advanced. And you should see his work with blast-ing agents!

Abe offered plenty of legitimate opportunities for bragging, Jen reminded herself. He was smart, he was creative, he had goals—currently to program an entire video game from scratch. He could be thoughtful, too. He'd reminded her about tonight's meeting.

And he had never tortured their cat. At least so far as she knew.

"Someone's communing with her Lolita Lemondrop," Janine sang out, and Jen realized that all of those politely inquiring faces had turned toward her.

"Jen," Janine said, "surprise us! Tell us your secret!"

None of them, Jen was certain, could even begin to handle her secret.

"I'm Jen Chun-Pagano," she managed to say. "And I love Regency fiction. Bodice rippers. The steamier the better. I'm hoping that's embarrassing enough to also qualify as my something unexpected."

Jen's chest melted into liquid warmth at the group's kind laughter.

"Last but not least," Janine trilled, "our hostess with the mostest. What's your favorite book, Harriet?"

Harriet, another book club mainstay, had lived in Cottonwood Estates longer than anyone else in the club. She had a severe gray crop, a perpetual frown, and the belief that every book had one correct interpretation, which it was her job to understand. Ostensibly to further this goal, she brought a yellow legal pad to every book club meeting and spent the entire discussion filling the thing with furiously handwritten notes, as though she were anticipating a test.

"One favorite book?" Harriet said with skepticism. "That's impossible to answer."

"Genre then? You love your mysteries."

"I suppose any amateur sleuth story," Harriet said. "Or the classics. Can that be our segue, Ms. President, to get on with this month's selection?"

Jen largely ignored the *Lolita* discussion. She had studied the book in high school and college and was already familiar with the role of games, the metacommentary about how Nabokov played with the reader.

As per usual with *Lolita,* there were two camps: those who couldn't get past the molestation and murder and those who thought the ugliness was exactly the point—that the book was a master class in unreliable narration and satire.

Jen had probably argued both sides in her life, but who cared?

It had been a mistake to call Scofield. Jen already regretted it. She wasn't even sure that Abe had smiled in the car; he had been subdued all afternoon. And he seemed so relieved to not have to go back to Foothills.

School must have been even worse for him than Jen had realized.

Jen didn't know what exactly had happened to make Harper turn on Abe, but the aftermath had been awful—whispers on line for PE, shoves in the cafeteria, "not it"'s during group projects for school, all perfectly timed for when the teachers' backs were turned.

Find a new friend, Jen had urged, but Abe explained with resignation that everyone had already heard he was a freak. If only he smiled more, Abe had said, but he was always nervous there and could never remember to do so.

Jen had tried to tell the school, but they were over Abe at that point. When Abe found a note in his drawing kit that said "Satan's Minion," Jen brought it up to the art teacher. *Are you sure he didn't draw it himself,* Mr. Marley had said in his infuriating stoner's drawl, *Abe can get pretty dark.*

What her son needed, more than anything else, was protection. Foothills had not provided it.

Jen's career ambitions were not the cause of Abe's issues— linking the two was misogynist draconian nonsense—but part of Jen had always wondered deep down, oh so very deep down because she knew it was crazy, plenty of parents worked, but—

If Janine *were* Abe's parent, she might brag about him, but she also would have been a solid, irrefutable daily presence, there in his corner from preschool on. Janine would have volunteered to be room parent and signed Abe up for Scouts, organized a troop if there weren't one in existence. She would have served punch at the class parties and dances (assuming that was an actual job and not just something Jen had seen on TV). She would have thrown him into social situations, and maybe he'd have developed better skills.

Paul said that Jen couldn't help but compare herself to other parents because she was a fundamentally competitive person. All parents compared themselves to other parents, though. People operated in relation to each other, just like wolves did, or prairie dogs or meerkats.

Or birds.

Lately, Jen's research had been heavy on the birds—there was a lot of recent work in the avian-navigation field—and reading about a flock's inexplicable telepathy, how it majestically ascended to the skies in one coordinated rush, Jen could not help but picture her neighbors, similarly in thrall to the mandates of a group soul.

At book club, differences were not celebrated, they were barely acknowledged. Last year, Jen had initially been pleasantly surprised to note that she was not the only book club member with a multicultural background. There was Priya and also Athena, who was half Liberian, half French.

Not that race or heritage was ever truly discussed. Everyone worked to gently herd the conversation toward safe common ground: opinions about the book, families, work stress. Teasing was always delivered with a smile, to emphasize that it was all in harmless fun.

Even amid tonight's rowdy *Lolita* debate, you could see the women striving to agree, their nods of reassurance toward whoever was speaking little pigeon neck-bobs of support.

The real currency at the Cottonwood Book Club wasn't literature, it was *sameness*. And Jen craved this feeling of belonging even as she hated what it confirmed: there was safety in numbers.

And danger in being an outlier.

The book club was really getting into *Lolita*. Annie kept clapping her hands together like a teacher trying to get control of a recalcitrant class and inadvertently elbowing Jen in the ribs.

"People," she shouted. "He's a pedophile. Sorry, Jen."

"You don't have to be friends with the characters, Annie," Deb said.

"Well, what a relief *that* is."

"*Lolita* is a classic novel," Harriet Nessel repeated stubbornly.

"*Good grief.* Who in the heck cares that it's a classic? Or that he's funny? We've spent hundreds of pages listening to the point of view of a murdering pedophile. Whoops, sorry, bumped you again, Jen, but if you all just *think* about that girl trying to put back her life together after this monster broke it into pieces, and then tell me: Do we need his perspective on anything?"

After a swell of dissent, the conversation grew even livelier.

Jen sipped her Lolita Lemondrop and rubbed her ribs where Annie kept jabbing her. She let the discussion wash over her until it died down and the women broke into small groups. Next to Jen, Annie Perley heatedly told Janine that if she liked Humbert Humbert so much, why didn't she hire him as a babysitter.

"Oh honestly," Janine said. "I'm changing the subject to our savior."

Religion was usually Jen's cue to politely excuse herself, but Janine was watching her with an unnerving soupy smile.

"Me?" Jen said.

"Yes! For volunteering to host November's meeting in my place."

Crap. Crap. Crappity Crap.

Jen *had* volunteered. She recalled the email plea—S.O.S. LADIES! We are DESPERATE for a host—from a million years before in the summer, when Jen had been full of optimism about her research grant and seventh grade.

"Oh, right," Annie said to Janine. "Your floors."

"I'm redoing my floors," Janine explained with a sigh, "so I can't host, and I know it's probably stupid, because our dogs are old and we'll wind up with a new puppy at some point soon and that puppy will of course ruin the floors, but then tell me, Jen, will there ever be a good time? We're probably perpetually three years away from a new puppy! You get the impossibility, of course you do!"

"It's amazing you can even function." Jen's tone was tart enough that Annie meowed and formed her hand into a claw. Janine's giggle made clear that she couldn't be less offended.

"Right?" Janine said with great enthusiasm.

Jen imagined gesturing to a waiter—*I'll have a bucket of whatever she's having, please.*

"The group will be much smaller next month, cross my heart," Janine said. "All the book club lookie-loos will be gone."

"Jen lives in the Stollers' old house, right?" Annie said.

"Which has that amazing great room," Janine said.

"With the wood beams and vaulted ceilings," Annie said, with a dreamy look on her face.

"Thank you?" Jen said, although the compliments did not seem directed at her.

"We'll do everything," Janine promised. "It will be barely any work."

"When are we going to talk about the vandal?" Deb Gallegos said. She and Priya Jensen had appeared behind Janine, and everyone shifted to let them into the circle.

Despite tonight's eighty-degree weather, Deb wore suede boots that came up to almost her waist. She had Disney princess hair, coiled perfectly over her shoulders in glossy waves.

"What vandal?" Jen said.

The women regarded Jen as though she'd announced that books were stupid, especially when you could just see the movie.

After a cycle of *how did you miss this, where have you been?* Deb explained worriedly that someone had graffitied not only the Cottonwood signs by the entrance but also—she lowered her voice, infused it with pathos—Lena Meeker's mailbox.

As in Lena Meeker, *of all people.*

Jen wasn't entirely fluent in neighborhood lore, but fragments of Lena's story had come up in some of the meetings—her husband had died in a horrible car crash years before in the neighborhood, and Lena had apparently responded by sealing herself off in that big house on top of the hill.

How would someone like Lena Meeker parent Abe?

At last an answer that Jen liked: *Not as healthily as Jen Chun-Pagano, who made it a point to leave the house and go to book club every single month.*

"Even if it is just bored kids," Priya said. "They're cruel. I've been pregnant four times, ladies. When my bladder sees a sign screaming PEE each morning, it thinks 'great idea!'"

"Hey," Annie said. "When did you guys get here?"

Annie's daughter Laurel, who was roughly Abe's age, had appeared behind Annie. "Five minutes ago," she said. In a gesture of casual affection, she'd draped her arms around Annie's middle, pressed her chin into Annie's shoulder. "Dad and Hank are saying hi to Mrs. Nessel."

Laurel smiled at Jen. She held excellent eye contact with those alert upturned amber eyes. Her mass of long curly hair was captured haphazardly by a scrunchy. Everything about her said *middle school is a breeze!*

"Mike," Deb Gallegos cupped her hands around her mouth and shouted across the room to Annie's husband. "Come here."

Jen stifled an eye roll. Whenever Mike Perley stopped by book club, everyone acted like they were on vacation and he was the hot scuba instructor who was making them feel twenty-one again.

He was different from the other husbands—because of his youth and that cheeky grin, because of his shaggy shoulder-length orange hair, occasionally swept up into a man bun, because of his penchant for accessorizing: rope bracelets around his wrists, leather cords with beads around his neck, ornate tattoos, one on each forearm. Because instead of leaving at seven thirty each morning for the office, he owned a struggling restaurant and seemed to be around a lot.

As he approached their group, the women's faces turned toward him like sunflowers.

"Mike Perley." Janine beamed. "Be still my beating heart. How was the blood drive?"

"Excellent!" Mike said.

The women swooned and tittered as he and Laurel jointly narrated the highs and lows of the school blood drive they'd just attended, after which Laurel was dispatched to protect the food table from Hank. Before she left, though, she referred to Hank by an affectionate nickname—Jen didn't catch it—that made Annie and Mike dissolve in laughter.

Tonight, proximity to the Perleys was a little too much for Jen to take. She suddenly felt a burning need to find cracks in their family dynamic. There had to be cracks. Didn't every family have cracks?

She had become a total jerk.

"Did you donate blood?" Janine asked Mike in a teasing lilt.

Mike gestured to the Band-Aid in the crook of his elbow, shrugged with false pride.

"I won the blood drive, actually," he joked. "Great veins, universal donor. They actually invited me back for next year and"—Mike raised his eyebrows and—"I don't think they do that with everyone."

Janine threw back her head in laughter. Her hand, Jen noted, lingered on Mike's arm, patted that defined bicep.

How would the Perleys have parented Abe?

They'd be unruffled, Jen guessed, which would probably be excellent for Abe. She and Paul both could get uptight and they tended to care too much about even the unimportant things.

At the food table, Laurel handed cheese cubes to her brother, who had the same bright orange hair as his dad and was hamming it up, overstuffing his mouth with the cheese.

Jen still occasionally questioned whether she and Paul should have tried for a second child. Abe had always seemed too fragile, and they'd been exhausted and worried it might disrupt his ecosystem. But maybe it would have been exactly what he needed.

Would Abe be more adaptable if he'd had a sibling looking after him, feeding him cheese?

Probably. And he'd have strong bones, too. All that calcium!

"Your son's not at Sandstone, right?" Deb asked Jen.

"Abe goes to Foothills," Priya said before Jen could respond.

"Great school," Janine said. "People love Foothills. That principal, people rave about him. What's his name, Denton? Talk about cult of personality—"

Because Jen was working so hard to keep her expression measured, it took a moment for her to recognize that the ringing phone was hers. Saved by the bell!

When the ID flashed her former area code she realized she hadn't been saved at all.

She managed a scrambled "excuse me," and pressed the phone to her ear as she rushed out the front door to Harriet's front steps.

"Hello?"

"Scofield here."

"That's some prompt service." Jen paused for Scofield to laugh, which he didn't. "I'm sure you don't remember us, it's been years since you saw our son, seven if I'm counting right, he was in kindergarten—"

Jen lowered her voice as the Perleys walked past her and Laurel paused on Harriet's porch for Hank to hop on her back. Annie and Mike linked arms and Hank chanted a pop song and they all joined in as they strolled across the street to their house, not even bothering to check for cars.

"Eight years," Scofield corrected. "He's just turned thirteen, right?"

"Right, I don't know if you keep notes or not, but his name is—"

"Abe. The guinea pig killer."

"It was a hamster," Jen said, already annoyed, "and no one died."

"Riiight," Scofield said in an indulgent ooze that made clear that the rodent's well-being wasn't the point.

"But I'm wondering," Jen said, "if you might have been right about him."

"Which part?"

There was a long, empty pause.

He was a horrible man, sadistic. He was going to make her say the word aloud. There was a difference between thinking it and tasting it on her tongue, slithery and rotten.

"The part—" Jen held her chin high just on principle, and

realized in a flash that Dr. Scofield was inconsequential. The man was not some oracle. He was an asshole, and always would be. The important struggle had always been the one between Jen and herself. Could she even consider this about own son, let alone say it?

It turned out that she could.

"The part," she said, "about Abe's being a sociopath."

OCTOBER

To: "The Best Book Club in the World"
From: proudmamabooklover3@hmail.com

It's that time again, Ladies!!! Put down that pumpkin carving knife and open this month's read . . .

The book: IN SICKNESS AND HEALTH. Paige Smithson is a pediatrician, married to the love of her life, with the career of her dreams, two beautiful young children, and a diagnosis of terminal cancer.

The story of a woman, mortality and how to say goodbye, written by the husband who loved her, has been called "as heartbreaking as it is life-affirming." "A treatise on what it means to be human."

I've read this twice now—am-A-zing!—and will warn you: bring tissues!!!

The place: Deb Gallegos's house, 5552 Frontview Way. Deb would like me to warn you about the hole in the front yard due to an issue with the pipes, so please watch your step, especially in the dark! And also, please leave your shoes in the front hallway when you come in.

I am just realizing, Deb, that all of your instructions are feet-related! Fetish anyone? ;) ;) ;)

The time: 7:30*

To bring: Tissues, drinks and snacks (so many great offerings last time, let's keep those themed masterpieces going!)

Until then, readers!!!!! (Who's with me in not believing it's October?? Where is the year going???)

*Is anyone else open to pushing the start back to a little later in the evening? (Just maybe like eight? Soccer mamas, are you with me? Katie's sport schedule is killing us this year!! #Goaliemom)

CHAPTER SIX

Annie's first appointment on Tuesday morning was with Deb Gallegos's daughter Sierra, whose science teacher had written her up for yet another dress code violation. Annie would have told Deb regardless—Cottonwood parents kept each other informed—but this offense, Sierra's third, triggered a mandatory call home.

Phone to her ear, Annie tapped her pencil's eraser against the yellow legal pad on her small desk. Most of the time, Annie wasn't bothered by how much younger she was than her neighborhood friends, but occasionally, from Deb, Annie felt an undercurrent of amused condescension that rankled.

Anticipating this, when Deb picked up, Annie blurted out the news abruptly and officiously.

"Sierra cannot wear denim underwear to school."

Deb snorted. "Oh my god, Annie. Your *tone*."

Annie felt herself blush. She had sounded rather harsh. "They've got to be at least mid-thigh. And no rips."

"Who makes this stupid rule?"

"The—"

"Middle-aged sexist pigs. And where is the rule about what a boy can wear?"

"I know," Annie said. "But kids *label* each other, Deb. I care about Sierra and her reputation—"

"Your innocence is adorable, Annie, if you haven't figured out that everyone wears short shorts. Stores don't carry anything else. Boys get those knee-length parachutes and girls get hot pants." Deb sighed. "What on earth is she supposed to wear when it's hot out?"

"It's not *me*," Annie objected, feeling like a nerdy hall monitor. "It's the school's dress code."

"Which is entirely sexist."

Yes, but so was life.

Annie wanted Sierra—all of the students—to be treated like whole human beings, not objects. If that meant adhering to an occasional double standard and buttoning an extra button, wasn't it worth it?

Before she'd sent Sierra back to class, Annie had tried to explain to her that the rules of fashion were not written to benefit teenaged girls, but rather to *objectify* them. *I remember that feeling of power, Sierra, and it's a ruse.*

Sierra had nodded gently and unconvincingly, as though Annie was the lonely local curmudgeon known to yammer on about how great life had been before that dang rock 'n' roll music ruined everything.

Only once did Sierra's eyes, heavily lined in turquoise pencil (when had *that* come back into style?), flick desperately to the door.

Annie had been tempted to grab her by the shoulders and bark that sex was evil.

Wasn't life just hilariously ironic, because teen Annie would have rolled her eyes *so hard* at such out-of-touch advice from a grown-up.

(Nor did Annie truly believe that sex was evil. It was fantastic, at least until you were a grown-up and really thought about how *young* pubescent kids were, how underdeveloped emotionally. She would never understand why biology handed out hormones to the young. Might as well send paper dolls to fight wildfires.)

"So," Deb said. "Do I need to pick up my little fashion victim?"

"I gave her a pair of Laurel's sweats and sent her back to science.

There was some big finger-pricking blood lab that she didn't want to miss."

"Bless you, Annie, because I have to show a house in half an hour. Are we done with the boring stuff?"

What had Annie expected from Deb? The woman had once worn a crop top and leggings to book club.

"It's not boring, Deb, it's—"

"Yes, I know, of premium importance. How ever can those poor, weak boys learn while our daughters' outfits distract them? So"—Deb's voice lowered to a conspiratorial tone—"are you visiting Lena Meeker again today?"

The day after that first visit, Annie had returned to Lena's with paint thinner and Lena had invited Annie in for some shortcake granola cookies. There had been two more visits after that, always with baked goods. Hank had tagged along on the last one and Lena had given him cupcakes and let him draw all over her patio with sidewalk chalk.

"You're a good person," Deb said. "She must be so lonely."

"I enjoy her," Annie said simply. And although there was more to the situation, it was true. "Math club was canceled tomorrow, so I'm taking Laurel up."

Seriously? Mike had asked. Again?

I don't pull up a chair and start confessing things, Annie had assured him. But she understood his raised eyebrows.

"Great idea," Deb said. "Older people love being in the presence of youth."

"Lena's not *old*."

"Isn't she? Anyway, I picked up some cute plaid fabric for the girls' Halloween costumes, but," Deb teased, "those skirts are far from dress-code-compliant. Postage-stamp-sized. I'll check with Laurel before I cut the fabric."

Annie laughed.

Deb still frequently told the story about how during their toddlers' play group, Laurel had waddled over to Sierra, who'd been happily eating dirt from a bucket. "No, no," Laurel had said with a grab of Sierra's hand. "Dirty!"

Designated hall monitor right there, Deb had said. *She'll keep 'em on track during high school.*

"Thanks, Deb," Annie said. "Just let me know what I owe for the fabric."

"Pish," Deb said blithely. "It's like fifty cents. Talk later."

As Annie hung up, she tapped the eraser against the notepad again.

When Laurel was a newborn, it had occurred to a horrified Annie that this pure and perfect infant would probably make some of the same mistakes Annie had: trust the wrong people, run headfirst into danger.

Thank goodness Laurel turned out to be more risk-averse than Annie had been. It was better to be a rule-follower, wasn't it?

Although, sometimes Annie also thought that she would have at least understood a daughter like Sierra. Deb and Sierra Gallegos were besties—for Christmas they had gifted each other BFF necklaces with real diamonds. Even with all of the love between Annie and Laurel, Annie sometimes felt—

Not even a wedge. A *hint* of a wedge between them.

Does Laurel seem joyless, Annie sometimes asked Mike. Heavy?

In graduate school, Annie had learned about Jung's collective unconscious and the theory that stress in one generation could alter the DNA of the next.

Laurel sees right through us, Annie would whisper to Mike. *She knows my sins.*

Mike knew his job in that moment was to bring Annie down to earth. *She's an observer by nature,* he'd say. *People are who they are.*

Annie was willing to bet that Mike had forgotten where he'd first heard that little nugget of wisdom, but she never would. Thirteen years before, their labor and delivery nurse had been a woman who seemed to derive a large part of her identity from being a redhead. When she spotted Mike, sitting in the guest chair, she'd squealed with such glee that Annie assumed they'd grown up together.

"Fellow ginger," she'd whooped, holding up her hand for a high five. Mike shot Annie a confused look and hesitantly returned the slap.

In a stage whisper, the nurse said, "Don't tell anyone I said this, because I'm not supposed to play favorites, but there is nothing cuter than a red-haired baby. *Nothing.*"

Mike was more unnerved than Annie, who by Laurel's birth, was inured to the fact that some people felt compelled to confess their wackiest truths to pregnant women, like they were all involuntary priests.

But when Laurel came out, all pale milky skin and jet-black hair, the nurse had looked at Mike, her lips pressed into a tight line. *She's lovely,* she had finally said in a brisk tone that might as well have been an apology. *People are who they are, after all.*

Annie had lain on the hospital bed, annoyed less by the stings of the doctor's stitches and by the fact that her midsection was an accordion squeezing out a tortured "La Vie en Rose" than by the nurse's disappointment about Laurel's hair color, which seemed to Annie like disappointment about *Laurel*.

She almost said something defensive about how perfect Laurel was, but pandering to the foot-in-mouth set wasn't how she wanted to kick off motherhood.

It only occurred to Annie years later that this entire memory was less about the nurse and more about Annie's own fears of Mike's disappointment. Which was silly. He couldn't have cared less, didn't even react to the nurse's comment about Laurel's hair, was immediately besotted.

But of course he was. Mike was Mike. *People are who they are.*

Laurel had been born cautious and cerebral, while Hank had been born energetic and confident enough to push boundaries.

Just last week, Annie had come home from her walk to see him in the driveway, stripping a D-cell battery to find out what was inside. Mike's mom, hearing the story, had reminded Annie that in all of his childhood pictures, Mike was in a cast or on crutches. A bandage and a giant smile.

They're two peas in a pod, Mike's mom had said.

Who would Laurel turn out like? Who was her twin pea?

But Annie should stop pegging her children. They were too young for it, and even if their personalities seemed predetermined, things changed.

And kids soaked up that stuff. Parents were flawed human beings, who for a few years there had all the power of gods. How you were treated, experiences, mattered just as much as disposition.

Take Lena Meeker.

Annie found it almost impossible to reconcile Lena now with the woman she'd seen on that summer night fourteen years ago.

Light on her feet, tendrils loose around her face, Lena had been a vision, gliding around the party in that seafoam-green dress with floaty layers. She was here, there. A hand on an arm, her head tossed backward, mouth open in laughter.

And Rachel?

It was almost impossible to assess.

Based on what Annie could glean online, Rachel Meeker was living a full life in Boston. She had a boring corporate job with one of those meaningless-sounding titles—vice president of operations and sales blah blah blah—and a fiancé.

The way Rachel had fled home that summer, though, indicated a disruption in trajectory. She'd still been a kid then, and as far as anyone knew, she'd never returned, not even for summer breaks or Christmas or to show off her new boyfriend. It didn't seem healthy to Annie, but she liked to think that Rachel had good reasons for staying away—maybe her life on the East Coast was so chock-full of great things that she couldn't find the time to come back.

Annie wasn't aware of how hard she'd been pressing the pencil tip to the legal pad until its tip broke off.

The corollary to Mike's philosophy—*people are who they are*—was that life wore grooves in people. It changed them.

How very poetic, Annie. How *oblique*.

Life wore grooves completely glossed over Annie's part, how she'd watched from the shadows that night, poised to pounce.

Life's grooves may have eroded the Meeker women's vibrancy—sure, why not—but you know what had helped things along?

One swift impulsive push from Annie.

If it was murder: What happened between the two of them out there?

An hour before the party, I passed by Lena's house with the thought of catching her for an early drink, before the crowds. When I arrived, I saw that Annie appeared to have the same idea. She and Lena were outside, sitting next to each other on an outdoor sofa.

I was halfway across the lawn to them when I heard Annie's sobs, shaky and gasping, as uncontained as a child's.

Lena looked straight ahead, her back rigid. She wasn't comforting Annie or yelling at her or, from what I could tell, acknowledging her at all.

Even from several feet away, I could feel that the energy between them was deep and ugly. On the way home, I realized my arms were covered in goose pimples.

At the party, though, Annie and Lena were back to normal, thick as thieves.

So maybe it was nothing.

I can't exactly ask now.

CHAPTER SEVEN

"The wedding dress is gorgeous," Lena said.

"It looks okay?" On the video chat, Rachel's dark eyes were filled with skepticism and hope. "Even from the back?"

"Gorgeous from all angles."

After a thin smile—*I can't exactly trust* you—Rachel ducked her head. "Thank you for buying it."

"My pleasure."

Rachel's wedding dress was a slinky slip of a thing, done in Mikado silk. Its price tag had made even Lena's eyebrows hike up, but she'd been delighted to pay.

For years, Rachel had treated the money like it was toxic. She'd insisted on living in that tiny apartment, had taken out student loans for business school, and been unnecessarily pious about vacations and restaurants.

For the wedding, however, Rachel had relaxed the self-imposed budget. This had to mean that Rachel was deliriously happy, didn't it?

Marriage was a statement of optimism and Lena was relieved that Rachel was making it, even if Rachel's choice of groom seemed safe, a little stale. That Evan Welnik-Boose called Lena *dear* in their brief video chats, like she was some decrepit aunt—*Hello dear. How's summer, dear?*—seemed a tad creepy.

Maybe he thought Lena *was* a decrepit aunt. Who knew what he'd been told?

Evan's parents, Samara Welnik, Ph.D., and Miles Boose, M.D., were lovely, cultured, accomplished people who lived twenty minutes from Rachel and Evan, when they weren't at their beach house on Cape Cod. Miles was a pediatric something or other and Samara was a psychologist specializing in childhood trauma (neither Lena nor Rachel had articulated the ironies of *that* to each other), who sent Lena warm notes in a lovely cursive about what a blessing it was that their miraculous offspring had found each other.

The wedding was to be at their beach house, which meant something to Rachel and Evan, if not Lena. The current debate was whether the ceremony should be on the beach (too public?) or in the yard (private, but too small for a tent).

There was, in Lena's yard, an expanse of lawn that had been literally designed to fit a party tent. And years ago, Lena had thought that the spot under the bough of the cottonwood tree, between the garden and the gate, with that view out to the snow-capped Rockies, would be perfect for a wedding ceremony.

Lena understood that the fantasy had been imagined for another life, but it didn't mean she couldn't notice the loss of it.

Lena's own wedding to Tim, which her mother Alma had planned entirely, had been at Lena's childhood church. Lena had worn Alma's wedding dress, let out to fit Lena, and there had been a reception afterward in her parents' backyard. She recalled no choices, only traditions to uphold.

She had also felt the tiniest bit like a dress-up doll.

The doorbell rang and Lena peeked over the stairwell.

Annie Perley peered through the window by the door, hand shielding her eyes in an attempt to see inside the house. Hank stood to her left carrying a plastic container, and the girl next to him, one lanky leg wound around the other like a contortionist flamingo, must be Laurel.

Lena inhaled sharply.

"What?" Rachel said. She leaned close to the phone camera, so Lena could only see the top half of her face: giant troubled eyes and forehead zigzagged with worry lines. "What's happened?"

"Someone's at the door," Lena said.

"Who?"

In the years since Rachel had left, Lena had tried to be as honest with her as possible, but something had kept her from mentioning Annie Perley's visits.

Rachel was, for the most part, functioning beautifully in the anonymity of a big city. She had the job, the fiancé, the big group of friends. Dragging her attention back to Cottonwood Estates might defeat the purpose of their sacrifices.

"Mom." Rachel leaned so close to the camera that all Lena could see were panicked eyes. "You're freaking me out. Who's there?"

Just Annie Perley, and she has a daughter with long curly dark hair and a familiar innocent coltishness and if I squint, I can fool myself into thinking she looks like you did, back when we were like everyone else.

"Rudy about pruning the cottonwood," Lena said, which was only a half lie because she did need to discuss it with him soon.

"I have to go anyway," Rachel said. "Love you."

"Love you too."

The words had come out hard. Lena desperately clutched for a joke, a funny story, something to smooth that worried brow, but nothing came to mind.

Lena waited until Annie was settled on the sofa before she presented her with the wrapped box.

"For you," she said.

Annie eyed Lena suspiciously. "What have you done?"

"Open it."

Lena sat down and clasped her hands in anticipation as she watched Annie carefully remove the wrapping paper.

"Lena." Annie's nose crinkled. She unfolded the tissue paper and looked accusingly from the box to Lena, who could wait no more. She leaned forward and snatched the peacock-blue cashmere wrap, held it up to Annie's face.

"Your eyes pop," she said with approval. "Sometimes it's hard to tell online, but I had a feeling about this color."

"I can't keep this," Annie pleaded. "I don't own anything this nice, Lena."

"All the more reason why you must."

Annie lowered her voice, even though the kids were outside on the patio. "You're doing too much for us. The baking, the sidewalk chalk for Hank—I know you bought it—the camera you just gave to Laurel."

"It brings me joy," Lena said simply.

Even before the accident, the act of giving had brought Lena a sense of connection and purpose.

And now?

She'd felt a shot of giddiness when ordering the wrap for Annie, and an explosion of joy when Hank had barreled inside the house to grab one of the homemade biscotti. *The best I've ever had,* he'd said in earnest.

"We're here," Annie said firmly, "because we enjoy your company, not to . . . acquire."

"I know that," Lena said.

"It is stunning," Annie said. After a moment of hesitation, she looped the scarf around her neck, patted it.

"So"—Lena crossed her legs—"any improvement with Mike's restaurant?"

"It's the same," Annie said.

A year ago, Mike Perley had started his own restaurant, called CartWheel. It had been a lifelong dream of his, and although, according to Annie, Mike was working very hard and the chef was amazingly talented and the concept was fabulous—American bistro fusion fare served via dim sum carts—business was slow.

Now, Lena settled in to listen. Annie was trying her best to be supportive, she explained, and she wanted Mike to be happy. He deserved to be happy, and she didn't want to be a dream killer, but she couldn't help but struggle with his decision to open a restaurant *now* and to use their home as collateral.

Lena nodded sympathetically and nudged the biscotti plate across the coffee table to her.

Annie took one and bit into it frustratedly, speaking through the chew. She couldn't object because—again, Annie lowered her voice—Mike hadn't wanted to live in Cottonwood at all. They could have afforded something bigger and far less expensive on the other side of the hogback.

Annie had insisted, though. She had wanted to raise a family here. She looked guiltily at Lena. He had compromised back then. Didn't Annie have to now?

"Wanting the best for your children is hardly a crime," Lena said.

She had always been drawn to blurters, people like Annie who wore their hearts on their sleeves. The choice was: step back or get swept up.

Lena always chose to get swept up.

Freshman year of college, Lena had walked into the Psychology 101 lecture room and found an empty chair next to a stranger who announced that she had not done the reading, because there had been a party in her hall, and even though she hadn't planned on going she had, and did Lena want to know what had happened at this party because it was crazy.

Oh, she had said, I'm Melanie, by the way.

And later that same semester Lena had met Tim, who could have majored in authoritative proclamations. When he zeroed in on Lena it had been thrilling: This is the plan! You and Me!

Who was she to argue?

Rachel had it wrong: Lena wasn't a manipulative supervillain. She was, at heart, a people-pleaser. In early life, it had been Alma's opinion that mattered, then Tim's. Finally, even though Rachel would never want to see it this way, it was Rachel herself who had motivated Lena to act.

It wasn't that Lena didn't have her own opinions or goals, just that other people's seemed more important.

But maybe everyone thought of herself as a follower. So many book characters were victims of circumstance—Alice in Wonderland, the Little Princess, Hamlet. Poor Odile up in the tree. Things had happened to them, and then their reactions propelled the story.

Just like Lena. She had merely reacted.

"You should bring these to book club when you come." Annie took a rabbitlike nibble of her second biscotto. "Deb will flip."

"*If* I come to book club," Lena corrected.

Annie made a swooping motion with the biscotto to indicate she was dismissing Lena's *if*.

Book club was well-trod ground between them by now—Annie pushing, Lena demurring—and although Lena had no intention of ever going to book club, she found it flattering to be so vigorously recruited.

"Deb's the one who makes the drinks?" Lena said.

She knew this already, too: Deb Gallegos made the cocktails and was overly permissive with her daughter. Priya Jensen was the beauty who had moved here from India as a child, modeled lingerie in her twenties, and married that football player and had a ton of money and children and beautiful clothes but Annie said you couldn't hate Priya, even if the laws of self-protection begged you to, because she was so kindhearted. Janine was the organizer who was, based on those frantic emails and Annie's stories, well-meaning but a bit hysterical.

Lena had grown fond of the women, who she thought of as characters in another book. She could imagine having a cocktail with them and advising them in the way she might Hamlet. *For heaven's sake, pay some attention to Ophelia!*

"Deb's drinks will convince you to become a book club member," Annie said. "She plots in a libations notebook—I am not kidding, she buys a new one each year—and orders obscure bitters and all of this equipment online. She might be a little bit of an alcoholic, though. Highly functioning." Annie laughed nervously. "I don't know. I'm kidding, obviously."

Lena was by now used to the way Annie's eyes would habitually float over to Rachel's picture.

They had been seven years apart, Annie stammered last week. She'd barely known Rachel.

But Annie had wanted to ask about her, Lena could tell, so she'd changed the subject. As she did now.

"Do you think Laurel would like to see Waterfall Rock?"

Just beyond the back gate of Lena's yard were hiking paths that connected to the state forest system. Rachel had named the spot where the trail led to a giant boulder, perched above a majestic thirty-foot waterfall that roared and sprayed down to the creek below.

Lena hadn't been in years, but once upon a time, when Rachel was about Hank's age, they'd picnicked there frequently, and she'd thought to show Hank and Annie during their last visit. They'd acted like it was Valhalla.

How did we not know about this, Annie kept exclaiming.

"Let's," Annie said with enthusiasm. "I have to warn you, though, Laurel's been grouchy since she came home from the sleepover. I'm not sure if it's lack of sleep or some teen drama. Probably both."

This Lena understood.

It hadn't mattered how many times Lena had tried to get Rachel to lighten up, she had always taken the rules a bit too seriously, which had been catnip to a certain type of frenemy. There'd been a parade of them in middle school—the overly bossy, the excluders, those who wanted to knock Rachel down a peg. Lena suspected they were jealous of the money.

Rachel's overly strong sense of justice hadn't helped. She could never decide if she wanted to fit in with her peers or police them.

With urgency, Lena watched Laurel, who was slouched on the patio chaise, tooling with Tim's old camera.

"How are her friendships generally?"

"Very tight. Three of them have been together since elementary. Sierra, Deb's daughter, lives right up the hill. Their friend Haley is just across Highway Five in the Red Mesa neighborhood."

"Good. Girls can be quite cruel."

"I know, as a counselor, I see some really—wait, Lena, why are you smirking?"

Lena pressed her hands to her cheeks. Had she been?

"I was just remembering how Sarah Loeffler used to have parties for the sole purpose of inviting everyone but Rachel. She was a horrid human being, and worse, she always sold the most Girl Scout cookies—"

"The Sarah Loefflers of the world always do," Annie said.

"And one year, we were like, *Not so fast, honey.*"

"What did you do?"

"It's a little embarrassing. Two grown-ups competing against this poor child like it was the Olympics. At the time I thought it was a victory, but in retrospect, maybe it's better to not engage."

For weeks, their entire garage had been organized into inventory, and when they'd finally won, all three of them had celebrated by opening a box of every flavor. Tim had eaten two boxes of the coconut ones all by himself.

Always a man of appetites, her Tim.

"I wonder what happened to Sarah." Lena cleared her throat, fiddled with her earring back. The good memories always landed a little rougher.

Annie raised one eyebrow. "I'm sure she learned a valuable lesson about kindness and was never ever mean again." Her gaze slid again to the largest photo of Rachel. "How's she doing these days?"

"Amazing. She's got a wonderful fiancé, and a great job."

Annie made a short sharp noise—an exhale, a laugh? She pounded her fist to her chest, cleared her throat.

"I'm so glad," she said.

"Annie," Lena said. "About Mike's restaurant? My brother Ernesto is in a business group, and they have a monthly dinner. Would Mike be open to their booking CartWheel?"

"I'm sure there's space," Annie said sardonically.

"It's a bunch of muckety-mucks who like to throw their weight around and act like they run the city, but one of them is connected to *The Post,* so it's an opportunity for press."

"Really?"

"Yes, and you'd be doing Ernie a favor, because apparently their current venue doesn't have reliable parking. I'll have him call Mike."

Annie pursed her lips.

"Ernie can call, if. *If*"—she folded her arms across her chest—"you come to the November book club."

"Oh." The ultimatum was cold water splashed in Lena's face; she had expected a few more months of being pursued.

"Tell me exactly what you're worried about." Annie watched Lena with such concentration that two deep straight lines appeared between her eyebrows.

"It's that—" Lena lifted up her hands from her lap and placed them back down helplessly.

How had the tables turned so quickly? This moment was supposed to be about Lena's offer, which Annie should have accepted, happily, gratefully, and then Lena would feel good. The End.

"You like to keep things quiet," Annie said.

Lena nodded. She did like to keep things quiet.

On the night after the funeral, the house had felt like someone had vacuumed out all of the noise. Lena had stretched out on the couch in her black dress, watched the sun retreat behind the mountains.

Another person might have followed Rachel across the country, started over in a new town, but Lena didn't want—didn't *deserve*—that relief. The only way forward was to shed her old pleasures, like molting a layer of skin.

It had been easier than Lena anticipated. A few months of unreturned outreach, and her neighborhood friends had released her. They had probably been grateful: no one knew how to treat her anyway. Lena herself had no clue how she should be treated; nothing felt appropriate.

She didn't become a complete monk. Melanie called from Newport Beach every morning like clockwork, willing to accept whatever Lena told her at face value, too far away to observe anything to the contrary. Lena's brother Ernie was more likely to forward emails about stocks and politics than initiate a meandering conversation about grief, mistakes, and regret, but he was there for her in the ways he could be. And he and his wife Trista always checked with her before the holidays, and if Rachel wasn't available, or Lena couldn't bear to travel, they made it a point to stay in town so that Lena wouldn't be alone.

Beyond that, Lena had her books and her shows, her online shopping and her maintenance projects and a rotating cast of paid friends necessary to dispatch them—landscapers, cleaners, Gregoire for her hair, and every few years, the painters and architect and the renovation crews—all of whom were legitimately good company.

There were bad months that sometimes stretched into bad years: Rachel's off-and-on anger, palpable even across the country, Lena's intermittent fear of travel and the panic attacks, which usually yielded to sessions with Dr. Friendly, a local therapist, and occasionally required prescriptions.

But all in all, the soundlessness diet had been effective. Lena's life shrank down to something manageable. That this worked for her—as an appeasement of guilt, as punishment, as a method of forgetting—she could barely explain to herself, let alone another person.

Annie was still leaned forward, elbows on knees, number-eleven wrinkles even more pronounced between her eyebrows. (Should Lena offer Annie Botox? She had a delightful woman who came to the house every three months.)

Lena didn't honestly believe one book club meeting would turn her into a social maniac.

What, exactly, was she worried about?

Neighborhood gossip and angering the gods and upsetting the balance by not respecting the thick red line that bisects my life into Before and After.

"I don't really like to go out," Lena said finally. *I'm supposed to have a shell of a life now.*

"It's not going out. It's like this." Annie's open-palmed gesture swept over their china teacups. "Cozy. And November's book is a laugh riot. There's suspense and sex and we'll just all have Deb's drinks and giggle about it."

Annie had once mentioned a Deb Gallegos cocktail concoction: pepper-infused vodka. The thing was that Lena could see herself on a sofa, sipping it, nodding in response to Deb's or Priya's point, asking Deb for the recipe.

"And Harriet Nessel, bless her, will try to bring the discussion back to the book."

"That sounds just like Harriet."

Harriet had been the first to arrive to all of Lena's summer parties, and her hostess gifts were inevitably regifted molded hand soaps in holiday themes. Once, Lena had made the mistake of opening the box in front of Harriet. Two out of the four Christmas trees had been missing.

Lena had been mortified on Harriet's behalf, but Harriet was only outraged at the rudeness of her cousin Amity, who had apparently been the original giver. "Who does that," Harriet had fumed, "who removes the soaps first?"

Lena's stomach quivered, her arm hairs stood at attention, as the memory of Harriet's face—stern eyes, pursed lips—swam in front of her. Odd that her body was behaving like she missed Harriet Nessel.

"Harriet can't wait to see you, by the way. I mean everyone can't, but she's very fond of you."

"That's nice."

"There has to be a quid pro quo, Lena." Annie stroked the cashmere throw around her neck. "I'll accept all of your ridiculous generosity, but then you have to do this one thing. You'll love book club. I wouldn't suggest it otherwise."

If Lena were to play devil's advocate, she would ask herself: Hadn't she already breached the social diet by opening the door to Annie, or to Gregoire, who usually stayed for dinner after ministering to Lena's highlights, or to Tommy the UPS man, who occasionally came in for coffee (black with so much sugar stirred in that Lena worried about his teeth)?

But on the other hand, Lena knew to ignore that grabby little voice piping up in her head: *You deserve, you want, take it, what's the harm?*

"It's all book nerds," Annie said. "Empathetic, openhearted readers. Our people, Lena."

Lena really wanted to go, was the thing.

"Come once. If you don't enjoy it, that's— Oh, Hank," Annie moaned. Annie's son had smushed his freckled face against the window, then pulled it away and smiled with delight at the greasy foggy smear he'd left: *I did that!*

"Lena, I'll clean that right up."

"Don't be silly," Lena said. "Let's go see the art."

Hank had drawn beautiful pastel mermaids with their hair flying behind them across Lena's patio, and after Lena admired them, they all went out to Waterfall Rock.

Lena made a big show of handing Hank the key to the gate and talking him through how to unlock it. They walked single-file down the hint of the path, which was nearly obscured by fallen pine needles, until they reached the large flat rock overlooking the falls.

Hank walked to the edge and cupped his hands around his mouth.

"Hello," he shouted over the rushing water.

"There's no echoes in a waterfall," Laurel said. "That's caves." The *dummy* was implied.

"Such an amazing view, huh?" Annie placed a hand on Laurel's shoulder and pointed with the other in the direction of the western valley below them, where the aspens' waving golden leaves covered the hills like fire.

"Please stop *touching* me," Laurel said. She shrugged out from under Annie's grip.

Watching Annie's face flush, Lena felt a sympathetic catch in her throat. It was something about the girl's profile—the sweet plane of cheek interrupted by those pinpoint round dimples. Lena had always loved Rachel's dimples, which broke up her default expression of sternness.

Rachel's hair had been so thick when it was long, it had grown out as much as down and it had taken Lena forever to figure out how to instruct the stylist to get the layers just so, and which products to use, and then, right after she'd gone east, Rachel had cut it all off.

She'd never grown it out again.

There wasn't a true resemblance. It was Laurel's age and what she was going through. Lena wanted to yell at her to be nicer to her mother, then throw her arms around those slouched narrow shoulders and lie that it would all be okay.

"Kids," Lena said. "Can I trust you with something?"

Hank looked uncertainly at his mother for the answer—*not sure, can I be trusted?*

"I'm giving you a key to the gate. You can use it whenever you want—on one condition. Your mother needs to give you permission first. And you have to share it with each other."

"Really?" When Laurel smiled at Lena, Lena saw into her future: with cleared skin, hair off her face, those braces off, standing up straight—the girl was well on her way to being as pretty as Annie. "Thanks so much, Mrs. Meeker."

Lena felt warm at having saved the moment. She'd always suspected that she would make an excellent grandmother: generous, a dash of wise humor.

"A-hem," Annie coughed, and nudged Hank.

"Thank you, Mrs. Meeker," Hank said.

"Laurel," Annie said slyly, "I'm trying to convince Mrs. Meeker to join book club."

Laurel managed to make eye contact with Lena. "You should go," she said in a monotone.

"There's always really good food there," Hank said.

"Just one meeting." Annie held up one finger. "Lena. You deserve to have some fun."

It wasn't the most compelling argument.

It's only book club, Lena repeated to herself over a quickening pulse.

She might choose to pretend that she gave in for the sake of Mike Perley's restaurant, but the fact was that Lena enjoyed Annie's visits a bit too desperately.

Lena wanted more. More warmth, more fun, more noise, more *belonging,* and it wasn't like Rachel was ever coming back.

Fourteen years and Lena's essence hadn't evolved. When she fancied something—like she did now, like she tragically had Gary Neary—Lena went for it, consequences be damned.

She suspected most people did.

CHAPTER EIGHT

D r. Scofield had referred Jen to Dr. Maggie Shapiro, who had a neat gray-streaked bob and warm almond-shaped eyes and, as fate would have it, a last-minute cancellation that meant she'd been able to start assessing Abe in late September.

Dr. Shapiro's office was decorated in calming shades of taupe and beige and was on the seventeenth floor of a glass office building. The HVAC system hummed soothingly and the yellow-tinted windows of Dr. Shapiro's office had a view of the jagged line where the mountains met the sky.

Over the past two weeks, Jen had filled out reams of paperwork for Dr. Shapiro about everything from the development of Abe's pincer grip right up to the Harper French stabbing. She and Paul and Abe had all met with Dr. Shapiro in various permutations, but today's meeting was the big one:

Ease into these comfortable chairs, Jen and Paul, so I can tell you just how broken your son's brain is.

Of all the experts Jen and Paul had been to, Dr. Shapiro was the very best at assembling a shit sandwich—neatly tucking the distasteful truth inside two slices of positivity.

I so enjoyed getting to know Abe this week, Dr. Shapiro now intoned in that soothing therapist's voice, *because he is a uniquely creative soul with deep interests and a searing intelligence.*

Abe fit the criteria for conduct disorder, a precursor to sociopathy. But: he was very lucky to have parents like Jen and Paul—present, loving, willing to do the work.

Even if Jen recognized the sandwich for what it was, her eyes teared, in part from the diagnosis's starkness, but also from the acknowledgment that she *was* a good parent. The proof tended to be in the pudding with child-rearing, and people looked at Abe and assumed that Jen and Paul, let's face it, mainly Jen—*if it's not one thing, it's your mother*—was asleep on the job.

But Dr. Shapiro, dressed in an expensive-looking fringy black-and-white sweater-blazer, assured Jen and Paul that they were up to the work ahead. There would be a lot: weekly individual therapy, possibly group therapy, all designed to bolster Abe's empathy skills, which were, well, not the strongest she'd seen. Ditto his impulsivity.

He had a pattern of lashing out when things didn't go his way.

"Having two involved, caring parents puts Abe in the minority, unfortunately," Dr. Shapiro said. "Many kids with this diagnosis come from serious abuse."

"What if Abe was abused?" The words emerged from Jen's mouth in a panicked rush. "He's been bullied. What if someone—"

Dr. Shapiro shook her head decisively. "This has been noticed from Abe's earliest interactions. The fact that he's grown up in a loving environment and still struggles with empathy makes me think this is about brain wiring."

"But no one in either of our families has anything like this," Paul said.

"Does anyone have anxiety or depression?"

There it was. From the stories he told about his childhood, Jen always suspected Paul's mother had undiagnosed bipolar disorder, and she was about to voice this when Paul spoke, his voice hopeful.

"Jen's mom is really anxious," Paul said. "You don't think it's just anxiety?"

Jen bit her tongue rather than subject Dr. Shapiro to an argument about whose mother was more emotionally stable.

Plus, she understood why he suggested it.

Anxiety was like the white wine of the diagnostic world: ubiquitous, assumed to be fundamentally harmless.

Abe suffers from anxiety, Jen would confide to friends, family, other parents at playgrounds and birthday parties (back when the entire class was invited).

Everyone would be *right there* with Jen—sharing how their own kids cared too deeply about grades, or got homesick on sleepovers, refused to eat any food that wasn't white.

Yes, Jen would nod, *it's exactly the same. We're all having such identical experiences.*

"He's never been violent with us," Paul objected. "I mean, he's never gotten physical."

"Which is good," Dr. Shapiro said. "But the behavior he's exhibited with others—squeezing a hamster just because, stabbing a classmate who he feels has wronged him—"

"But she did wrong him," Jen said. "If we're talking about Harper French. She was awful to him."

Dr. Shapiro nodded at Jen in a way that made her somehow feel both heard and dismissed before continuing.

"—challenging the teachers—we can see a cluster of aggressivity, an indifference to consequence. Talking with Abe, it was clear to me that he lacks remorse for this behavior. How is he with his chores?" Dr. Shapiro pressed gently, "Unloading the dishwasher, taking out the trash, mowing the lawn?"

Jen and Paul exchanged a guilty look. They never made him do chores. Getting through each day seemed to be enough of a burden for Abe.

"He might be so pleasant around the house because you guys are easy to manipulate," Dr. Shapiro said matter-of-factly.

So maybe they weren't such good parents after all.

"Give him chores and reward him for the effort with points

that allow him to earn something." Dr. Shapiro glanced at her notes. "Like that giant gaming monitor he mentioned to me approximately three million times. Most kids with these traits can learn to manage them, even grow out of them."

The HVAC hummed peacefully and Paul absentmindedly rubbed his beard. His eyes looked glassy as they once again met Jen's. She had a wild unhinged need for someone to tell her how to feel. Luckily, Dr. Shapiro was up to the task.

"Have hope, Paganos," she said. "Have hope."

Maybe it was Dr. Shapiro's kindness that made Jen want to meet her halfway. *Accept it,* she challenged herself. *Don't fight it like you always do.*

When they stepped into the empty elevator, Paul grimaced at Jen. "What's up next," he said, "couple's root canals?"

"Colonoscopies first," Jen said. "Then the root canals."

The silver doors dinged closed.

"Congratulations," he said, "we created a sociopath."

"A burgeoning sociopath. But with hard work, who knows?" Jen tugged her tote bag onto her shoulder. "Do you agree with her?"

"The thing is." Paul stared up at the tiles on the ceiling. "She seemed to really get Abe."

"I know."

On the tenth floor, the elevator lurched to a stop and a short blond woman with a green handbag stepped inside. She looked remarkably unburdened.

"Do you still want to stop at the farmers market before home?" Paul said formally.

"I do." Jen matched his stiff tone. "We need bread."

Paul sighed and once again regarded the ceiling tiles. "When I was six," he said, "I used to deliberately step on ants."

The blond woman stopped rummaging in her green bag and looked up with alarm. When the doors opened at the garage level and the woman was safely out of earshot, Jen said, "The ants aren't the same thing."

"We have to remember that even if this is right, even if he has this disorder, Abe is the same kid he was earlier this morning. He's still Abe."

"True."

"It doesn't even sound that bad. Conduct disorder. It sounds like—"

"Like you misbehave in class."

"Like borderline personality disorder." Paul pressed the key fob and their car beeped open.

"What?"

"It's just always sounded so gentle to me, like it's on the border of not being a problem. But apparently people with that diagnosis can suffer tremendously. I'll drive?"

They opened the car doors and got in.

"Have you been researching mental illnesses on Abe's behalf?"

Paul buckled his belt, looked at her bashfully. "It's silly."

"Not at all."

Apparently, this was how to romance Jen, because she'd never felt more like hugging him.

Jen tried to forgive Paul's distractedness: he was gone most of the week, traveling and working hard. Sometimes, though, when she'd report in on Abe, she felt like she was explaining a movie to someone who'd wandered in in the middle. *Keep up,* she wanted to scold.

Which was unfair. Paul's job was work, and Jen's was Abe, and this was the way it would be because Jen made approximately ten percent of what Paul did.

Even now, she wouldn't have wanted to trade. If someone was going to focus on the puzzle that was Abe, it had to be Jen. (She'd feel like a caged tiger, otherwise, probably call home fifty times a day and bark at Paul that he was doing it wrong.)

But it did feel sometimes—and this wasn't Paul's fault—

imbalanced. They'd started out on such equal footing, after their first date. Both of their careers had been theirs alone to manage.

Paul was very taken with you, Jen's friend Candace had told her after one of her crowded house parties.

"Me?" Jen said.

To be singled out like this was a new experience for her. There had been partygoers spilling out of Candace's house to the back-yard, and Jen hadn't been able to remember which one was Paul.

"You know," Candace answered, bringing her hand to about three feet above the ground, "short, slight, really prominent eye-brows, looks kind of like a Muppet—but in a good way. I'm giv-ing him your number."

It didn't sound promising.

When Paul called, he had a nice warm tenor and they made a date to meet at a restaurant in Chinatown. Jen hadn't expected much, but when she saw him there, in front of the king crab tank, she smiled. (Which was really saying something: those poor crabs, trapped in that murky crowded water, legs pressed help-lessly against the glass, always made her temporarily resolve to be-come a vegetarian.) Paul was short and slight, with the promised eyebrows—two thick caterpillars slanted downward, which gave him a stern, intense air.

Candace hadn't mentioned Paul Pagano's neatly bearded, even-featured face. Or those giant hazel eyes underneath the brows: the kindest eyes Jen had ever seen.

It was funny now to think that Candace, who later disavowed the Muppet comment—but come on, how could Jen have made that up?—was a social media friend who seemingly spent twelve hours a day filming and posting videos of her daughter's dance team, and Paul had become everything that mattered.

Jen often wondered if she was the butt of some higher power's practical joke. The part of life that she had expected to be difficult—finding a life partner—had landed in her lap, while the part she might have assumed easy—sending your school-aged child off to school—required Herculean effort.

Jen shouldn't even go there anyway: Paul would *never* say they weren't equals, and neither should she. They were a good team who'd made the only logical decision about resource allocation, and were both just doing the best they could.

Paul switched on the ignition. The podcast they'd listened to on the way to Dr. Shapiro's—about a man who purchased a DNA kit and found out his uncle was his father—blared over the speakers like the world's biggest non sequitur. Paul switched it off.

"It fits," Jen said. "I don't want it to but—"

"What?"

Jen's phone had started to ring and the Bluetooth announced *Mom calling* in a soothing voice not dissimilar to Dr. Shapiro's.

Jen looked at Paul helplessly. "I can't."

"Definitely don't," Paul said.

Jen hadn't even told her mother about Abe's expulsion from Foothills because she'd never felt quite strong enough to talk her down from the hysterics that would result.

Maybe her mother did have an anxiety disorder.

When the phone stopped ringing, Jen picked it up.

"Calling back so soon?"

"Nope, I'm looking up the school Shapiro mentioned."

Dr. Shapiro had mentioned three alternative programs for Abe. Jen had already visited one of them before the move, and had not been impressed—too big, too impersonal. The second was two hours away, but the third, the Kingdom School, was a small religious school close to their home. It wouldn't matter, Dr. Shapiro said, that both Jen and Paul were lapsed Catholics. Plus, sometimes the inherent structure and moral code of religion provided a helpful bright line to kids like Abe.

"There's just a picture of a shack," Jen reported. "And a paragraph about Jesus written by founder Nan Smalls. How do we know Nan Smalls?" Jen asked, as Paul turned onto to Main Street, which was as messy with traffic as usual.

"We don't." Paul stopped short on the brakes as a Mercedes jeep pulled in front of them.

"The name is familiar, though." Jen paused. "Maybe if we send Abe to the Kingdom School, our prayers will be answered."

Paul snorted but Jen hadn't been entirely joking. She hadn't prayed much before having Abe, not even as a relatively pure-hearted youngster, but at least once a week she would try to quiet her mind and channel a peacefulness and plead—not to God per se, but also not *not* to God—that Abe would find a sense of belonging outside of their family, that he would be *okay* in a vague general sense.

Jen was aware that by the dictates of fairy tales she was violating the rules of specificity. What was *okay*? Meaningful, reciprocal relationships? Or just not stabbing anyone?

The answer was a moving target.

The light changed and they inched forward, their bumper a little too close to the Mercedes's.

"When we die, he's going to be all alone," Jen said.

"Of all our happy topics, this one is always my favorite," Paul said.

"We can't die, you know. Ever."

"So you've informed me."

The Mercedes in front of them suddenly stopped short and began backing up in a fruitless attempt to turn left on a road that was mostly behind them.

Paul slammed on the brakes and then the horn. "*Asshole,*" he said. "There's no room behind me. Where do they want me to even go?"

"I'll run in from here." She opened the door. "Watch something calming on your phone."

The town park in the middle of Main Street was an ode to autumn, with clusters of pumpkins and red-and-yellow leaf garlands twined around the lampposts. People wore knit scarves and tall boots and everything appeared gilded by the sunlight, which was so thick as to look artificial.

A dozen kids around Abe's age had overtaken some of the picnic tables. Their laughter, the effortless way they bit into each other's burritos and leaned their gawky bodies against each other, gave Jen an ache deep within her body.

Not a sociopath among them, she suspected.

(Although Dr. Shapiro *had* told them that it was more common than you'd think. *A lot of CEOs,* she'd said matter-of-factly.)

Jen sprinted to the baker's stand, grabbed the last two baguettes, and then because the line was brief, and she and Paul deserved it, made her way to the good espresso cart.

Jen decided that she felt relatively calm. They had a plan now, which was good. It was always better to have a plan.

The two women at the front of the line left with their paper cups and waved at Jen: Priya and Janine from book club.

"Those beautiful pumpkins are a slap in the face," Janine said, after the cheek-pressing had been completed. She was referring to the crop of large pumpkins clustered around the gazebo.

"Why?" Jen said.

"Because of the vandal," Priya explained.

"What'd he do now?"

"Pissed all over Pumpkin Walk," Janine said.

Cottonwood had several Halloween celebrations and Pumpkin Walk was, if memory served, the one where everyone put an intricately carved jack-o'-lantern on their stoop.

"Oh dear," Jen said. "Not literally?"

"Metaphorically. As in he went house to house and smashed all of our carved pumpkins."

"Not *all* of them," Priya said.

"Enough of them," Janine said. "We called the police and they don't care. Wouldn't you think they would?" She eyed the baguettes under Jen's arm. "Is that from Glenwood Bakers? Did you happen to notice if there're any left?"

"These were the last."

The way Janine's face crumpled disturbed Jen as much as anything had this morning: the woman always seemed so impervious.

Jen handed her a loaf.

"You," Janine said, "are the absolute nicest. Is Foothills off too on Monday? Because we're all getting together at my house to make caramel apples. You and Abe should come."

Own it, Jen.

"Abe isn't at Foothills anymore."

"Why?"

Just a little conduct disorder.

"He's an anxious kid," Jen said. "It wasn't a good fit."

"Katie gets anxious too," Janine said. "She's a perfectionist. We've been really happy with Sacred Heart. Small and cozy. You should check it out."

"Do you guys know anything about the Kingdom School?"

"Nan and Wes's school?" Priya said.

"Nan Smalls, yes. Is it very religious?"

"I'd assume. They left my church because it was too loosey-goosey," Priya said. "Nan is amazingly compassionate."

"Does she live in Cottonwood? I was trying to figure out where I've heard her name."

"She lives closer to town." Priya grimaced. "And you've probably heard about her son."

Yes, that was it. Last year, Jen had sat down on one of the benches by the gazebo and noticed the gold plaque—IN MEMORY OF DANNY SMALLS, OUR ETERNAL ANGEL.

Who would have calculated his heartbreakingly short life span? Jen had found an article online about a memorial 5K in honor of Danny Smalls, drowned, age four, in a swimming pool. There had been a photo of an adorable chubby-cheeked boy.

Jen hated to use someone else's tragedy for perspective, but sometimes it worked that way, as a reminder that it could always be so much worse.

CHAPTER NINE

The cancer memoir was divisive from the start. Most declared it to be the world's greatest love story, but a small and extremely vocal cadre dismissed it as treacly garbage.

Jen Chun-Pagano led the Treacly Garbage group, whose main complaint was that the wife didn't seem like a real person.

But she is a real person, insisted the Greatest Love Story contingent. It's a memoir.

"What pediatrician do you know who rides a motorcycle," Priya said, "and swigs absinthe straight from the bottle? She's a *fantasy*."

Jen pumped her arms. *Yes! Exactly,* and Janine scolded them both for picking apart a man's memories of his dead wife, because some things should be sacred, and yes, the author had gotten remarried suspiciously quickly after his wife's death, but who was the Cottonwood Book Club to tell him how to grieve?

"Is it me or is everyone a little intense tonight?" Annie asked Deb Gallegos under her breath.

"Maybe it's the absinthe."

"I thought absinthe was illegal?"

"Not the domestic stuff. You can order it online."

"It just didn't seem real to me."

"The absinthe?"

"No. The marriage. I don't know any couple that *adoring*," Annie said.

"Really? Not Mike?" Deb said hopefully. "He seems like he'd be so attentive in bed. He's not afraid to *emote*. And those biceps. He could probably support you in any—"

"Ugh. Deb."

Deb winked exaggeratedly and fanned her hand in front of her face.

The way the women drooled over Mike was objectifying and inappropriate and felt disrespectful to Annie. She'd complained about it to him, pointed out that they certainly didn't talk that way about any of the older husbands.

Mike had seemed confident that it had less to do with age or profession than his undeniable sex appeal. He was probably right, even if sex was way down on Annie's list these days, usually after grocery shopping.

It was that way for everyone, she suspected. It had to be: Deb Gallegos's whole act about how the kids were always walking in on her and Salvador was a pile of baloney. Or at least an exaggeration.

"Where do they think they're going?" Annie pointed out the front window at Sierra and Laurel, who were supposed to be studying together in Sierra's room, but were instead, for some reason, walking down the driveway to the street, purses slung over their shoulders.

Deb and Annie exchanged a bemused look.

Deb knocked twice on the window, and with a crook of her index finger, beckoned them inside.

"Can we go to the mall?" Sierra said, once the girls were back in the entryway. Laurel could barely make eye contact with Annie.

"Nice of you to ask now," Deb said with a snort, "after you've left."

"I sent you a text," Sierra said. "We just didn't want to bother you."

"You can't just skip off shopping," Annie said, incredulous. "Without permission."

Laurel shifted her weight from one foot to the other, chewed a cuticle, obviously chagrined.

"Aren't you supposed to be doing that project on, um—?" Annie looked at Deb.

"Mesopotamian trade," Deb said.

"We finished," Laurel said. "Haley's mom can pick us up at the Cottonwood sign in fifteen minutes, and drive us home."

"It's a school night, though," Annie said.

"We really need a break," Laurel said. Her voice squeaked as she said it and Sierra nodded wide-eyed.

"We really, really do."

Annie and Deb locked eyes for a silent conversation.

"Home by eight thirty," Annie said.

The girls nodded and opened the door, darted out before minds were changed.

"Wait," Annie shouted after them, "don't you need money?"

They skipped down the hill, heads together, giggling.

What was that quote about a little rebellion being a good thing? Maybe Annie should be happy.

"Is school more intense this year?" she asked Deb.

Last week, Beth the librarian had stopped by Annie's small office, a comically high stack of science textbooks in her arms. "Laurel's interlibrary loans came in," she said. At home, Laurel had accepted the books with a terse nod.

"Seems the same as always," Deb said. "But if Laurel thinks it's too intense it probably is."

"You know the part," Janine's slurred voice broke through from the other side of the room, "the part, where they're tangled in the sheets and the way he touched her, the way he *touched* her."

Drawn back into her living room, Deb sighed again. "The love-making *was* beautiful."

Annie could feel the sick swirling in the back of her throat.

"I have an announcement." She rapped her fist on the doorframe until everyone turned around. "Lena Meeker is coming to book club next month."

There was a shocked silence, followed by hushed murmurs between the women.

"I've seen her car," Janine was saying. "But I've never actually met her."

"That's a lovely gesture." Harriet Nessel nodded her approval in Annie's direction. "Inviting Lena."

"I'm so glad she didn't come tonight," Priya said. "Can you imagine if she had to read this month's book? An ode to a beloved dead partner?"

Harriet Nessel shifted on the sofa. Next to her, Priya pounced.

"What's that face, Harriet?"

"I didn't make a face."

"You did. You guys saw it, right?"

Harriet pursed her lips, which emphasized the vertical lines under her nose. "It's not really my place."

"Spill the tea."

Harriet's palms skimmed over her legal pad.

"I have no idea what she thinks of him now," she said finally, "but even before Tim killed that young man, I'm not so sure it was paradise at the Meekers' house."

FIFTEEN YEARS EARLIER

Lena didn't care about the girls. Her attitude toward Tim's affairs had evolved through the years. What started out tender had callused.

She cared about the scene he was making at her party, though.

He was at the far end of the lawn, by the lilac bushes, broadcasting in a drunken foghorn voice to an audience of twenty-somethings that the beaches in Mauritius were otherworldly.

Oh, Tim, you urbane sophisticate, you.

Lena tried to figure out which young woman he was trying to impress. The well-endowed blonde, probably.

"The opposite of you," Mel had once pointed out helpfully, after Lena had described Tim's type.

Thankfully, Rachel appeared oblivious. She was distracted by something tonight. Lena suspected a crush on Jett the rented bartender, who was stringy-haired and too-cool.

Rachel had beamed when he'd showed up, and declared herself his assistant. Just a second ago, Lena had overheard Rachel telling Jett a made-up a story about partying with friends. A familiar note of worry had vibrated in Lena's stomach: Was Rachel still that desperate to impress?

Tomorrow, Lena would have a talk with Rachel about dissembling, but tonight, Jett was a harmless distraction. He was visibly disinterested in Rachel, which left Lena free to spend time with Gary Neary.

Someone in Tim's group shattered a glass on the ground. *Incoming!* There were shrieks of laughter.

Lena looked again to Rachel, who had propped her chin on her fists to watch Jett sloppily pour a vodka tonic.

Yes, tomorrow she and Rachel would have a nice long talk.

"I should probably clean up the broken glass," Lena said to Gary Neary, who had returned with two mojitos.

"Not your job." He handed a glass to Lena. "Have you seen my son? He's supposed to swing by to meet you."

"I'd love that," Lena said.

As a technical matter, Lena already knew Gary's son, just as she'd known Gary: for years, just another person in their small town.

But everything felt different now.

A few weeks earlier, when his divorce settlement had finalized, Gary had moved to Cottonwood Estates, into the small gray cape on Wildcat Court. Lena had whipped up a batch of raspberry-mocha brownies and knocked on Gary's door, because this was the type of neighborly gesture that was reflexive to her, and also because she wanted to talk to as many divorced people as she possibly could.

She had long fantasized about divorcing Tim but had always felt trapped. Alma didn't believe in quitting a marriage, and Rachel was generally horrible with change.

After Alma died, when Rachel entered high school, Lena realized that she no longer had to shield her so protectively. They had been curled up in Lena's bed one night, watching the *Pride and Prejudice* miniseries, when they'd heard Tim's sloppy footsteps down the hall. He'd stopped, one hand on the wall in the bedroom doorway.

"Alma's girls," he said. He was smiling and Lena registered the expression on Rachel's face: hopeful, surprised.

"You both got her jowls," he said, with a helpful swipe under his chin. "Alma's masculine jowls. Such a Mack truck of a lady."

Rachel's skin had flushed but she'd held her head high.

"Just think," she'd said, her voice wavering the tiniest bit, "if it weren't for Uncle Ernie, *that* would be my male role model."

She'd turned the volume up so loud that Tim had walked away.

Tim wouldn't leave as easily as that, Lena knew, but at the insistence of her family lawyer, he'd signed a prenup, and she was starting to feel strong enough for a fight. By the time Gary Neary moved into the neighborhood, Lena had already scheduled a few appointments with divorce lawyers and had started to taste her freedom.

Pace yourself, Lena thought as she waited on Gary's front step, brownie pan in hand. Don't bring up his divorce right away, no matter how inappropriately on fire you are about the topic.

When he opened the front door, something about the twinkle in his hazel eyes rendered her momentarily speechless.

Zing.

He had felt it, too.

Gary Neary, tall and rangy with bushy gray hair, was not half as handsome as Tim. He had an angular face and comically deep crow's-feet and a large nose, and giant, outsized grapefruit calves from all the cycling he did. Beauty was symmetry, they said, and Gary Neary's face might have been the least symmetrical Lena had ever seen.

But he had listened to her with his whole body, which Lena had never experienced before. It felt like being struck by lightning.

In the weeks before tonight's party, Gary had been Lena's savored secret. Even though Lena freely complained to Melanie about Tim, she had kept quiet about Gary. It was too new, too first-blush. She had been happy to wait for it to unfold like fate.

For a few more hours, Lena would honestly believe that life made sense in its own funny way, that its primary lessons were about perseverance and patience. Because she had suffered through a bad marriage and learned she deserved more, Lena had earned True Love.

By the next day, she would understand that this line of thinking was mythology—trying to see the narrative in a series of thoroughly meaningless acts.

It *had* been real with Gary, though. After the accident, even with everything else she had to grieve, Lena's heart still made space to mourn him. But just because something was real, just because you might deserve it, didn't mean you got it.

Every time she thought of telling Melanie what had almost transpired, Lena would imagine the silence on the other end of the phone.

Gary Neary and *you*? It defied belief.

And what was there to even divulge?

It had been nothing: a few weeks flirtation, and then one night of distraction, which had caused Lena to take her eyes off the ball completely.

It had been everything.

There was a parallel universe where Lena and Gary had a condo on a West Coast beach, and went for long sunset walks and hosted slightly awkward blended-family dinners. Sometimes, in the moments before sleep, Lena allowed herself to visit.

In the real world, Gary Neary was gone. And even if some magician were to bend the rules of time and space and deliver him to her, Lena was certain that Gary would take one look at Lena and run as fast as he could in the opposite direction.

CHAPTER TEN

"Please don't make me go in," Abe said.

He slouched in the passenger seat of Jen's car and flicked his finger to close the air vents before flicking them open again.

In front of them was the Kingdom School, a double-wide trailer with peeling white paint, located one mile down an unpaved road. The bright sunlight exposed the scragginess of the lot—the half-bare trees, the patchy brown grass. Across the street were a rusted tractor and a fenced-in trio of malnourished horses swooshing their tails.

Even with their car windows rolled up, Jen could smell manure.

"Think of all the points you'll earn if you try it for the day," Jen said. She watched conflict play across Abe's face. Dr. Shapiro's bribe offensive had been almost too easy to implement.

Abe had created a shared spreadsheet and in the past week had enthusiastically taken out the recycling and the trash and neatened his room. The monitor would be his by summer, he'd promised.

"Ugh," Abe said. He flicked closed the vents. Flicked open the vents. "Why can't I just homeschool?"

"Ms. Smalls, the principal, is supposed to be wonderful."

Although when Jen had talked to her, she had sounded vacant, maybe not all there.

Prior to the call, Jen and Paul had discussed how best to explain Abe's conduct disorder diagnosis to Nan Smalls in a way that didn't scare Nan, but provided sufficient notice of what she was getting into.

But Jen had never gotten the chance. During their phone call, Nan Smalls only wanted to talk about Faith—her Faith in the children and the children's Faith in the teachers and the teachers' Faith in Nan. The Kingdom School, Nan seemed to want Jen to know, was one giant inescapable circle of Faith.

Whenever Jen tried to interject, there had been painful pauses, into which both of them would speak at once, and then Nan would say, "After you," and Jen would say, "No, please, after you."

"Well," Nan had said finally, "he's free to spend the day and we'll take it from there."

"You're dropping me into a horror movie," Abe said. He flicked the vents quicker: open, close, open, close.

Jen saw his point. On the lawn was a hand-painted off-kilter sign, THE KINGDOM SCHOOL: TAKING TRUTH FROM SCRIPTURE. It was begging for a chilling breeze in which to creak ominously.

But back in the Bay Area, they had looked at gorgeous schools with landscaped campuses and endowments and state-of-the-art libraries and mission statements that separated church and state.

Abe hadn't been a fit there. Or anywhere else.

This was their reality: sitting in the car outside the Kingdom School with whispered prayers of Faith.

A beaten-up blue sedan pulled into the spot next to them. The banjo strains of bluegrass streamed out the open windows. Jen bobbed her head along to it, but Abe didn't even crack a smile.

A young man with a chin-length bob and a bandana headband hopped out of the car and, whistling, went around to the trunk.

"Does he go here?" Abe said.

"Maybe?"

They watched him hoist a guitar case from the trunk, loop it over his shoulder.

"Is he wearing eye makeup?" Abe said in a low voice. He slunk down even further in his seat. "He saw us. *He saw us.*"

Indeed, the young man, who did seem to be wearing eyeliner,

was waving at them through the windshield. Jen zipped down her window.

"Morning," he said. "I'm Colin."

"Hi," Jen said in a bright phony voice. "This is Abe. He's visiting today."

"Awesome," Colin said.

Abe scowled. Flicked the vent.

Colin pointed to the graphic novel on Abe's lap. "What's that?"

"Gothracula."

"Never heard of it."

Abe looked skeptical. "Seriously?"

"Cross my heart. What is it?"

"The best vampire fantasy battle series in the world. There are, like, seven books. You've really never heard of them?"

"Nope."

"I'm going to turn the books into a ten-level video game," Abe said. "Like Foxhole. You know Foxhole?"

"No," Colin said. "But maybe you can show me sometime?"

"Are you a student?" Abe asked suspiciously.

"In graduate school. I'm a new assistant teacher here. I like it."

"It's creepy," Abe said. "It looks like a horror movie."

Colin considered the outside of the double-wide as if seeing it for the first time. "It totally does. There's nothing scary inside, though. I promise. You know we do customized curriculums, like that video game could be part of your homework."

"Video games as a class," Abe said suspiciously. "Is there a decent Wi-Fi connection?"

"Come check it out."

Before Jen had gotten out of the car, Abe was following Colin up the steps.

"I'll get Nan," Colin promised Jen, as he opened the door. "Abe, follow me, there might be snacks in the back if you're hungry. Emma, she's the other teaching assistant, usually bakes something over the weekend."

Inside, the schoolroom looked small and spare: a few desks,

a small kitchenette, mostly bare-walled but for a world map taped to the wall and some quotations stenciled in a flowery cursive.

I will instruct you and teach you
in the way you should go; I will counsel you
with my eye upon you. Psalm 32:8.

"Jen?"

Jen looked up from reading and was face-to-face with a tiny woman, swaddled in a gigantic olive cardigan. She had short bushy gray hair, vampiric pallor, and stern brown eyes.

Colin hovered closely behind her, like a cautious grandson who'd been tasked to watch that grandma didn't fall and rebreak her hip.

"Hello," the woman said. "I'm Nan."

Their handshake felt dry and delicate, like a tight squeeze from Jen might break Nan's thin bones.

"Abe made himself at home," Colin said with a half laugh. "He's back there trying to boost the internet connection."

"Computers are his passion," Jen said.

"Nice."

Jen broke the awkward silence. "Nan, is there any more information you need from us?"

Medical records, Dr. Shapiro's report, transcript from Foothills? Anything?

"No," Nan said. "Let's just see how he feels being here."

Jen decided that if Nan wasn't going to ask, she had no obligation to share Abe's diagnosis, at least not at this early stage. First, give them a chance to get to know *Abe,* minus any labels. After all, Jen still hadn't decided if the diagnosis truly fit.

Nan nodded solemnly. "'My God is my rock, in whom I take refuge, my shield and the horn of my salvation.'"

It was just unexpected enough that Jen panicked. She looked

desperately at the ceiling, then the floor, then Colin. It was almost indiscernible, his teensy nostril flare, the way he widened his eyes at Jen as if to say, *Better get used to it*.

What stopped Jen from a torrent of giggles was the sobering realization that she was leaving her son under the responsibility of a woman who seemed—all due respect—not entirely there.

"Don't worry," Colin said, as if reading Jen's mind. "We'll take excellent care of Abe, I promise."

To: "The Best Book Club in the World"
From: proudmamabooklover3@hmail.com

The book: This month's pick, THE GIRL IN THE WOODS, promises to be quite controversial!*

When Fiona wakes up to find herself in a remote alpine forest with no idea how she got there, can she piece together what happened in time to save her son? And is it just a coincidence that her ex-husband has recently bought a log cabin in the very same remote woods where she is found?

Reviews have called it "a taut psychological thriller" and "the literary page turner of the year!"

The place: Our lovely Jen Chun-Pagano is saving our bacon by hosting this one last minute (mwah, mwah Jen!!!! Forever grateful!) and she has asked for a start time of **seven o'clock sharp.**

PSA: The Thankfulness Turkey is looking a little bare!!! Please, everyone, remember to take your kiddos to tape on their "Thankfulness Feathers"!!!!!! (Red, yellow, or orange construction paper only, please and black markers work the best. You can't miss it— It's the Giant Wooden Turkey right by the Cottonwood Welcome Sign!)

Katie will be selling BRACELETS at FALL FEST to raise money for her MOCK TRIAL TEAM'S trip to SUNNY CALIFORNIA! WE APPRECIATE ALL OF YOUR SUPPORT!

And speaking of THANKFULNESS, as always, I remain thankful for YOU, my wonderful book club family! xoxoxoxoxo

*True story: two members of my sister-in-law's book club almost came to blows when they discussed this!

Although my SIL swears the tensions had been brewing before

And I know from firsthand observation that they are not as refined as are we, the classy ladies of Cottonwood ☺☺☺

CHAPTER ELEVEN

Annie used her fingernail to scrape off the last stubborn spot of marinara sauce caked onto the lasagna pan. She set it on the drying rack.

The house was so quiet.

It was only seven thirty on Friday night. Mike was at work. Laurel was sleeping at Sierra's house, and Hank had just gone to bed to be well-rested for his Fall Fest performance.

Annie stretched out on the couch and picked up the book club book. She couldn't get into this one, had spent ten minutes rereading a single paragraph describing the gnarled tree branches in the deep dark forest. When her phone binged, she eagerly grabbed it from the side table.

A social media post from Janine.

> *PSAT prep:* ✔
> *Fall Fest set up:* ✔
> *Time to curl up with a good book and a cuppa, ladies!*
> *#livingthedream #momentofcalm #bookclubmama!*

PSAT prep?

Even though she was alone in the room, Annie shook her head. Katie was in middle school.

Childhood should be preserved, Annie always counseled parents, don't tangle up your ambitions in their futures. Laurel was at the top of her class, but working hard, Annie had always believed, was an honest expression of Laurel's identity.

Last week, though, Laurel had failed to turn in an English paper.

Annie only learned about it when Laurel's teacher referenced it in the teachers' lounge. He'd assumed it was a mistake. Questioned about it by Annie, however, Laurel had shrugged.

I'll take the fail, she'd said.

With great self-control, Annie had managed not to spout clichés at Laurel, but they'd been right there on her twitchy lips: *you're not seeing the big picture, ninth grade is right around the corner and it COUNTS, these are the mistakes that IMPACT YOUR FUTURE.*

And, ugh, the feelings that churned inside Annie for the rest of the night: disappointment and frustration bordering on hysteria. The sinking pit-in-her-stomach certainty that Laurel was perhaps like Annie after all.

Annie picked up the book again. Deb called this kind of novel dingbat lit.

The main character Fiona was so hysterical that she could barely make a pot of coffee without fainting. When she suspected someone of being a murderer, did she call the police?

No, Fiona went alone to visit the murder suspect, and Annie hated herself for caring when Fiona wound up chloroformed and bound in the trunk of a car. What did you expect, Fiona?

These are the mistakes that impact your future.

Some of Laurel's recent decisions would fit well in a dingbat-lit novel.

Skipping off to the mall without telling a parent, her surly *I'll take the fail.* And she had started to dress like Sierra. Teeny miniskirts. Caked-on eye makeup.

Well, that was a little dramatic. Laurel had worn that outfit once.

Fiona, Annie reminded herself, was a fictional character. Laurel was nothing like Fiona: she was smart, much smarter than Annie ever had been.

Well—Laurel was book smart, which didn't mean she hadn't inherited a self-destructive streak.

That was the flip side of Cottonwood: these kids were adored, but they were coddled house cats. For all of Annie's complaints about the benign neglect of her own childhood, at least she'd had freedom to learn by trial and error.

Annie was so grateful to hear Hank's footsteps in the hall that she didn't even tell him to get back to bed.

"What's up?"

"I'm too excited to sleep."

The second graders always performed a few song-and-dance numbers at Fall Fest, and Hank and his classmates had been practicing since September.

He spread his arms wide. "I have the whole room to myself. I don't really miss Laurel. At all."

"I won't tell her."

"She can't try to lock me out, and before bed, she won't play that stupid song fifteen million times and she won't wake me up at two in the morning either."

"Laurel wakes you up at two in the morning?"

"She turns on her bed lamp and types all night."

"What is she typing?"

"She said it was research."

"Homework?"

Hank shrugged. He had a well-earned reputation for hyperbole. Laurel had probably woken him up once at ten. Nonetheless, the Perleys' one big rule was: no screens in the bedroom.

"Want another tuck-in?" Annie asked.

"Okay," Hank said agreeably.

She followed him into the bedroom, smoothed the covers over him with one gentle yank. Annie felt a tug of guilt about how small the room was.

Maybe Laurel's recent prickliness was about lack of privacy. Annie had always told herself that Cottonwood Estates was worth any sacrifice in space. But an almost fourteen-year-old having to share to share a bunk bed with her seven-year-old brother wasn't ideal.

"Did you invite Mrs. Meeker to Fall Fest?" Hank asked. "She's really excited about my dance."

Too crowded, Lena had said to Annie, and her eyes had begged for the conversation to end. "She can't make it," Annie said, "but we'll send pictures."

"She told me she's going to buy me a skateboard."

Annie sighed. "You have to stop asking her for things, Hank."

"She said it makes her happy."

"Even so." Lena and her brother Ernie had done enough for the Perleys. Due entirely to Ernie's connections and word of mouth, Mike's restaurant was booked through next month. *There's definite buzz,* Mike had said, *buzz buzz buzz.* Hank had pretended to be a bee for the entire rest of the night.

"At least try to limit your requests," she said.

"I'll try," Hank said, in a tone of voice that made clear he couldn't promise anything. "Night."

"Night."

Annie flicked off the light and, on her way out of the room, lifted the grab handle of Laurel's backpack, which had been left by the door.

An eighth grader a few years back had—unbeknownst to her parents or therapist until the girl fainted in world history—spent hours each day studying evil websites that glamorized anorexia: how to abuse laxatives and count calories and binge and purge. She'd missed the entire rest of the school year. It always struck Annie how entirely clueless the parents had been.

The friends had known, though. The friends always knew.

But Laurel didn't have an eating disorder. Her appetite, larger than even Mike's, was a running family joke. Last night, she'd downed three helpings of lasagna with a huge side of salad and then belched healthily, because she'd known it would make Hank laugh until he fell off his chair.

Unless it was disordered to eat so much? Had they drawn too much attention to her big appetite, made it a *thing*?

That swirling anxious feeling Annie had while reading about Fiona was because she knew something was off with Laurel. She just didn't know what.

Laurel did seem self-conscious in her body, at least compared to Sierra. When she'd worn the miniskirt, she'd hunched over, tugged down the skirt.

And when Annie had asked Laurel what flavor cake she wanted for her birthday in a few weeks, Laurel had claimed to not need a cake at all.

Most teenage girls were uncomfortable in their bodies, though, and maybe Laurel was experimenting, trying to shed childhood traditions in favor of more grown-up ones.

None of it meant that Laurel had an eating disorder.

Annie shouldn't make up issues. Laurel enjoyed food, she wasn't obsessed by it.

(Which is probably exactly what the family of the girl who had been hospitalized had thought.)

The computer part—the late-night typing—was troubling. And what did *research* mean anyway? There were any number of horrible places on the World Wide Web where a teenaged girl might conduct "research."

Annie had just seen a news report about a police officer who'd made a fake profile for a fourteen-year-old girl. Within hours, literally hundreds of creepy older men had contacted her.

Laurel knew all of the stranger-danger rules, had sat through a billion school assemblies about internet safety and Annie had drilled them in at home, of course—but what did every parent say after their child had emptied her piggy bank to run off to some motel room with a total stranger?

If this happened to us, it could happen to ANYONE.

But it didn't happen to anyone. It happened to kids with distracted parents. Kids without boundaries. Kids who had a hole of need inside of them.

A memory broke free from deep inside of Annie, floated up to consciousness.

His cold hand pressed against her bare knee. A mocking peal of laughter slipped through the open window from outside.

In a frantic swoop, she zipped open Laurel's backpack and shook out its contents on the couch, fired up her computer, typed in the password—the family rule was that passwords were shared, and even though now Annie wanted to congratulate herself for sticking to that rule, she didn't deserve any praise.

Why had she not checked over Laurel's shoulder?

Parents were instructed to make clear to their children: this is *my* computer, not yours, but Annie and Mike believed that their children deserved privacy, which was a form of respect, and Laurel was a good kid and—see? Look.

Her online search history seemed innocent and appropriate: Wikipedia. Science journals and how-to videos about makeup application and bleaching her hair to better hold dye. Her school notebooks still told the story of an engaged student: equations and paragraphs about Greek mythology and a complicated table with rows and columns of letters: A, A, AB.

Cryptology? Some sort of Boolean language?

Now that Annie could see all of Laurel's homework—the books and the notebooks and that chart spread over the couch—she had to agree it was a lot.

The leftover lasagna was a brick in her stomach. Annie turned on the kettle for mint tea.

Laurel was almost fourteen. It was normal to be moody with her family. She had solid friendships, and had failed to turn in one assignment. There was no eating disorder, nor any evidence of a lurking predator.

Scurry off, chickens. Nowhere to roost here!

The whistle on the kettle blew and Annie switched off the stove, reached for a chamomile bag instead of mint to better ease the acidic burn that had risen in the back of her mouth.

But even after she sipped it, the sour taste in the back of her mouth grew thicker.

CHAPTER TWELVE

"Fall Fest." Melanie's voice through the phone was raspy from a cold. "I'll never forget Fall Fest because that's where we saw the Nearys. The mom and son, remember?"

Lena closed her eyes.

She regretted how she'd presented Annie's invitation to Melanie like a little gift. *My new friend Annie wants me to go to Fall Fest.*

The subtext was that Melanie didn't need to worry so much about Lena's loneliness because, see? Lena had been invited to something!

(Maybe Lena had also been showing off. Hearing about Melanie's social calendar—her golf dates and cocktail and girls' lunches and couples' cruises—gave Lena a hollow left-out feeling.)

"You can't remember?" Melanie sounded worried. "It's happening to me too. I couldn't think of my second-grade teacher's name last week. I loved her so much, I wanted to be her when I grew up, and it's just—poof—gone."

"It's okay, Mel."

"Let me help. Bill had a conference downtown, so I came to stay with you, and Rachel was three or four. We got to the park early, before all the events started and there they were, the Nearys. The boy had golden hair cut in bangs and a bob, like Little Lord Fauntleroy. It seared into my mind because you don't see that haircut every day."

Lena wished she remembered the haircut. She had a different memory of the boy seared into her mind.

"Remember," Melanie continued, "that Rachel was obsessed with clamming, because of that book you read her every night, you know, *Goodnight Sam the Clam* or whatever it was called?"

"I remember the book."

"And she insisted on bringing this little red bucket to the riverbank to fill with clams, which were really rocks. The boy thought she was hilarious. His mom said something like, *creativity in motion* and then complimented you for nurturing it. It was sweet but a little woo-woo, you know. You and I managed to keep a straight face, but when she left, excuse me, sneezing—"

For a brief and merciful moment, Melanie stopped talking.

"Where do unsneezed sneezes go? Anyway—you told me she was one of those magical supermoms, who sewed her own clothing and baked bread and probably made daisy crowns instead of turning on the TV. Meanwhile, you'd just screamed at Rachel for tracking in mud on the white carpet, and oops, excuse me, sneezing—"

Melanie sneezed, neat and tidy, three times in succession. "Ugh, this cold."

"Bless you. I told you all that?"

"You tell me everything, sweetie."

No, I don't.

Once, Lena had believed Melanie to be the type of friend to accept deep dark secrets without judgment, but back then, Lena's secrets hadn't been particularly dark or deep. There had been moments when Lena had felt a pull to come clean to Mel, but it had never been worth the risk of losing her.

"Do you remember it now?" Melanie said. "I *hate* that feeling, one black hole where there used to be knowledge. It's irrevocable proof that it's all downhill from here, baby."

Lena did remember how, for Fall Fest, she and Rachel would wake up early and get a box of éclairs from the French pastry place on Main Street. They set up chairs and a blanket on the banks of the river, a safe space away from the gazebo because when Rachel was little, crowds made her tense.

And she could never forget the clamming phase.

"Only child," Lena would explain with a laugh, but Rachel really had been exceptionally creative, before Lena messed with her head—or maybe all parents thought their children were creative.

Probably all children *were* creative.

Lena certainly remembered Gary Neary's not-yet-ex-wife and son: how they had the same compact peppiness, the way they always seemed delighted with each other.

She even remembered thinking Gary's wife gorgeous, not because of her features, which were a little too pointy, but because of her vitality—that outdoorsy glow and sparkling eyes and her obvious unabashed love for her son. Lena had once bought a ridiculous pair of patterned tights after seeing Gary's ex look adorable in a similar pair. (A look, it turned out, that Lena could not pull off. The tights had worn Lena, not the other way around.)

Lena wanted to ask Melanie if she'd mentioned Gary at that Fall Fest. Back then, she had only been vaguely aware of him as a dry and craggy local dentist. Once, when Dr. Marconis was out on maternity leave, Gary Neary had subbed in, put his gentle gloved hands right in Lena's mouth. Gary remembered that, too; they laughed about it.

When Lena had taken the time to think about the Nearys' marriage, she had incorrectly thought that they must complement each other in the way a steady rock would ground a free spirit, that their family dinners were full of song and laughter and that on summer evenings they all went outside to make fairy traps out of dewy spiderwebs, play in the sprinklers, make those daisy-chain crowns.

Nope, Gary said later. The marriage was never horrible, but even the divorce had been more plodding than fiery. When Lena painted the picture of his ex as a free-spirit earth-mother pioneer, Gary had replied that whatever personality Lena had dreamed up, it was nothing like the woman he'd been married to.

Still, there had at one point been love between Gary and his ex. The bonds of family certainly had been stronger than Gary made it sound—Lena had observed that by the way they had leaned against each other at the funeral, bound forever by a joint grief no one else could understand.

"Games are supposed to help with memory loss," Melanie said. "Crosswords and anagrams. We should start doing them."

"Maybe."

"Are you okay, Lena?" Melanie's voice was tentative. "I was being an idiot, wasn't I, prattling on about poor little Brian. I should've stopped myself."

Even if she had amnesia, Lena would never forget his name.

"It was Bryce," she whispered. "Bryce Neary."

"Wait," Jen said. "Abe *wants* to go to Fall Fest?"

"The whole gang is going," Colin said. "It's supposed to be great."

Gang? There was a gang?

Jen and Abe had been about to start dinner when their doorbell rang.

"That's probably Colin," Abe had said.

"The teacher?" Jen said, but Abe was already at the door and indeed, there, under their portico light, stood Colin from the Kingdom School. He held up a giant book about video game programming.

He had, he explained, promised Abe that he'd look for it in the used book shop right by the music store on Main Street and bring it by if he found it.

"Ten tomorrow, right?" he'd said.

Apparently, the Kingdom School kids had planned to meet up at Fall Fest. The group would find each other on the riverbank. Colin would bring a picnic blanket and some instruments because everyone seemed pretty excited about learning some chords, and he'd heard there was an epic burrito stand.

"You know that Fall Fest will be crowded?" Jen asked Abe. "Crowds and gross porta-potties and children who sing loudly and off-key?"

"It'll be fun, Mom." Abe patted her arm as though *she* were the persnickety one. "Colin, do you like rotisserie chicken? We were just about to eat dinner."

"Abe, it's late," Jen said. "Colin might have already eaten."

"He's always starving." Abe snorted. "He eats my leftovers at school every day. Don't get mad, Mom."

"Why would I get mad?"

"You got upset when Isabella would eat my lunch."

"That was different." Jen felt a low throbbing in her sinuses at the memory. "Isabella was taking advantage." Colin grimaced as if he'd had a bag or two of chips stolen by Isabella, too.

"If you truly have enough food," he said, "I'd love to join you guys."

Jen opened the front door as wide as it went. "Come on in."

The Paganos did not excel at putting things away. The surfaces in their home were crammed with piles of books and cords for electronics and hastily discarded layers of clothing. Jen always told herself that it wasn't dirty, just overstuffed, but seeing it now, through the eyes of a guest, she had to admit that it wasn't exactly clean either.

Someone needed to do a deep clean before Jen hosted book club next week. Melissa Stoller, who had lived here before, had been a regular member of book club, and the entire group appeared to be creepily invested in Jen's house.

Your countertops aren't granite, Janine had once corrected Jen, *they're soapstone. Melissa selected them to be maintenance free.*

Thank goodness, because now, those soapstone counters were littered with half-empty glasses (or half-full depending on the day), dinner takeout from Breadman's, and opened boxes of cookies, because sometimes the cookies were the only thing getting Jen through the day, *and there was nothing wrong with that,* thank you very much.

"We're always a little less formal when Paul is traveling," Jen said by way of apology. She left out that Paul was *always* traveling.

"You have a beautiful home," Colin said with earnest politeness. His affect was Boy Scoutish beneath all the grunge: floppy plaid shirt, faded jeans, the chin-length hair, the cool black nail polish on both pinkies. Again, the kohl line under his eyes.

"Is Mr. Pagano somewhere exciting?"

"California," Abe said with a frown. "I told you that yesterday when we were sitting under the tree outside."

"You did?" Colin said. "You can't blame the rest of us mortals for not having a photographic memory."

"Abe, will you set the table?" Jen heard her voice, a little higher, a touch tentative, and wondered if Colin had noticed.

She wasn't scared of Abe, she *wasn't,* but after thirteen years of treating him with kid gloves, she felt sheepish suddenly demanding he do chores.

"How many points will I earn?" Abe watched Jen with a hawk's sharpness.

"Um. The usual."

If their exchange had been awkward, Colin didn't appear to have noticed. He had drifted over to their banquette to examine the painting above it, which was an abstract triptych, also selected by Melissa Stoller.

The Kingdom School had not yet asked for any medical records or diagnostic history, and Jen had not yet volunteered Abe's diagnosis. Every week, after Abe's therapy session, Dr. Shapiro asked whether she should be in touch with Nan, to provide guidance on Abe's incentives or challenges.

Nope, Jen lied. Nan's on board. She gets it.

Jen would schlep Abe all over town for whatever counseling Dr. Shapiro recommended. She would break down his chores in charts and point values, but still—something was stopping her from sharing the diagnosis.

Dr. Shapiro was smart and kind and wise, but she'd spent maybe five hours with Abe before slapping a label on him. Maybe it was accurate, maybe not, but either way, telling Nan was pointless.

The woman spoke in psalms, and any conversation about conduct disorder would turn into one about lambs or loaves or turning the other cheek or how we were all God's children.

So, no. Jen didn't even feel bad about the omission.

(Maybe she felt a little bad.)

"I love this," Colin said about the abstract triptych.

"Came with the house," Jen said. "It's a mountain." Janine had informed Jen of that, and also that Melissa Stoller had ordered the piece from a SoHo gallery.

"Can I show Colin Foxhole?" Abe said.

"Please," Colin said, "I've heard so much about it and Holla123."

"I'll go summon him," Abe said.

After Abe bounded upstairs, Jen said, "Please let me know if Holla123 turns out to be a creepy fifty-year-old man."

"What?" Colin's face was stricken.

"No, no." Jen sometimes forgot how to act with people who weren't Paul. "It was a joke in very poor taste, mostly about how Paul and I should be a little more careful supervising Abe's online time. Holla123 is a kid from Michigan. Seems sweet enough. So, it's going okay? At school?"

"Abe is a *great* addition."

"He is?"

"Are you surprised?" Colin's brow crinkled. He raked his hair behind his ears.

"I've never seen him so . . ." Jen reached for a word that wouldn't make Abe sound like a total freak. "He's usually not a fan of big group activities like Fall Fest."

"Maybe he's been overwhelmed at other schools? He's a really good fit with Kingdom. It's small, which for a kid like Abe can be much easier to navigate."

"A kid like Abe?"

"Anxious," Colin said. "Shy. Into his passions. I didn't mean to assume anything—"

"No, no," Jen said, "that's Abe."

"Creating a five-level video game from scratch is pretty ambitious, but I have every faith he'll do it."

"I thought it was supposed to be ten-level."

Colin grinned. "We're in negotiations."

"I bumped into Nan the other day," Jen said, "and she quoted a psalm that I think was about patience? I worried it meant he wasn't fitting in."

Colin bit his lip. "Nan is amazing, but sometimes . . . I don't know . . . the psalms are a little—"

"Vague," Jen said diplomatically. Inside, she was screaming, *Yes, exactly!*

"Abe is doing fine. I was like him when I was younger—you know, other kids didn't know what to do with me—and I would have thrived at a place like Kingdom."

"Abe might have something called conduct disorder," Jen said. "We're still figuring it out."

"What's that?"

"He has to work a little harder than others to learn empathy and consequences."

"Oh." Colin shrugged. "Doesn't that describe like half of the people in the world?"

"It might." Jen smiled.

"I don't mean to make light. People are complicated, though." Colin swallowed roughly and forced a smile, but it was wistful. "And folks sure do love their labels."

"Don't they just," Jen said.

CHAPTER THIRTEEN

The weather for Fall Fest was aggressively perfect: sunny with a razor of chill in the air. Annie and the other second-grade parents were clustered in front of the gazebo for the best views of their children, who were being ushered up the steps by their teacher, Mrs. Jalonski.

Hank waved at Annie and she waved back.

"Annie, Hank's bow tie is *adorable*."

"Where did you all find such bright green pants? Seriously, all I could find for Finn was that drab olive, poor guy."

"Finn looks great," Annie said with a half glance toward the stage. She scanned the crowd for Laurel and her friends. "All of them do."

Mrs. Jalonski approached the microphone, tapped it once officiously, and delivered the annual warning about how all applause must wait until after the *entire* performance.

"*I love you*, Fall Fest," a lone voice shrieked from over by the river. "Woo-hoo!"

Light laughter rippled through the crowd. Someone whooped. The two square speakers in the gazebo's corners crackled and, as if they were zombies controlled by a hive mind, the second-grade parents lifted their phones and pointed their cameras at the stage.

The background music blared through the town square.

Form the corn, form, form the corn.

The moves were pretty simple—jazz hands extended overhead, kick ball change, turn to the side, repeat. Hank was better than a lot of his classmates, Annie noticed with a surprised pride. One of Mike's sisters had majored in dance in college, and Annie made a mental note to send her the video, ask if Hank was as good as she suspected.

"Dying," one of the parents said. "I'm dying."

"'Form the corn,' though?" someone whispered. "Are they teaching them science?"

"More to the point: Are our children glorifying GMOs?"

"Shhh."

Annie snapped a photo and sent it off to Lena and looked around again for Laurel, who really should be here by now.

People applauded as the song ended, then stopped abruptly as they remembered that clapping was forbidden.

An exuberant voice broke through the quiet.

"Live from Fall Fest, the FALL FEST DANCERS. WOO-HOOOOO! WORK IT, Fall Fest dancers! Give us some MORE!"

A murmur surfed through the crowd. Heads craned toward the noise.

"YAAASSS. Shake it, shake it, SHAKE IT, FALL FEST DANC-ING DANCERS!"

"Yikes," Finn's mom said. She arched an eyebrow at Annie, who was too stunned to respond.

She knew that voice.

Laurel was on the bank of the river with one hand cupped around her mouth. In her other hand was her pink water bottle, held overhead like a pom-pom. Behind her, her friends were dou-bled over in laughter.

The second-grade parents had lifted their cell phones toward the gazebo, where their children were rearranging themselves in a large imperfect circle for the next number.

Annie's gaze was pinned to whatever the hell was happening on the riverbank.

Sierra was attempting to contain Laurel in a clumsy hug as Laurel wriggled in protest. She broke free, shook her arms overhead in a victorious V, and her T-shirt rode up to expose her belly button.

Sierra tried again, and they toppled in a tangled heap on a family's picnic blanket. Plates spilled, the parents jumped up, and as Sierra started to help clean up the mess, Laurel crawled on her hands and knees toward their toddler, then rose on her hind legs, hands clawed like a grizzly bear. The child's mouth opened in a wail as the crowd began to cheer for the second graders, who were taking their final bows.

Annie glanced guiltily at the stage before looking back toward Laurel, who kneeled in the center of the plaid picnic blanket. She swigged from her pink water bottle, wiped her mouth with her sleeve.

There was a cold pit of comprehension in Annie's stomach. Laurel was *drunk*.

The text that Annie had sent to Lena showed Hank in the town's gazebo in the throes of a dance step, his knees bent inward awkwardly. It wasn't fair to blame Annie for sending the picture. She thought she was being nice.

Which didn't mean Lena wanted the thing.

The oven timer buzzed. Lena should check on the cupcakes, but she ignored them. She pressed delete and watched the gazebo and Hank's knees and the slice of river and the crowds of people gathered for Fall Fest swirl together and swoosh into the trash.

Very satisfying.

This was the problem with new friends: they might breezily send pictures of off-limits places, unaware that there were rules to be followed.

No main street, no town green, no high school, no riverbanks. Places are tricky, Annie. Memories barnacle to them.

This was the problem with old friends, too. That one conversation with Melanie about Fall Fest had been a signal whistle to long-buried memories: emerge and attack!

Like the year when Rachel was in middle school and Tim, for some reason, had decided to crash their mother-daughter tradition and tag along to Fall Fest.

He had acted like a bratty child, sulked when Rachel wanted to hang out with her friends and insisted that they make a leaf pile like they had when she was little. Rachel had played along dutifully, watching patiently as he fell dramatically backward into the pile with a too-loud laugh. He stayed there for a long moment, playing dead.

Middle school was difficult enough and the last thing Rachel needed was to worry about placating her embarrassing dad. Lena recalled being furious, wishing that Tim wasn't just playing dead.

It wasn't out of the realm for him to have fallen on a rock and knocked himself out, was it? And if he was left there for long enough . . . well, given hypothermia, rattlesnakes, bears, might he just disappear?

She remembered feeling a little burst of happiness at the thought. Life would be so much easier without him.

It started there, Lena's granting herself permission to imagine, when she needed to, Tim slipping off Waterfall Rock, Tim's car with failed brakes. The game was figuring out how to off him in a way that would keep her hands as clean as possible.

All that preparation apparently served her well: when she succeeded in killing him a few years later, Lena didn't even break a nail.

"That girl is crazy," Abe said.

"What?" Jen asked. She was trying to collect errant burrito wrappers into an empty doughnut box and the wind kept blowing them away.

Jen had purposefully set their blanket down as far away from the stage as possible, but even so, Fall Fest was a sensory explosion. A tiny child had wandered over to the Kingdom School picnic blanket to repeatedly slam the tambourine Colin had brought, and there was a line of kids patiently waiting for a turn with his guitar. And from the gazebo there were the chants of the second graders and the feedback of a PA system that was circa 1952.

People were shouting and cheering and despite it all, Abe had neither melted down nor insisted they leave.

"She fell down again," Abe said with a snicker. Colin and Jen both turned in the direction of his pointed finger.

About twenty feet away, a teenaged girl lay on her back, singing loudly, her arms raised upward in an attempt to conduct the clouds.

One of her friends filmed her with a camera phone, while another tried repeatedly to get her up on her feet.

"Is that Laurel Perley?" Jen said.

"What is she *on*?" Abe said.

Laurel was now upright and sashaying in their direction. She stopped along the way, extended her hand to an older couple sitting in camping chairs. "*Madame and Monsieur, voulez-vous enjoy Les Fall Fest Dancers?*" she shouted.

"Oh dear," Jen said. She stepped in Laurel's path, and was hit by the sour smell of alcohol. Colin appeared on the other side of Laurel, and together they coaxed her over to their blanket.

"Laurel, I'm Jen, a friend of your mom, from the neighborhood."

"Lucky for *you*," Laurel said. "She's a blast."

"Here," Colin said. He handed Laurel a water bottle. "Take a sip."

Laurel held up hers. "I'vealreadygot."

"This one is water, though. Good to hydrate."

"Excellentidea," Laurel said. "Big French test on Monday. *De l'eau!*"

"Right," he said.

She sipped and closed her eyes and then leaned over and got sick on their blanket. Jen awkwardly patted her back.

"Gross," Abe said. "Colin, it's on your pants."

Jen hadn't noticed Annie run up, but suddenly she was on their blanket, too. She yanked away Laurel's pink water bottle and un-screwed the top, sniffed and gagged.

"Where did you get this?" Her voice was a hiss.

"L.L. Bean," Laurel said. "It's right on the bottle." Her laugh-ter turned into ungainly hiccups.

"She's going to puke again," Abe said in a warning tone, "and it's still on Colin's pants."

"I'm so sorry," Annie whispered to Jen.

There were pink spots of humiliation on Annie's cheeks and her eyes were mortified. Jen felt a complex mixture of empathy and relief that this time, at least, it wasn't her kid everyone would be talking about.

"Don't even worry about it," Colin said. "It happens."

Jen nodded lamely, wished she'd thought to provide reassur-ance before judgment.

"I don't know what you're thinking," Annie said to Laurel. She sounded bewildered as she wrapped her arm around Laurel's waist and led her away.

"How old is she?" Colin said.

"Eighth grade I think," Jen said.

"Yikes." Colin shivered. "That's messed up." He'd removed his plaid shirt to dab at the sick stain on his jeans. In his thin white T-shirt, he looked skinny as a teenager. "I had an interview in twenty minutes at Breadman's Market. Probably better to just bail?"

"Would it help if I go and explain that you were doused in the name of Good Samaritanism?" Jen said. "They know me. I shop there all the time."

"Why are you interviewing?" Abe's mouth was an accusing straight line. "Are you quitting school?"

"Never," Colin said. "Assistant teachers don't get paid a lot is all. It would just be an after-school job."

It was becoming clearer by the day that Colin was good for Abe, and it hit Jen that they could be good for Colin, too.

"Wait," Jen said. "What if we hired you from time to time?"

"You own a market?" Colin said. He and Abe shared a goofy smile.

"No, but I could use help with pickups and drop-offs and Abe would probably benefit from some help with his independent project—"

"We could pay Colin to compose music for my game," Abe said. "He's actually a decent musician."

"Thanks for the compliment," Colin said. "And I'd much prefer that to bagging groceries. But I'll do it for free."

"Why don't I at least ask Nan if it's okay to hire you?"

If Nan didn't require medical forms, Jen was pretty sure she would have no objection to helping one of her teaching assistants earn a few extra dollars after school.

There was probably a perfect psalm for the occasion, something about sharing your wheat bounty with your neighbors.

"Really?" Colin said. "I wouldn't want to impose."

Jen would later try to reassure herself that her motives were anything but selfish. That warm effusive glow in her chest was the manifestation of *generosity*. She wasn't *using* anyone.

But for the rest of her life, she would never be entirely sure.

CHAPTER FOURTEEN

When Lena Meeker arrived at her very first book club meeting, she handed Jen a lovely bottle of Sancerre and a long white pastry box, both of which were slightly damp. With that meticulously flouncy brown layered hair and perfectly applied makeup, Lena sure didn't look like Cottonwood's Great Hermit.

And she smelled amazing, like vanilla roses.

"The box got rained on," Lena said. "I'm so sorry."

"Don't be silly," Jen said. "Annie, how is everything?"

"Fine, fine." With noticeable effort, Annie forced her mouth into a tight smile. "Sorry again about the scene at Fall Fest."

"Don't be. The apology note from Laurel was totally unnecessary—"

"I should introduce Lena around," Annie said quickly. She placed a proprietary hand on Lena's shoulder and steered her into the living room.

Jen followed them, and set down Lena's box on the coffee table. Deb Gallegos was on the couch, wiggling her fingers in greeting.

"How's Annie doing?" Jen asked.

Deb hiked her eyebrows. "Apoplectic. Poor Laurel will be in lockdown until she's thirty. I told Annie that they'd *all* been drinking, including Sierra. Laurel just put on the biggest show."

Jen nodded.

"They need to be punished, *obviously*. But we've all been there, and we turned out okay, right?"

THE NEIGHBOR'S SECRET 115

"Right."

"Plus"—Deb lowered her voice—"it's a teensy bit hypocritical because I've heard her school stories, and Annie was no saint. So. What do *you* think is inside that box?"

It sat in front of them on the coffee table, low and long. Pastries of some sort, Jen thought.

"A severed limb," Jen said, sotto voce.

They both started to chortle at the image: perfect Lena Meeker with the off-the-shoulder cashmere and those giant diamond earrings and the shiny pink manicure getting splattered as she sawed through bone.

"What are you two laughing about?" Janine said. She was carrying a tray of martini glasses filled with Fiona Stolis, which she carefully set down on the coffee table.

"Dismemberment."

"Obviously, with this book," Janine said. She handed them each a martini glass and waved over Lena, handed her one, too.

Lena accepted it with a grateful *thank you,* and folded herself into the love seat opposite them. Her skin sparkled in a way that seemed unnatural for November.

"I'm opening it," Deb said, and she hummed a burlesque accompaniment—ba-dum-dum—that drew the others over to watch her unloop the string and ease open the box top.

"Wow," Deb said.

"Unbelievable," Priya said.

"I've never seen anything like that," Harriet Nessel said.

"Isn't she amazing?" Annie said.

Lena smiled, pink and pleased, and spun around the box so all could admire the two dozen cupcakes inside, frosted the same hunter green as *The Girl in the Woods.* On the top of each one, with sugar and icing, Lena had perfectly replicated the cover art: the forest, the female silhouette, the ragged red font, the whole shebang.

"Did you make those from scratch?" Janine asked in awe. "How long did it take?"

"It really wasn't too bad."

A massive clap of thunder broke in a loud crack. Janine shrieked, loud and piercing, and clasped her hand to her mouth.

Everyone froze.

"*Janine*," Deb Gallegos said. "Calm yourself."

"Sorry." Janine took a shaky nervous gulp from her martini glass. "I am on *edge,* ladies, since the vandal's pyrotechnics."

Janine had put the entire book club on her vandal text chain and bombarded it with updates about the vandal's latest—he'd torched the Thankfulness Tree erected near the playground every November. The blaze hadn't spread, but the tree was charred enough that they'd dismantled it for the season.

"This one seemed more political," Deb said. "A statement against the tyranny of forced gratitude." Deb glanced worriedly at Janine. "Not that I didn't love the tree, because I did."

"Sure, Deb," Jen said with a wink.

"Deb," Annie said with an impish grin. "Are you trying to tell us that you're the vandal?"

"Trust me," Deb said. "I could light a better fire than that."

"Don't joke. Something is off," Janine said. "With this neighborhood. I can feel it. It's building. He's probably out there right now, watching."

"It *is* getting out of control," Harriet said.

"It's minor property damage."

"That's how it starts, though. Property, then animals, then people. Remember how they cut down on graffiti in New York City and the murder rate decreased? It's all connected."

"I'm not happy about it either, but let's keep things in perspective."

"My kids are terrified. The whole point of living here is so they have a space to be safely independent. The moment Nick and I decided to move here was when we saw Sierra and Laurel walking down to the playground by themselves—"

"We know," Deb said.

"They were only nine."

"They were six, Janine, remember, because Katie was five and you were pregnant with the twins."

"Oh, lord, I was so nauseous after the drive out here, all the twists and turns, but as soon as we saw Laurel and Sierra carefully crossing the street, I knew it was worth it."

Janine's Cottonwood Origin Story usually made Annie feel good about her insistence on moving to the neighborhood. The Perleys were short on space, but look what they had gained for their kids: first-class education, a wonderful community.

But tonight, when Deb chuckled and said, "They're *still* sneaking off to the playground together, this time with stolen vodka," Annie felt a blizzard of loss, even though Deb put a supportive hand on Annie's arm.

Were they supposed to laugh about it?

When Laurel and Sierra had been six, the worries had been: Was she eating a rainbow plate? Was she saying *please* and *thank you*? Was she trying her best in soccer practice?

Before Fall Fest, Annie had been worried, yes, about the moodiness, the lapse in grades, but her concerns had been speculative. The drinking made it real: Laurel was in crisis.

Sierra told Deb that Haley had stolen two bottles from her parents' liquor cabinet—so the idea hadn't been Laurel's alone. But only Laurel had gotten so out of control. Only she had been powerless to stop.

What if a lifetime of nurturing was no match for the steady pulse of nature?

"Let's talk about the book," Harriet said.

"No one sane would kill as many people as Fiona did," Priya said. "Not even for their child."

"But it's the height of sanity," Jen said. "What better reason to kill than for your child?"

"I call BS," Deb finally said. "To actually kill someone? To take a life? You couldn't go through with it."

Jen shrugged. "Probably not."

"Deb"—Harriet paused her frantic note-taking and looked up

briefly—"do you mind repeating for the notes, what did you say after 'I call BS'?"

"Um, that none of us would be capable of killing somone," Deb said.

The night's one bright spot was that Lena found the discussion riveting. There was a spark of curiosity in her expression that Annie had never seen before.

"Everyone was so nice," Lena said as she and Annie walked down Jen's dark driveway to Annie's car.

"I told you," Annie said.

The storm had moved east and left behind a warm mist. Lena felt the evening's exhilaration evaporate off her. "And those drinks were very strong."

"Don't worry." Annie paused meaningfully before she opened the passenger door. "I'm fine to drive. I only had a sip."

As Annie backed out of the driveway and turned onto the road, Lena looked out at the blur of lights below them. She rarely went out at night, and forgot how cozy the neighborhood could look after dark, how the house lights dotting the valley seemed so inviting.

"It's a fun group," Lena said. She had not admitted to even Melanie how nervous she'd been about book club. She was glad to have brought the cupcakes—they had loved them.

"How was it to see Harriet?"

"Good. She's still a prolific note-taker."

"It's probably mostly gossip," Annie said dryly. "She's a bit of an information hoarder. Once, Deb peeked at her notepad and Harriet had scribbled down everything we'd said *before* the book discussion. Deb said, 'Harriet, you can't do that,' but Harriet wasn't even embarrassed."

"She hasn't changed a bit. Everyone seemed so familiar. They remind me of—"

"Who?"

They reminded Lena of *her* friends from the neighborhood, a generation before. That zinging heady energy of a group of women at ease with each other. Most of Lena's friends from before had moved away, which was part life cycle and part, Lena suspected, a reaction to Tim's accident, which had certainly popped Cottonwood's bubble of safety.

Life—people—did succumb to patterns and rhythms. The neighborhood was an assembly line. Miniature fungible dolls on a conveyor belt, moving in, moving out. Low-stakes drama and routines year after year after year.

People thought their lives were so important, but they were tiny specks, ants. There were decisions that had seemed mammoth to Lena before, and she saw now they hadn't mattered in the least.

She swallowed the rough lump in her throat. Sometimes the abstract thought of time passing, all that normalcy, all that minutiae that she'd missed out on, made Lena unbearably sad. Even with a bad marriage, she'd had such a nice little life.

Once she admitted a version of this truth to Dr. Friendly, who had given her a coping trick: look ahead to the concrete future, not back in the rearview mirror.

(Not very sensitive of you, Dr. Friendly, to rely on a car metaphor.)

In the immediate future, Lena would write Jen a thank-you note. She had done a lovely job hosting and decorating, although Lena wouldn't have picked the floral print wallpaper in the powder room, which was too dark and overpowering for the small space. She knew from her design magazines that the pattern was on-trend, but something softer would have worked better.

They had pulled into Lena's driveway, but Annie's pensive expression kept Lena from reaching for the door handle.

"Is it normal?" Annie said. "The drinking? Because everyone acts like it's some rite of passage."

As Lena weighed her response, the car's front seat seemed impossibly tiny.

"I'm not going to lie about the dangers," she said. "But teen-agers are idiots. They try things, they move on. You gave Laurel consequences, and you're talking to her about it. That's all you can do."

Annie's face screwed up, as if she was collecting courage to confess something. "There's a family history of alcoholism," she said in a rough blurt.

"Well," Lena said gently, "I understand that."

"You do, don't you?" Annie's mouth zipped tight, her eyes alight with a realized bond.

"It's fairly common. People manage." Lena felt her cheeks get hot and was glad for the darkness. She desperately wanted to return to the silliness and camaraderie from tonight. The group's conversation had felt as welcoming as a warm hearth.

"I think they liked the cupcakes," Lena said quickly. "Do you?"

"They loved the cupcakes," Annie said. Sharp drops of rain had started up again, plopped onto the windshield.

"I'm planning to go again next month," Lena said. "And maybe on one of those weekend walks Janine organizes."

Annie snorted. "Janine will hunt you down if you don't."

"She seemed energetic enough to do just that."

Annie smiled. "She has a confession, you know."

"What?"

"Sorry. Inside joke." Annie glanced at Lena. "Every time she gets tipsy and we read a steamy book, which is a lot, Janine confesses that she made out with a woman in college and it was *hot* and then she laughs about it for like a half hour. No one can figure out why she acts like it's such a big deal, but fifty bucks she's doing it right now."

"Why do I feel like this." Jen was aware that her voice was emerging in a Rex Harrison—esque sing-chant. "I only had two Stolis."

"Two Stolis, two Stolis," sang Janine.

They were all, except for Harriet, drunk. Jen felt floppy-limbed and silly as she finished Saran-wrapping the Brie, swung open the door to her refrigerator.

"That's about six shots," Deb sang, and her voice went up with a screech, like at the end of *my dog has fleas*. Jen smiled in appreciation before it hit her.

"Six shots? You're kidding."

"Six shots," Deb confirmed with a hiccup.

Harriet, who'd been dutifully stacking into a Tupperware the homemade buckeyes Athena had made in honor of the book's Ohio scenes, made a disapproving harrumphing noise.

"What did you guys think about the tunnel scene?" Janine said, her voice a little mumbly as she slumped into Jen's banquette. "With that, what was her name? One thing I'll say about our girl Fiona. Verrry equal-opportunity. Did I ever tell you guys about in college, when I—hello, and what do we have here?"

Colin and Abe, both in heavy wool coats, had come into the kitchen. Their cheeks were flushed from the cold, and their faces were too serious for the room.

Abe fled upstairs abruptly, but if he'd been rude, the women didn't seem to notice. They beamed at Colin.

"How was the movie?" Jen said carefully. It felt inappropriate to act tipsy in front of Colin.

"Fine," Colin said. "Can I help you guys clean up?"

"Don't worry about it," Jen said at the same time that Janine hissed something that sounded like, "Yaassssssss."

With a messily dramatic point of her arm, Janine directed Colin to carry the folding chairs to the closet. When he turned his back, she mimed grabbing his rear.

Cute, she mouthed, and dissolved into giggles. She pointed sloppily under her right eye and mouthed, *He's wearing makeup.*

"Janine," Jen said. "Control yourself."

Janine saluted and lost her balance and laughed even harder. "Sir," she asked Colin, "are you in college?"

"Grad school," Jen said.

"How *old* is he?"

"Twenty-five," Colin said quietly.

Jen smiled at him in a way that was intended to transmit it was all silliness, not harassment in the least.

"Twenty-five," Janine sang. "I remember twenty-five."

"We're very pleased for you," Jen said.

"Wait. Do I?" Janine sounded lost as she stood up and wobbled over to Colin, cupped his chin with her hand. "You are an itty-bitty Goth baby."

It would have been an awkward moment for most anyone, but later that night, Jen would think of all the different ways that Colin might have reacted.

He might have stepped backward to free himself, or smiled politely or tried to laugh it off or even pushed away Janine, who was half his size. But whether a person became predator or prey had nothing to do with size or strength. It was all mindset.

Becoming a mother—Abe's mother—had turned Jen into a vulnerability detector. She couldn't stomach watching someone flail, even fictional characters, even cartoons. Every Bambi, every Dumbo: *It's Abe,* her body would scream. *That could be Abe.*

So, when Colin froze in response to Janine's touch, when his spooked eyes met Jen's, she snapped into action.

"Janine, are we going to have to enroll you in sensitivity training?" Jen pulled Janine off Colin and pushed her in the direction of the banquette. "Who's driving her home?"

"I will," Priya said.

Collapsed against the soapstone countertop, Janine blew a big sloppy kiss in Priya's direction. "My hero."

"I'm so, so sorry," Jen said to Colin as she walked him to the door. "Are you okay?"

"Fine," he whispered. "Thank you."

It took all of her strength to not rub his back as she would have with Abe. Some people just needed a little more help.

.   .   .

Annie stayed in Lena's driveway until she saw the lights go on inside.

Whenever Annie brought up Rachel, Lena's canned reaction reminded Annie of her first job after college, which had been assisting a public relations department.

Yes, Rachel is doing GREAT. And . . . topic pivot. When someone answered like that, there was always more to the story.

Did Rachel have friends? An explosive temper? Had Rachel's personality ever changed on a dime? Did Rachel have a problem with addiction?

On the night of the party, Rachel had been tending bar. Even from feet away, Annie could feel her storminess, her general dissatisfaction.

Not to mention that ugly scene at Bryce Neary's funeral.

Annie wanted Lena to level with her, because she was pretty sure that Lena had insider information: What was regular teen angst and what was something more?

When Annie got home from book club, she found Laurel stretched out on the couch in the darkened den that smelled faintly of nail polish. Laurel's headphones were plugged into Mike's old MP3 player.

"You got that thing to work?" Annie said.

"Necessity is the mother of invention."

Annie perched on the couch's arm, squinted at Laurel's toes. "Is that polish turquoise?"

"This is my life now. Boomer music and painting my nails."

"You got off easy."

They had grounded Laurel for only two weeks. Annie wasn't sure how effective it would be—Laurel still seemed disinclined to reflect on *why* she was being punished.

"Is it because I work at school?" Annie asked. She lifted Laurel's feet and scooted underneath them.

"Sure."

"Really?"

Annie had had the thought just this morning: how stifling to be almost fourteen and have your mother always down the hall—at school, at home.

"No, not really," Laurel said. She propped up on her elbows. "We were all drinking because we're teenagers. There's not some mysterious reason."

"Okay, but—"

"And you don't need to punish me. My body punished me enough. My headache is like, just now gone. Do you think you're making such a big deal about this because you're the school counselor?"

"What you did is dangerous, Laurel."

"You don't need to make some example out of me. *Everyone's* done something like this." Laurel's lips twisted as though she was trying to squelch a smile. "People thought it was hilarious."

"Anyone who found it funny isn't your real friend," Annie said. A pinched quality had crept into her voice.

Laurel's sigh—indicating Annie was the one who'd never get it—made Annie want to grab her by the shoulders and shake comprehension into her.

"You have no idea how dangerous alcohol can be," Annie said. "There are people who don't have an off switch, do you understand?"

Laurel bent over to tap the pad of her index finger against her big toenail, check its dryness.

The dark shiver Annie had felt when Laurel was a watchful toddler, the slight wedge between them had been *this*. On some subconscious level, Annie had been bracing for the time bomb in Laurel's DNA.

"Look me in the eye, Laurel. Like *that*"—Annie snapped her fingers—"what starts as fun becomes a lifelong struggle. I've seen drunken mistakes literally ruin lives."

Laurel kept silent, but from the way she held Annie's gaze, Annie suspected she'd finally gotten through.

"Like your friend?" Laurel said. Her eyes moved from Annie's to the wall behind them, filled with framed family pictures. "The guy you went to prom with? Bryce?"

"Yes."

Annie tried to hide how his name sliced through her, left behind a dull ache.

If she ever found herself trying to rationalize Laurel's performance at Fall Fest, all Annie had to do was think of Bryce Neary.

FIFTEEN YEARS EARLIER

It occurred to Annie, as she spied on the Meekers' party from behind a cistena plum, that this could all go horribly wrong.

For starters, was he even here?

The lawn was a sea of indistinguishable middle-aged guests: men in pastel linen button-downs and women with expensive pashminas draped around their shoulders.

And, if he was here and she managed to find him, the band was so loud. Was she supposed to shout the news in his ear, over that weighted bass line?

Surprise! You're going to be a father!

In the plum bush, branches tickling her arm, Annie considered for the first time that just because she could see the future laid out in front of them did not mean he would.

He liked late nights more than early mornings. He prized spontaneity. They'd been talking about taking a real trip together—somewhere requiring immunizations and a visa—and so much for that.

Most people Annie's age wouldn't be excited about an unplanned pregnancy. There was something wrong with her, and why was she just realizing that now? She had driven all the way out here on a whim.

But it had seemed like fate, the way Annie had been half watching a daytime talk show about vision boards and seen the post on Bryce's MySpace page: a party, tonight. The more the merrier!

At the *Meekers'* of all places.

They had plans for the next day, and she'd been planning to wait until then to tell him, but screw it, she'd decided, she would drive to the party, tell him tonight.

You're insane, Mike grumbled over the phone, that's way out in the boondocks. Still, he had promised to try and make it after work, so that Annie wouldn't have to "go it alone."

Annie felt painfully, deliciously exposed at the phrase: she would never ever have to go it alone again.

It was horribly cheesy, but now, in the bushes, Annie closed her eyes and visualized it, just like the daytime television show had instructed.

He was here somewhere—or he would be soon—and he'd find her and they would sit in that gorgeous garden, on a stone bench. She would fish out of her pocket the flimsy ultrasound print and she would watch him looking at it, and they would be together, encircled in joy.

Annie opened her eyes, reached into her jean jacket pocket, pulled out her phone.

There was an uncrowded spot near the house, far from the liveliness of the dance floor.

If u r here, she texted, I'm waiting by the house.

CHAPTER FIFTEEN

"A neighborhood book club," Rachel repeated. "Well, why not?"

"That's what I think," Lena said. She opened the oven and peeked under the foil. The turkey legs were still pale.

"What happens if you don't approve of their selections, though?" Rachel's voice grew ominous. "Watch out, ladies of Cottonwood."

When Rachel attempted jokes about how dangerous Lena was—never gracefully, never with any actual wit—Lena felt like snapping at her. But she hadn't ever.

"Did you know anyone at book club?" Rachel's voice was back to normal.

"Just Harriet Nessel, and she didn't miss a beat. It felt like I saw her just last week. What time are you and Evan's family meeting at their club for the big meal?"

"Seven. What time is Uncle Ernie coming over?"

"Four. He's got an early flight tomorrow."

Ernie apparently no longer felt sorry for Lena and had already grumbled at length: friends of theirs spent Thanksgiving Day *in* Hawaii. He didn't understand why Lena was commanding him to stay here and go through the motions.

You're a grown man, Lena replied. I can't command you to do anything.

He and Rachel probably had long, unjustified conversations about how incorrigibly bossy Lena was.

Alma had had a very strong personality, and her mantra was: family is everything. That's why Ernie was sticking around. It had nothing to do with Lena. And as far as Rachel went, Lena had called the shots fourteen years ago, in a moment of crisis.

It was the very definition of parenting, and Lena had always hoped that as Rachel matured, she'd understand that life wasn't always so black and white. Sometimes, laws must be broken for a greater good.

But Rachel was already in her thirties. The lesson seemed to have eluded her.

"Do you remember the Thanksgivings we used to have?" Rachel said.

"I remember cooking for a full month before."

They'd used to host almost fifty people—Alma and all of her relatives, a few locals from Tim's side, plus whatever strays he'd dragged along.

And then suddenly there had been no one.

During Rachel's angry years, Lena had forced herself to fly east for meals at hotel restaurants that never felt right. Once, Lena had arrived to find that she was being punished and Rachel had made other plans, so she'd ordered room service and eaten Thanksgiving dinner alone on her bed.

"Not the big family meals," Rachel said, "how we used to go to the Bahamas. Just you and me."

But that had only happened twice—a slippery attempt at a tradition in the years before Tim died, when it was still the two of them against the world. Lena opened her mouth, about to correct the memory before stopping herself.

There had been a time that Rachel had trusted Lena more than anyone or anything. Lena wondered if every parent had that window at some point, and if they all, inevitably, exploited it.

"I made a friend at book club," Lena ventured. "Annie Perley. She's older than you, but she said she'd been to our house for a swim-team dinner."

"Annie Perley," Rachel repeated. "Does she have brown hair?"

"Light chestnut," Lena said. "Chin length. She's pretty. Her face has very delicate bone structure."

"Maybe I'm thinking of someone else."

"I bet your paths didn't really cross. Her husband owns a restaurant downtown and they've got these two kids—"

"Was she there the year we had paella? Or the year there was the big thunderstorm?"

"That wasn't the same year?"

The skies had turned ocean gray, the wind tipped over the outdoor umbrella, melamine plates with food were rushed inside, and kids had grouped around the window to watch lightning flash over the mountains.

"Paella's an odd thing to serve children," Rachel said.

"People loved it."

"If you say so."

"You'd like Annie. She's sharp. And kind. And closer to your age than mine."

"But she—Annie—had already graduated when—" Rachel paused.

Hearing the familiar tremor in Rachel's voice, Lena sprang into action. She'd mostly lost Rachel long ago, but there were still moments like this, of reliance.

"If Annie had any clue what I did, Rachel, do you think she'd want me at her book club?"

"Right." Rachel's laugh was small. "I don't suppose she would."

"He's here!" Abe said. He had been stationed at their bay window for the past fifteen minutes, watching for Colin's blue car.

"Colin's here," Jen repeated to Paul, who had the oven door open and was squinting suspiciously at the precooked turkey.

We barely know this kid, he'd said.

Paul wanted a Thanksgiving like they usually had: the three of them eating takeout on the couch, treating the holiday as a breather before the frantic bounce of Christmas—from Jen's mom in northern California to Paul's sister in the middle to Jen's dad and young stepmother in Los Angeles, worrying all the way, *ha, ha, ha,* about whether Abe was going to behave, and were his cousins being little jerks.

The official arrangement with Colin, what he was being paid for, involved his driving Abe home after school four days a week and staying until dinner so that Jen could work. But Colin seemed desperate for family time and tended to stay longer. He ate with them most nights and always helped clean up afterward and had even volunteered to come over on any weekend, really, he was never doing anything anyway. Like them, he was relatively new in town and didn't know many people.

And he was so good for Abe: reasoned and calm, but he gently challenged him to venture outside of his comfort zone. Last weekend, they'd walked to the Cottonwood playground and shot basketball hoops.

Unprecedented.

When Colin chewed on the cuff of his plaid flannel shirt and mumbled that he had no plans for Thanksgiving, all Jen could think about was Abe as a lonely young adult.

She had extended the invitation to Thanksgiving dinner, and Colin's entire face lit up with disbelief. *You mean me?*

Obviously, the women of book club—with their chocolate turkeys and kids' tables and Thankfulness Trees and traditions up the wazoo—were getting to Jen, because she'd ordered the full catered Thanksgiving dinner from Breadman's Market.

And as she opened the door to Colin, Jen felt a wash of genuine thankfulness toward him.

"Colin," she sang, "come on in."

To: "The Best Book Club in the World"
From: proudmamabooklover3@hmail.com

Tis the Season, Ladies!

The book: THE GIVING MITTENS, a "heartwarming tale of one pair of mittens passed through ten different owners over several decades."
 Follow THE GIVING MITTENS from the Great Depression to a closeted 1950s housewife, from a homeless son reunited with his parents in the 1970s, to a present-day single dad, newly laid off, and unable to purchase the "it" toy for his disabled son.
 It has been called "emotionally resonant" and "touching" (literally, ladies, this one is not for the germophobes among us, am I right?) and:

 "kind of like the sisterhood of traveling pants. But with mittens.
 And strangers. And even less realistic."*

 Like last year, we acknowledge our own #luck and #blessings with a clothing drive for those in need! Please collect all outerwear (mittens, scarves, coats) prior to the meeting.
 Jen Chun-Pagano has volunteered to deliver everything to the Kingdom School and will be parked in PRIYA'S DRIVEWAY (8323 Red Fox Way) to collect your bags and boxes so dig deep into those closets, Ladies!!!
 Whew! You still with me or are you all still hung over from last month's club meeting??? (Hahahahahaha! But seriously Deb, maybe you could bring an aspirin chaser this month?)

*Okay Deb said this, but I thought it was perfect ;) ;) ;)

CHAPTER SIXTEEN

t was a tale as old as time: being in the "in crowd" required so much more effort.

This was why Jen found herself standing in Priya Jensen's driveway, huddled against a cold so bitter that she could feel the tiny hairs inside of her nose freeze, listening to Deb Gallegos talk about air mattresses.

After the November book club, Jen had been initially tickled to be included on the "inner circle" text group, which so far had consisted of reports of coyote spottings, an invitation to an exercise class called Feel the Burn, and a long discussion about which wines were safe for a Paleo diet.

But there was a quid pro quo to all this information sharing: assumptions of availability, demands on Jen's time. Nobody had asked her about tonight, it had been: *Jen will be in charge of the clothing drive!*

"The platforms don't make a difference," Deb, who amazingly hadn't yet exhausted the topic of air mattresses, said. "In price, yes, but comfort no. You're still sleeping on what is essentially a plastic balloon."

Jen felt a surge of hope for a topic change when Annie Perley drove up, her hatchback full of Lena's boxes for donation. As soon as Annie stepped out of her car, though, Deb cupped her hands around her mouth. "I brought the air mattresses!"

It turned out Deb was lending them to Annie because Mike's

family was staying with the Perleys over Christmas. Not only did Deb have some strong opinions about the quality of the borrowed air mattresses, but also several thoughts on where Annie should place them.

Jen, increasingly desperate, asked the first thing that came to mind. "Annie," she said, "how's Laurel been?"

Deb shook her head slightly, shot Jen a warning look.

"Hey wait," Jen said clumsily, trying to save the moment. "If these are Lena's boxes, where's Lena?"

Another misstep.

Even though Annie was wearing a beanie, Jen could tell her brow had furrowed beneath it. There was a weirdness when Annie talked about Lena, like Lena was a favorite porcelain doll and couldn't be jostled. Jen wasn't sure why this protectiveness annoyed her so much, but, like everything else, it did.

"Lena's not here yet?" Annie said. Her blue eyes were big, her voice tremulous.

"She's probably just running late," Jen said. "Deb, do your air mattresses have remotes, because I saw that once?"

"You know, though," Deb said, "I always lose remotes."

"Guys, I'm worried," Annie said. Stuffed into a winter coat, hands hanging at her sides, she looked like a lost child. "Why isn't Lena here?"

"She'll come," Deb said. "Who would donate all this and not show up?"

"There she is." Jen pointed down the dark road toward a figure walking in their direction.

Annie squinted. "No, that's Harriet."

When she reached them, Harriet thrust a brown paper bag in Jen's direction.

"Hats," she said. "All knit by my sister and itchy as heck. She gives them as gifts."

"Thanks?"

"I'm happy to get rid of them, actually. So. I assume everyone heard about the Donaldsons?"

"What about them?"

"The vandal cut up their Frosty the Snowman inflatable. Snipped off the little carrot nose like a psycho." Harriet scissored her gloved fingers. "Their grandkids found the remnants this morning and are traumatized."

"Don't the Donaldsons have that doorbell camera?" Deb said.

"It didn't catch anything." Harriet eyed the boxes they'd stacked in Jen's trunk. "Is someone moving?"

"These are Lena's donations," Annie said. "Most of it still has tags. She snuck two brand-new pairs of gloves to Laurel, and I'm like, thank you, Lena, for teaching my fourteen-year-old about cashmere."

"She's always been very generous," Harriet said. "Money's never been her issue. They sold the family's company for hundreds of millions, apparently."

Annie peered fruitlessly down the street. "I should call her."

"I wouldn't count on her coming, dear," Harriet said.

"She had fun last month!" Annie insisted.

"She's different now. *Tentative.*"

Jen was unable to stop the exasperated sigh that escaped from her mouth in a puff of vapor.

She was too cold and irritated to care about the shocked looks. Everyone had their shit: Jen certainly did, and she'd brought her own donations and managed to come early, thank you very much.

"I'm sorry," Jen said impatiently, "it's tragic that her husband died, but wasn't it like years ago?"

"He didn't just die." Deb sounded scandalized. "He killed Bryce Neary in a hit-and-run. He went to jail for it."

"That's horrible." Jen frowned. "Was Bryce—did he live here too?"

"How do you not know this, Jen?"

"I thought I did," Jen said.

"Apparently not," Deb said.

CHAPTER SEVENTEEN

"First of all," Deb said, "I'm not the best person to tell the story. Annie went to high school with Bryce."

"A million years ago." Annie's lower jaw spasmed, which briefly altered her face into something ugly.

"And Harriet was literally at the accident," Deb said. "It happened in her front yard."

"About fifty yards up the hill," Harriet demurred. "I didn't see it."

Deb paused for either of them to pick up the story, but when neither did, she shrugged and continued.

"Bryce's dad lived in the Yung's house, you know, the gray cape on Wildcat that backs up to the red rocks? No? God, Jen, next weekend I am going to give you a personal tour of the neighborhood, it's like you don't even live here sometimes.

"Anyway, Bryce had just graduated from college a few weeks before, and was about to move to Chicago. The night was supposed to be a reunion of sorts for a bunch of them who'd gone to high school together, and they started at the Meekers' party before moving the celebration to a classmate's parents' house just across Highway Five.

"Meanwhile, after the Meeker party ended, Lena went to sleep and Tim drove off to God knows where to do God knows what. When he drove back—at the same time Bryce was walking home from the house party—"

Deb pushed the tips of her fingers into the other hand's flattened palm, to indicate the crash.

"Tim didn't even stop. Lena woke up when she heard his car, saw the cracked windshield and managed to, I don't know, interrogate him successfully enough that he admitted he hit something near Harriet's. When Lena knocked on your door in the middle of the night, her eyes were like a wild animal's. Just filled with pure grief and shock, right, Harriet?"

"It was forever ago," Harriet said briskly.

"You told someone that, Harriet. I couldn't make up that detail, it's so chilling." After a shudder, Deb continued. "Lena screamed at Harriet to call the police, that it was Tim, and you did, right Harriet? And they came for him a few hours later. He had a record, which we don't think Lena knew—DUIs—I think even an outstanding warrant or something. The police dumped Tim in a cell and he had a heart attack that night, they think from alcohol abuse. Anyway, he died in the jail cell, only a few hours after he hit Bryce."

"Oh my God."

"Awful, I know. And Lena's daughter, Rachel, fled for boarding school after that, and as far as we know, she's never deigned to come back, not for Christmas, or her mom's birthday or anything, she's just frozen out Lena, and oh my gosh, Harriet are you okay? Do you need some water? There's a cold going around, Sierra's started just like that with the gunk in the throat and—oh, hello Lena! I didn't hear you walk up, how are you? So glad you came! We were just talking about all your fabulous donations, weren't we, girls?"

Deb finally stopped talking, slammed her lips together. Even in the dim moonlight, Jen could see her face flush with embarrassment.

Lena's guilty eyes made clear she had heard, if not all of the story, the tail end.

Annie sidled close to her and squeezed her arm and started

babbling something about all the boxes and Jen chimed in and then Deb said she had egg whites waiting inside to froth for the drink, and was desperate for Lena's help with getting the spices right and it's so cold, what are we doing out here, let's all go inside.

Deb Gallegos's hands were a whirl of measuring and pouring. Every few minutes she shoved a shot glass filled with test cocktail at Lena: *too sweet/bland/weak?*

Lena wanted to comfort her, and all of the other women, so sweetly frantic in their attempts to make her feel better. They thought they'd hurt her feelings, but she'd been riveted.

"The Story"—Lena's story—had been reshaped into a neat little package: beginning, middle, end.

It wasn't the first time Lena had heard a version of it. *It's a small town,* Dr. Friendly had admitted in their initial consultation. *I already know what you've been through.*

In Dr. Friendly's reverent retelling, Lena had sounded like a movie heroine: the burdened widow with an impossible choice! Her family . . . or the greater good?

In the gossipy neighborhood version, though, Lena had sounded more like a victim. And a little mad with grief, thanks to Harriet's graphic detail about her wild animal eyes.

Lena felt the teensiest bit defensive hearing the part about how Rachel stormed off to the East Coast in a huff, angry at Lena for unintentionally killing her father. It made Rachel sound like some immature brat who couldn't cope, when in truth, her anger was righteous and complicated. If they had only seen Rachel's hysterics when Lena had dropped her off in New Hampshire.

Lena could never correct them, though. If people thought they knew The Story, it meant they had accepted it, plot holes and all.

There had been not quite four hours between when the last guest had left Lena's party and the police officers knocked on her door looking for Tim. They were the defining moments of Lena's life.

The fewer questions about them the better.

FIFTEEN YEARS EARLIER, 12:01 A.M.

Jett the bartender was the last to go, with a fat tip in his pocket. He had nodded tiredly when Lena slipped it to him, as if in agreement that he'd earned every last cent.

Lena leaned against the front door, stepped out of her heels. Always such a bittersweet feeling when a party finally ended, a little relief, a little sadness mingled with the contentment.

She surveyed the kitchen. Alma used to say you could gauge an event's success by the mess, in which case tonight had been epic: wineglasses and stacked dirty plates and half-empty platters covered the countertops.

Lena stole a cube of Manchego from a platter on the island and popped it in her mouth before going upstairs.

Behind the door of her room, Rachel sang along to loud music in an unselfconscious falsetto. Lena thought against knocking, did not want to ruin the carefree moment.

In her bathroom, Lena smeared cold cream on her face, carefully slipped off her dress and pulled on a nightgown, sat down at her vanity to sponge off the cream.

She heard the mechanical whir of the garage door.

Through the years she would agonize: Why hadn't she really listened?

She'd have realized that Tim was in no position to drive, and she could have run downstairs to stop him, stop all of it.

Because Lena was too selfish to see past her own happiness to care about anyone else, too filled with thoughts of how, right before Gary had left to drive his son to meet friends, he'd said a casual *I'll call later,* twisted his pinky finger around hers and held it a little too long.

She pressed in her face oil with light upward sweeps of her

finger, climbed between the sheets and fell into a dreamless heavy sleep that was interrupted by the ring of her phone.

The clock said 1:15. Her heart sprinting, she fumbled the cordless receiver off its stand, pressed the phone to her ear.

"Hello?"

"Did I wake you?"

"No," Lena lied. Her eyes adjusted to the darkness. Indulgently, she stretched her arms above her head. "What are you doing up?"

"Waiting for my son to call for a ride home," Gary said. "Want to sneak out and wait with me?"

Lena paused.

"Don't say no."

Lena didn't. She was already getting out of bed.

CHAPTER EIGHTEEN

"Do you think Colin is gay?"

Paul ignored Jen's question. He took a sip of wine, swallowed. Carefully cut another bite and pushed it onto his fork and slid it onto her plate.

"You have to try the lamb," he said.

They were at a restaurant that had once been a ranch house, and was perched atop a winding road on acres of farmland, deep in the Foothills. Paul and Jen were in front of the giant stone fireplace, with a view outside to the rows of evergreens, Christmas lights strung through their branches.

Jen had decided they should split a bottle of champagne. Since book club started in the fall, she'd found herself adopting the club's attitude to alcohol, which she could best describe as: *Why not? I deserve it!*

And it was true. A glass of something now and then made everyone seem more fun and every problem a little more bearable. Even Jen's mother couldn't find the worry in her new habit.

You go girl, she'd told Jen clumsily, *uncork a little.*

"Or do you think Colin's bi?" Jen said. "And before you accuse me of stereotyping because he's got the hair and the eyeliner, I asked him this afternoon whether he ever thought of dating Emma and he said, 'Not my type.' Have you seen Emma?"

Paul nodded. Yes, he had seen Emma, the other assistant teacher, who was gorgeous with that long shiny hair and creamy skin and the boobs and *get positive* boppiness. Jen guessed that Emma would be anyone's type.

"Maybe Emma's simple?" Jen said. She held up a hand. "Not dumb. I don't mean dumb. I mean not complicated. Colin is complicated."

"If you say so." Paul forked another morsel of lamb.

She sighed. The problem was that alcohol made *Jen* uncork and Paul brood. It really wasn't as much fun when you were the only gabby one.

"I know Colin's young, but he's got a wise soul. Bruised, though."

"A wise, bruised soul," Paul repeated.

Colin's "um, no" when Jen had asked if he wasn't going to Texas for Christmas had been sardonic, like he'd rather be touring Superfund sites.

She had a picture of his parents that *was* admittedly very stereotyped—Jell-O salads and plastic-covered La-Z-Boys and Colin hiding behind a hay bale, strumming the Cure on his guitar and being told to stop listening to that devil music.

He wasn't as religious as Nan, that was for sure. And while Jen knew he was a student at the seminary, she wasn't sure how ardently he believed.

"I bet he's like, a real Christian, you know? It's not about the politics or the repression, but about the principles. Maybe he's asexual too," Jen said. "There's an entire generational movement now. I read an article. They're all above mortal urges."

"I think you've pegged him," Paul said. "A real Christian asexual with a bruised soul."

"Don't be like that."

"What?"

"Condescending."

Paul arched an eyebrow. "I'm not sure why we have to spend this entire meal talking about Colin's romantic preferences. We pay him enough to not have to think about him in our free time."

"It's not about the money with him."

Whenever Jen took out her wallet at the end of each week,

Colin blushed and ducked his head and did one of his nervous tics—Jen knew them all by now—the sleeve chew, the hair push back behind the ears (always repeated at a tortured double-time clip). Jen had started leaving the money in a drawer to avoid the entire dance.

"That's pretty naive," Paul said, "it's always about the money."

"It's really not." She popped the lamb bite in her mouth. "Oh, this *is* good."

"Maybe it's not about the money. Maybe you're the appeal."

Jen, who'd been taking a sip, swallowed wrong, ending up sputtering. "Um. No," she said, after a cough.

After sixteen years of marriage, Paul still thought Jen—who had (and she was being objective here) only become older and slower and nuttier and more square-shaped through the years—inexplicably desirable.

There was no logic to it: Jen had just been lucky enough to marry someone equal parts devoted and stubborn. This, she had come to learn, was no small thing. Some of the book club women talked as if one hundred percent of their romantic moments came from the books they read.

"I'm changing the subject," she said.

"Thank god."

"The vandal struck again last night, and this is actually pretty creepy. He attacked an inflatable snowman on Wildcat Court. Like, took scissors and snipped off its little carrot nose and then stabbed the body until it deflated."

"Jeez."

"Agreed, but at this point I don't know which is more disturbing: the vandal or Janine's obsession with him. Thirty-seven texts." Jen held up her phone to Paul and scrolled through Janine's endless group-broadcast panic. "You know what I keep thinking?"

Paul shook his head.

"Whoever this kid's parents are, they'll probably just shrug it off. They'll make a deal with the police, or whomever, that's it.

They're not going to be up all night, unable to sleep, worried that they're about to unleash a psychopath on the world."

Jen cut herself another piece of Paul's lamb, stabbed it onto her fork.

"I don't know about that."

When Jen railed against other clueless parents, Paul frequently reminded her that everyone had their shit to go through.

But this was a lie. Jen had been to enough book clubs, scrolled through enough social media to understand that she was having a fundamentally different parenting experience from anyone else.

She'd gladly trade her vital sex life for a little more boring, a little more *normal*. The lamb in Jen's mouth, which she had been chewing angrily, suddenly tasted like straw. She looked down at her plate.

"I should just count my blessings that Abe isn't the vandal," she said.

At the funny look on Paul's face, Jen felt a ping of warning vibrate inside her.

"What?"

"Nothing."

"*What.*"

"It hasn't crossed your mind that burning the Thankfulness Tree might possibly derive from the same great criminal mind that brought you last year's boys' bathroom trash-can fire?"

"No way." Jen shook her head stubbornly.

"Think about Abe's school career: the hamster, the fire, the locker-bank destruction? The patio-furniture topple. The Harper French stabbing."

Paul was saying it like a litany, like there had been an inexorable progression when in fact those had been isolated incidents, all triggered by cruelty and separated by years.

"It's not him."

"How can you be sure? I travel and have no idea where he is," Paul said. "You go to bed totally depleted—and rightly so—from working and being a single parent most weeks."

If he was so worried that Abe was the vandal, how could Paul fly off every week? How could he sit there eating his lamb shank like it was nothing? Why hadn't he tried to do anything?

And his tone—light and disinterested, like he found it all slightly *amusing,* like it was somebody else's problem and not the thing that kept him awake at night and slapped him in the face every morning and was a steady hum in the back of his head all day?

Jen swilled her champagne but didn't sip. "No, everything's different with this school. We have Colin now."

"That's what you said about Harper, even whatshername, the bratty one—"

"Isabelle."

"Right. It's the same pattern. It's only a matter of time before it all goes to pieces. You loved Harper, and her mother, and remember, you took them to all of those plays, because Harper loved theater? Sometimes I think I could replace Colin's name with Harper's and poof, it would be last year."

"I never *loved* Harper, Paul, that's— No." Jen's fork clattered down to the plate. "You're not paying attention."

"I pay attention."

"You try. But you're not here. If I'm telling you it's different, you have to *believe* me, you cannot just sit there and judge, when you don't have any firsthand information about—"

"Okay."

"You're not here half the time." Her voice had hiked up, come out loud and shrill. "You have no idea what's happening."

"You're right. I'm sorry."

She stabbed her trout with a fork. Her hand was shaking and her eyes were filled with tears.

"Should I not have hope? Should I give up trying? What are my alternatives here, Paul?"

She'd spoken too loudly. Diners at some of the tables near them had turned their heads.

"I'm sorry," Paul said. But the apology wasn't enough. When

he extended his hand across the table, she was physically incapable of reaching across and taking it.

She understood how unfair she was being, that the avalanche of fury burying her had little to do with Paul, but she was in too deep to see a way out. She pushed back from the table, grabbed her bag.

"Well"—she flashed him an icy smile—"thanks for ruining dinner."

And then she stalked outside into the cold.

CHAPTER NINETEEN

It was Christmas Eve and the Perley house was filled with garlands and tea lights and poinsettias and presents and Mike's family, who had arrived from California a few days before.

They'd managed to find a spot for everyone to sleep: Mike's sisters and a brother-in-law were in the unfinished basement, on the Gallegos's air mattresses, and Hank and Laurel were with their cousins, in a pile of sleeping bags on the floor of the den. Annie and Mike had given his parents the master bedroom and themselves the kids' room, where they were both trying to change into pajamas in the narrow space between bunk bed and desk without colliding.

"How on earth do Hank and Laurel peacefully coexist in this room?" Mike said.

Annie could hear her father-in-law's snores through the wall like a buzz saw. She knew their house was too small, but whenever Mike pointed it out, she got an uncomfortable guilty feeling in the pit of her stomach.

"I don't know," she said. "I would've given anything to be close to my brothers, or have a giant cousin sleepover every Christmas Eve."

Her childhood Christmases had felt quiet and empty. Holidays like the Perleys'—with traditional recipes and group karaoke and gingerbread houses and skating—were so much more fun for a kid.

According to the therapist Mike had dragged Annie to after

Laurel was born, Annie's lonely childhood explained a lot of her bad decisions later in life. She had been an obvious accident, born twelve years after her next-younger brother, and when Annie was four years old, it was decided she should move to her grandmother's silent two-bedroom apartment from August through June—ostensibly for the superior school district. But even as a small child, Annie had felt her parents' relief each August when she'd left.

Once, Annie had been recounting this feeling to her therapist, and the woman had shrugged in a way that communicated impatience.

"What do you think your baby is about?" The therapist had undereye creases as deep as canyons and a rough accent from somewhere on the East Coast.

Annie didn't understand the question. Were people ever *about* anything? Weren't they just people?

"The pregnancy wasn't planned," the therapist said. "You were young and unmarried. You had other choices, but you didn't even deliberate. Why?"

Annie looked down at her still bulging lap. "Love?" she said.

The therapist snorted.

"What?" Annie had wiped her wet cheeks with the back of her wrist.

"It's okay to want to be the parent you wished you had, Annie. There are worse child-rearing techniques."

Sometimes when Annie took stock of what Hank and Laurel had—big family, loyal neighborhood friends, packed schedules—she understood that the secret of life was seeing your children take for granted what you had once ached for.

Laurel was surrounded by security and love, and Annie was certain that this would be enough to keep her anchored. It had to be.

"Oh," Mike said. He reached into his pants pocket. "My mom gave me the necklace for Laurel. I promised my parents that we wouldn't put it under the tree, though. They haven't told my sisters yet and there will be drama when they find out they're not getting it."

His jeans were flung over the desk chair, and he reached into their pocket and pulled out a jewelry box in worn navy velvet. The hinges opened with a creak.

Annie touched a finger to the small gold circle on a delicate chain. Saint Nicholas's face, etched into the pendant, looked slightly creepy, bare as a skeleton.

"It's beautiful," Annie said. "She'll love it."

"I know." Mike snapped shut the box and tucked it back into the pants leg. "So. We'll save it for eighth grade graduation?"

Annie nodded.

There were light footsteps in the hallway. The bathroom door creaked open. Over the sound of the running faucet, Annie heard the toilet flush once, then again.

Mike hiked his eyebrow.

After a third flush, Annie went out into the hall, knocked lightly on the door. "Everything okay in there?"

"Fine."

"Laurel?"

The door opened a crack.

"I thought you were asleep," Laurel said. Her eyes were puffy and her breath smelled like toothpaste.

Annie pushed open the door. Laurel had on sneakers and a vest.

"Where are you going?"

"I need some fresh air."

"It's eleven o'clock."

"These people are just a little much," Laurel said. She scratched at her sleeve jerkily. "And I'm not grounded anymore."

"These people?" Mike said. "It's your family, Laurel. They came all this way to see you."

"I'll come with you," Annie said.

"No. I need *space*." Laurel shook her head stubbornly. "And it's not that late." She dragged her fingers down her face. "*Please*. You have to start trusting me again."

"Take a breath," Mike said. He put a hand on her back, traced a circle, and she leaned away.

"I'm going to go crazy," Laurel said. "You two are going to drive me crazy."

Mike frowned, looked at Annie for a long moment. "Bring your phone," he said. "If you see the vandal, run straight home."

"Thank you," Laurel said. There was a horrible crack of desperation in her voice. "Oh god, thank you."

After she slipped out the front door, Annie and Mike stood at the bay window and watched Laurel be enveloped by the darkness.

"It's weird," Mike said. "But running is better than going out there to get wasted."

When they looked at each other, it was clear that both Annie and Mike were imagining that exact scenario.

"I'm going to follow her in the car," she said.

"Don't. She already feels suffocated."

"Then I'll call Lena," Annie said. "I'm pretty sure she's home."

"I see her," Lena said. She was on the upstairs balcony peering through a pair of opera glasses to the street below.

"Where?" Annie said.

"The hill on Coyote Lane. She's keeping to the shoulder, don't worry, and running up the hill and walking down. I'll pretend I'm out for a walk and just happened to bump into her.

"Are you sure?" Annie said. "I feel like we're ruining your Christmas Eve."

"I'm putting my jacket on," Lena said.

"But—"

"I've had years to consider this, Annie," Lena said, her voice tight and neat. "Better to intervene than have regrets."

I think it started a few months before the party.

I was up late one night with my nose in a book and heard muffled voices from outside. When I peered through the blinds, I saw movement: shadows darting through the blackness.

It must have been them.

Although I didn't hear anything that sounded like violence, I sensed danger, or at least its potential. I've always been one to trust my hunches, but that night, I chalked the feeling up to the thriller I was reading.

If only I'd turned on the patio lights, used their illumination to drive away the dark, it might have changed everything.

To: "The Best Book Club in the World"
From: proudmamabooklover3@hmail.com

Happy New Year Ladies!!!!

The book: PIONEER PARENTING, or as Deb Gallegos calls it, our annual Mommy Guilt Book:

- Did you know that suicide rates of 12-to-15-year-olds have increased by two hundred percent?
- Did you know that one in five kiddos has mental health issues?
- Did you know that there's a forty percent increase in depression in teens?
- Are you as terrified as I am by all of this? Ladies, we need to become part of the SOLUTION!

PIONEER PARENTING by Dr. E. Leona Flimsba examines how implementing a few golden rules from the pre-industrial times WILL translate into a happier, healthier, well-rounded child. We're talking less screen time and Red 40 and more stories around a campfire!

The place: MY HOUSE!!! 5423 Coyote Trail Road

CHAPTER TWENTY

"Abe *might* be doing the vandalism," Dr. Shapiro said. "It's possible."

"He says he's not"—Jen leaned against Dr. Shapiro's black leather couch—"and he's never lied to me."

Jen had asked Dr. Shapiro if they could chat after Abe's regular individual therapy session. Even if Jen still wasn't fully committed to the conduct disorder diagnosis, Dr. Shapiro was an excellent listener. The beige walls of her office, the bonsai garden on the coffee table, the gently burbling water feature—Jen found it all very relaxing. When Dr. Shapiro pressed Jen on an issue, it didn't feel like a slap so much as the welcoming stretch of a tight muscle.

"You sound certain." Dr. Shapiro's shiny bob stayed in place even as she cocked her head. "Why do you really need my opinion?"

"Paul and I had a huge fight before the holidays about it," Jen admitted. "I need a reality check."

Jen still felt guilty for the fight, and for the silent treatment she'd given Paul the entire next day. She'd tried to apologize, but Paul had assumed all the blame, and sent Jen two dozen roses and a gift card for a spa day at a luxurious resort in the mountains. She was pretty sure she didn't deserve him.

"Everything's fine with us now, but am I in denial?"

"You strike me as a good citizen. If you really thought Abe was hurting other people, you'd do something about it."

Jen shifted in her seat. The assessment seemed too generous.

"If Abe were the vandal, is that even the end of the world? It's just a little property destruction."

Dr. Shapiro eyed Jen gravely. "Is that what you really think?"

"No," Jen admitted.

The property destruction in and of itself wasn't the problem, even if there was something creepy about how holiday-focused it was. If the vandal was another kid, it would probably be a blip in his development. Through work/music/church/sports, he would find a path back to mainstream functionality.

The problem was if Abe was lying to Jen.

The only time she had felt smug during book club gossip was listening to some of the women talk about their teenagers, who apparently lied all the time, about everything. Abe did not lie to Jen. What was between them, she knew on a cellular level, was pure and true.

But if he was getting thrills from sneaking out alone, if the innocent expression on his face was a mask, well then, Jen had lost touch with something intrinsic to her.

"How's the rest of your life?" Dr. Shapiro's voice was as richly resonant as a Tibetan gong. "The non-Abe part, like your ethology research?"

"Work's a bit of a slog right now."

An understatement.

Last week, Jen was supposed to read a new study about leatherback turtles, who, in their lifetimes, navigated eight thousand miles from Indonesia to California and back. How they managed it without getting lost, how scientists went about trying to locate the turtles' biocompass to understand the connection between animals and environment, was the kind of thing that fascinated Jen.

That used to fascinate Jen. Her brain, usually reliable, had been incapable of latching on to any of the concepts. The words on her computer screen slipped eel-like out of Jen's mind as she thought about Abe, groceries, the need to get the sidewalk shoveled, anything other than those amazing turtles.

She'd been in front of that computer screen for seven hours, and she didn't have a single note.

Colleagues of hers who had claimed writer's block or requested deadline extensions for reasons of vague personal strife had never elicited any sympathy from Jen. There were excuses, she had believed, and then there was just putting your butt in the chair and doing the work.

She wasn't herself anymore. She was a leatherback turtle with a broken biocompass, swimming thousands of miles in the wrong direction.

Dr. Shapiro's smile was kind. "May I suggest a New Year's resolution?"

"Not if it's going to therapy."

One side of Dr. Shapiro's mouth lifted.

She'd tried therapy, Jen had explained to Dr. Shapiro, more than a few times since Abe's problems became apparent. Dr. Shapiro might not be aware of this, but there were a lot of hacks out there.

One had asked, with a disturbing enthusiasm, for details of Jen and Paul's sex life, another had insisted on mining the pain from Jen's parents' divorce thirty years ago (and there was pain, but triage, folks, *triage*). A few were probably excellent, thoughtful practitioners, but they all advised the same thing: *You're too closely identified to Abe's problems.*

They weren't wrong.

Jen knew all the clichés: put on your own oxygen mask first; help yourself before helping others; happy mom, happy baby. From a psychological standpoint, she *was* too wrapped up in concern for Abe, to the detriment of her own well-being.

But what was the alternative?

Abe's well-being was Jen's well-being. They were unhealthily tethered, which was exactly how biology wanted it. So, Jen would ask the therapists, I'm supposed to understand Abe, and read his hieroglyphics—I'm blamed if I can't—and then skip off to work and meet friends at one of those canvas-and-cocktail nights?

It's about balance, they would counter, try and take a holistic approach to your life. Frequently, they'd offer medication, which as far as Jen could tell would force a state of numbness.

Jen was all for people doing whatever they had to to get through the day—medication included—but if the world kept insisting her son might be a sociopath, didn't everyone *want* Jen's edges sharp and vigilant?

"I'll gladly see," Jen had told Dr. Shapiro, "any therapist whose own child has been diagnosed with conduct disorder."

Who else would understand?

Dr. Shapiro now watched Jen with a delicately wrinkled forehead.

"What about hobbies?" Dr. Shapiro said. "Something fun?"

Talking to you is fun, Dr. Shapiro. Does that not count?

"Book club," Jen said confidently. "I'm going there straight after this."

Dr. Shapiro's frown lines deepened. Jen couldn't stand her pity, which disrupted the pretense that she and Dr. Shapiro were just two girlfriends talking.

"How often does your club meet?" Dr. Shapiro asked.

"Every month."

Wrong answer. Dr. Shapiro pursed her lips in a way that told Jen she was a pathetic and isolated creature.

Paul would say: *Why on earth do you care what Abe's therapist thinks of your social life?*

Because, Paul, even if we disagree with her diagnosis, we still need to show her that it's not all our fault!

"I see people," Jen said, "don't worry. My grad school friend Maxine is coming from out of town to give a talk."

Maxine Das deserved every ounce of success she'd achieved. She'd spent eighteen months living among the elephants in Mali and was very successfully milking it for as long as she could: two books, the newspaper column, and now the second documentary, for which she was currently touring.

Jen had planned to decline Maxine's invitation, which wasn't until next month, and not because she resented Maxine's success— okay, maybe she did a little—but because what was the point?

"What's the talk about?" Dr. Shapiro asked.

"Elephants."

Dr. Shapiro straightened up. "It's not Maxine Das? I just read an article about her new documentary."

"It is."

"If I gave you a book, d'you think she'd sign it for me?" Dr. Shapiro suddenly looked girlish. Her frown lines had erased and she reached a hand up to fluff the back of her perfect bob.

Apparently, Jen would be attending Maxine's talk after all.

"She'd love to," Jen said.

Dr. Shapiro's fangirl smile made Jen feel a little more on equal footing, enough so that she circled back around to the real issue.

"So, you don't think I need to worry?" Jen asked. "About Abe's being the vandal?"

"You have good instincts," Dr. Shapiro said. "Trust them."

It was settled, then.

Jen knew her son.

CHAPTER TWENTY-ONE

" Janine? This list that you typed out summarizing the Pioneer Parenting laws leaves out *never mention body/food/weight, especially to girls.*"

"That wasn't in this book, Priya, but the one from last year, does anyone remember the name, it's going to bug me—"

"*The Unconditional Parent.*"

"Yes! Thank you. I never figured out how not to mention food. What would you like for dinner, Taylor—oh, I'm sorry, I meant let me just present you wordlessly with this plate of . . . matter you can put in your mouth and chew."

"These books are a *conspiracy*. They *want* to muddle our minds."

"Yes, it's like that quote about giving our children roots and wings. It sounds so great and poetic, but as a practical matter, it's a recipe for evisceration?"

"Who picked this book?"

"I did and don't look at me like that. We're not supposed to take this literally."

"Roots *and* wings? I mean, that's physically impossible. Are the roots retractable? But then they're not really roots, are they?"

"Deb, what's in the Pioneer Parent Punch?"

"It's based on a mulled hard cider. Cloves, cinnamon, and I mixed in a fresh apple puree."

"Harriet, did you just write down what's in the punch?"

"Katie, love, can you bring in the other pitcher?"

"Didn't last year's mommy guilt book tell us unconditional love was the most important thing? And now it's 'make them plow the fields'?"

"I'm telling you, it's a *conspiracy,* making us think there's one right way to do things. Guess what, ladies? There are no rules in life."

"Well, technically there are. They're called *laws.*"

"Who's conspiring?"

"*They are.* Them. Society. *People.*"

"You're all being too literal. No one is supposed to actually plow a field."

"Thanks, Katie. Congratulations on the big mock-trial win, by the way."

"Katie, dear, some more napkins, please."

"Lena, have you opened the cupcakes yet?"

"Ooooh, they're so cute. Look at that tiny little pioneer."

"With his tiny raccoon cap!"

"You know who needs Pioneer Parenting? Our vandal."

"We should have Laurel look out for him."

"Laurel? Why Laurel?"

"Sierra told me she's been running the loop after dinner? We should fasten a GoPro to her head to catch any night activity."

"She's not out there at two in the morning."

"The vandal doesn't need Pioneer Parenting, ladies, he needs incarceration."

"The stockades! Jeez, Harriet, don't write *that* down. I was joking."

"Or, and this is a radical thought, maybe we should just ignore him."

"Seriously, Jen? I can't tell if you're joking or not."

"He hasn't done anything major, you guys. It's been a little aggression toward holidays. If this is the best he's got, I'm not really impressed."

To: "The Best Book Club in the World"
From: proudmamabooklover3@hmail.com

Happy Month of Love, Ladies!!

The book: ROSA OF KRAKOW, which reviewers have called "moving, lyrical, powerful." The story of Rosa, a Polish seamstress coming of age in 1939 and torn between three men: her Jewish childhood friend Abel, Gunther, a Cadet in Hitler's SS Youth—and Gary, an idealistic American Soldier.

> Who will be a victim of history?
> Who will win Rosa's love?
> Will Rosa use her sewing skills to join the resistance, or be pulled
> into the Kinder Kirsch?

"Passion, death, the triumphs of the heart and the siren song of family obligations . . . ROSA OF KRAKOW is a fascinating historical journey about a woman *just like us*, born at a pivotal time in history."

(It is SO important, ladies, to take a moment and realize how #blessed we are.)

Steel yourselves, ladies! You will swoon over this Holocaust love triangle.*

The place: Priya's House

The rest: Y'all know the drill by now: start time is 7:30, creative snacks appreciated and bring tissues to spare!!!!!

*Square?

CHAPTER TWENTY-TWO

M iddle schools were supposed to be dingy, depressing places with humming fluorescent lights and peeling mustard paint. The one Annie had attended, five miles east of Sandstone K-8, had an appropriately soul-sucking institutional feel.

By contrast, the Sandstone kiddos sprinted on landscaped sports fields and swung from monkey bars on an award-winning sustainably sourced playground. They skipped to class on bamboo-wood floors, through warm beams of sunlight refracted down by pyramid skylights, past student artwork that had been professionally framed.

Today, Annie walked slowly down the main hallway: balanced atop her overfilled steel coffee mug was a red velvet cupcake that she'd snagged from a platter in the teachers' lounge.

She'd been gluttonous to take it: Lena was coming to dinner and had hinted that she was bringing something rich for dessert, but Annie used her slow pace to appreciate the new student art, which had been switched out over the weekend.

The rotating Student Art Gallery was a Sandstone point of pride, which didn't mean the art was any good. Annie suspected that most of it wasn't, certainly not the giant blurry photograph above the water station, which seemed to be a close-up of a dog's nostrils.

The quality didn't matter; what mattered was that everyone acted like it was the creative expression of geniuses, and the dog-nostril photographer—a self-aware sixth grader who'd come to Annie last year for strategies to cope with "perfectionist tendencies"—would feel valued, which would lead to good posture, strong eye contact, boosted self-esteem, and the courage to try new things.

Or she'd graduate feeling entitled to accolades she did not deserve, petulant and thirsty for external approval.

That was the risk of a Sandstone education, Annie supposed, and the rewards far outweighed them. The first time Annie had walked inside of the building, she had felt like one of those parasitical birds—Jen Chun-Pagano would know the name of the species—who laid their eggs into other birds' nests.

I don't belong here, Annie would sometimes think when she spotted Laurel on the kindergarten playground, *but she sure as hell will.*

There seemed to be a pet theme to this month's art gallery. Up ahead was a painting—a slightly better piece, Annie suspected—that gave the Warholian faces treatment to someone's Siamese cat. Sierra and Haley were deep in conversation against it, their heads framed by neon pink and green.

From Sierra's hip jut, the way her mouth moved nonstop, interrupted by only Haley's nods of agreement, Annie could identify an impassioned rant.

She crossed to their side of the hall, hovered a few feet away from them, inched close enough to hear Haley's voice, clear and loud, punch her in the ear.

"She's *out of control.*"

One wide step and Annie was between the girls, inches from the painting, close enough to smell the not-quite-dry acrylic. "Who's out of control?"

Haley's eyes narrowed. Sierra blushed.

"Who?" Annie repeated. She didn't care about the boundaries she had just bulldozed through, because she knew exactly who they were talking about.

The moodiness, the night "runs," after which Annie would surreptitiously sniff her daughter's jacket, check its pockets for bottle caps.

Who else could it be?

Laurel was out of control. The apple didn't fall far from the tree. And, as Lena had said over Christmas: better to intervene.

"Sierra," Annie said in her best strict-teacher voice. "You're coming with me."

"Someone needs to do something," Sierra said. She took a bite of the red velvet cupcake and held it out to Annie. "Splitsies? It's so good."

"All yours," Annie said.

Annie had bribed Sierra with the cupcake from the teachers' lounge, but it hadn't been necessary. Sierra was an open book, happy to miss a few minutes of English to spill everything about Señora Bemis, the new Spanish teacher, who was apparently *totally out of control.*

"Two tests in two weeks isn't helpful to anyone." Sierra spoke with her mouth full of frosting. "No one is learning, no one understands what she's saying because she only talks in Spanish. And she hit Joshua Flake. In class."

"Señora Bemis *hit* Josh?"

"Well, she tapped his backpack. With a pencil. But hard. I could hear it three rows away. Teachers should *not* be touching students. Isn't that, like, a violation of Me Too?"

To move things back on track, Annie tilted her head, pretended to silently contemplate how to solve a problem like Señora Bemis.

She waited a beat before asking, "How's Laurel doing?"

"She's taking French." Sierra didn't bother to disguise her pity at how out of the loop Annie was.

"Yes. I know, I mean—is she drinking?"

"No." Sierra's eyes widened. "We all got the message, Annie: Alcohol *bad*. Very, very bad."

"I worry about Laurel. About all of you guys."

"Aw." Sierra's brow furrowed in sympathy. "But she's so healthy, with all the marathon obsession."

Marathon?

Given that her daughter had grumbled through every cross-country unit in PE, it had not occurred to Annie that Laurel was genuinely passionate about running. She'd assumed it was a cover for alone time. Or sneaking into neighbors' garages to steal from their coolers.

Laurel was planning to run a *marathon*?

"Laurel's planning to run a marathon," Annie said haltingly.

Sierra nodded. "If anyone can do it, it's Laurel, but a marathon is, like, twenty-six point two miles? Did you know that?"

Was it even *legal* for a fourteen-year-old to run a marathon? Wasn't some sort of parental permission required?

"But don't worry, Annie, because she's being so healthy, like no junk food, tons of vegan protein bars and water. She wouldn't get drunk, even if, like, Haley and I pushed a bottle in her hand and chanted, *drink, drink, drink*."

Sierra laugh-snorted, then quickly stopped herself, straightened her posture and made her face angelic. "Not that we would *ever* do that."

"Hm," Annie said.

On its face, running sounded like a perfectly healthy hobby, but alcohol abuse and exercise abuse were both addictions.

"She really loves running," Sierra said in a "Scout's honor" tone. "Like really." She peeled the cupcake's pink wrapper, popped the last bit in her mouth. "Did my mom tell you, I think I'm going to dump Zack? He's nice but a sloppy kisser."

Good grief.

Sierra blinked myopically, waiting for advice. Really, you could dole it out until your face went blue, but they never took it.

"Don't ever waste time kissing someone you don't like kissing," Annie managed.

"I know, right?" Sierra nodded with enthusiasm.

"Let's not tell Laurel about this conversation? I just don't want to make her feel—"

"Like you're crazy?" Sierra said a little too quickly. She had a sly smile and her eyebrows had arched high.

I'm not crazy, Annie wanted to scream. *I'm the only one paying attention.*

CHAPTER TWENTY-THREE

Twenty minutes before dinner, Annie found Laurel cross-legged in the laundry closet, her back wedged in the crack between the washer and dryer, her head bowed over her science textbook.

"You can't be comfortable," Annie said.

Laurel shrugged.

Last year, Annie would have just blurted out the question—what's this insanity about a marathon?

But their entire relationship had been different last year. Laurel had been reachable. There had been hugs. *Voluntary* hugs, right up until October.

Annie was no scientist, but she did not think genes flicked on with the suddenness of a light switch. Since Fall Fest, in between surreptitious checks of the levels on the liquor bottles and sweeps of Laurel's pockets, Annie and Mike had asked her—repeatedly—whether something had happened. Big or small, Laurel, you can tell us whatever it is.

Are things slow at work? Laurel replied. *Not enough middle school drama?*

"Hey," Annie said finally. "Do you need new running gear?"

Laurel looked down at her baggy gray shorts. "No."

"Shoes, maybe? The restaurant's doing better. We could buy new."

"Okay."

"Mrs. Meeker will be here soon for dinner."

"I thought she didn't leave her house."

"Don't be silly," Annie said. "But we need to be welcoming, and this is technically a thank-you dinner for her help with Dad's restaurant, you know, getting that good review in the paper and—"

Laurel rolled her eyes. Annie wasn't certain at which part.

"So," Annie tried again, "I heard that Señora Bemis is tough." Laurel's eyes registered confusion for a moment.

"Right," she said slowly. "People are upset about her."

"She hit Josh with a pencil?"

Laurel shrugged.

"I can't believe it," Annie said. "It's so wrong."

Poor Señora Bemis, whom Annie had met once at a potluck. She'd seemed like a lovely person and probably did not deserve to be fodder for whatever this phony attempt at connection was.

"I need to finish this," Laurel bowed her head over the book.

"One more thing," Annie said. "Grandma P. is scheduled for a hip operation your graduation week."

"So?"

"Would you be hurt if they missed the ceremony?"

Almost imperceptibly, Laurel's shoulders hiked a centimeter. Annie felt a connection fuse. The running had started on Christmas Eve, when their house had been overrun by Perleys.

I have to get away from these people, Laurel had said.

Her in-laws were active in their church, founders of an orphanage in Haiti, and all you had to do was spend ten minutes with Mike to know he'd grown up loved and adored. It seemed unimaginable that they could hurt Laurel somehow.

But how many well-meaning parents had made assumptions just like that and unwittingly betrayed their children?

"Laurel." Annie crouched down, ignored the doorknob in her back. "Did something happen with Grandma and Grandpa P.?"

Laurel looked up, startled. She swallowed, stared at a spot just over Annie's shoulder.

"Over Christmas," she said.

"What?" Annie's heart thumped.

"I don't want to—"

"You can tell me anything, Laurel."

With one finger, Laurel traced a crooked line in the linoleum. "They burned the gingerbread men," she said in a rising voice. "Like twenty of them, god, it was so sad. Families were torn apart."

When she looked up, Laurel's sly smile was an almost exact replica of Sierra's: *Crazy Annie Perley.* Annie felt like slapping it off her face.

"It's only eighth-grade graduation," Laurel said in her most insufferable voice, "I don't give two shits about it."

A spark of defiance had flared in Laurel's eyes as she'd cursed. *Reprimand me. I dare you.*

"Fine," Annie said. "I'm giving our extra ticket to Mrs. Meeker."

"Fine," Laurel said.

The bell rang.

"Fine," Annie repeated. "We can invite her right now."

ena stood on the steps of the Perleys' tiny red brick ranch. She clutched the handle of a cake carrier in her right hand. In the crook of her left arm was a bouquet of peonies and a bottle of wine.

"Let me help," Annie said.

"This," Lena said, handing over the wine, "should go with the steaks, which smell divine even from here. I also made an ice cream cake, which will thaw during dinner."

Annie pursed her lips in disapproval. "Can we take a rain check?"

"On the dinner?"

"Gosh, no. The wine."

Lena tried not to frown. Annie clearly did not understand how special the bottle, a 2000 Château Pétrus, was. "Why don't you and Mike hold on to it for later?"

"Honestly?" Annie clutched at her throat with her free hand. "I don't even want it in the house."

"Because of Laurel?" Lena said. She'd sounded too judgmental. Spots of color had appeared on Annie's cheeks.

"You think I'm going overboard," she said.

"No," Lena said quickly. But Annie was.

That night, Lena had been drinking mojitos, and whenever she thought of the drink—even if someone mentioned it in a movie— Lena would taste in the back of her throat that once-refreshing mint sweetness and feel a wave of nausea strong enough to knock her off-balance.

She would love to be able to blame what she'd done on the mojitos, but alcohol was just an easy scapegoat.

"Rain check," Lena said with what she hoped was an understanding nod. "I'll run the bottle back out to my car."

"Laurel," Mike said, "you're completely missing out on this ice cream cake."

She sat spine rigid, sweatshirt zipped up to her chin, beanie pulled down over her forehead. Hank reached over to his sister's plate and spooned off a large mound from her untouched piece, popped it in his mouth. The rest of them laughed too hard, in compensation for Laurel's lack of reaction.

"Do you want to ask Lena now," Mike prompted her gently.

"We have an extra ticket to my graduation," Laurel said to Lena. Her leg jiggled *updownupdown*. "If you want it."

"We'd all go out afterward," Mike said. "The five of us, for a lunch."

The wash of emotion was so overwhelming that Lena felt almost sleepy. She gripped the sides of her chair, pressed her back into its slats.

"I'd love that. Thank you, Laurel."

"Yeah." Laurel shrugged. Her amber gaze skipped around the table.

"Can Laurel point me to the ladies' room?" Lena asked.

"I could tell," Lena told her, when they were out of earshot, "that you were dying for an exit."

"It's fine." Laurel fumbled with the zipper of her track jacket. It didn't take an expert to observe that Annie and Mike's heavy scrutiny was not working: the girl was miserable, itchy in her own skin.

"It's out of love, you know," Lena said. "All of the breathing down your neck is out of love. They just want to know what's going on with you."

Laurel's face shuttered. She looked down, suddenly absorbed with the zipper.

"How's the running going?"

"I'm slow."

"Not true," Lena said. "I see you working those hills. Are you getting enough fuel?"

"Yes." Laurel's head lifted up and those light eyes sparked to life. "Grams of protein equal to half of my body weight, so I don't bonk."

"Well, whatever bonking is, it sounds like something to avoid."

Laurel giggled. "Can you tell them I went for a run and that yes, I took my phone?"

"Of course, dear," Lena said.

"Thank you, Mrs. Meeker."

"And if you ever need some space, Laurel, come over. My house is a certified nag-free zone."

Laurel smiled gratefully.

Lena shook her hands dry, rather than use the threadbare bath towel hanging on the back of the bathroom door.

She was worried about the Perleys.

Fall Fest had been an embarrassing one-off. To brand Laurel as an alcoholic seemed an overreaction, no matter the family history.

As Lena had told Rachel years before: Yes, horrible things could—and had—happened because of alcohol abuse. But enjoyed in moderation, wine could be one of life's great pleasures.

Laurel, and Hank, too, eventually, needed to learn how to drink responsibly. There was a reason you didn't hear historians touting Prohibition as having been an especially effective movement.

The family was moving toward a crisis, but Lena had gotten Laurel to laugh for a moment. She felt a pulse of excitement: they needed her.

Other widows, Lena had read, mourned the loss of human touch, and while she respected their truth, it was not Lena's. She was more than fine without sex. When characters in books got hot and heavy, Lena would catch herself thinking with impatience that they were all such young idiots. Lust was nothing but an embarrassing lack of control.

Lena craved feeling *necessary*. Melanie and Rachel would share things with her, but they didn't need to. No one had truly relied on Lena for years and there was something healing about the naked way Annie solicited Lena's opinion.

Lena opened the bathroom door and a heightened prickly energy directed her gaze to the collection of framed family photographs on the hallway wall.

Bryce Neary.

Lena would be able to recognize his image in the busiest crowd, from miles away. She took several steps closer, fumbled in her sweater pocket for her readers.

It was a group photo, taken after a track meet. Bryce was bottom left, in their team uniform; his maroon singlet matched his ruddy cheeks. His hair mushroomed out from beneath a baseball cap. A grinning face peeked over his shoulder. Lena recognized the Adriatic blue of Annie's eyes, her pert nose.

Tucked inside the frame was a frayed wallet-sized picture of Bryce. He was smiling from the passenger seat of a tan jeep, binoculars around his neck.

"Found you," Annie sang out. She stopped when she realized what Lena was looking at, clapped her hand over her mouth.

"Oh shit. Lena. I didn't think."

"It's all right," Lena lied.

"He was a year behind me in high school," Annie said. "We were in the same group of friends, but I never brought him up because I thought it would—and see, you are upset."

There had been a circle of young women at the funeral, neat dark suits and shining hair. Their high-pitched sobs of disbelief had lassoed Lena with shame. Had Annie been among them?

"It's fine," Lena said. She felt and sounded cross. "Don't worry about me, Annie. I'm the last person you should feel sorry for."

Feel sorry for Gary Neary. Feel sorry for Bryce, and the life he might have constructed, given the chance.

Lena could still feel, all these years later, the sickening soft bump under her tire late at night, see the boy's empty blue sneaker planted upright in the middle of the road.

CHAPTER TWENTY-FIVE

Jen sat in a garnet-cushioned hotel chair, in the empty front row of the ballroom where Maxine Das had just completed her Q and A. Maxine was still onstage, trying to extract herself from the group of overly enthusiastic elephant fans grouped around her.

Maxine's latest documentary had been framed by the heart-pulverizing story of Flower, a baby elephant born with a birth defect, and consequently ostracized by his herd. Jen still felt slightly sick from watching poor Flower desperately wander the savanna to the soundtrack of mournful violins.

Nature was brutal.

So was the nasty little voice in Jen's head. It sounded a lot like Scofield and tended to lie in wait, piping up when Jen was weak and shaky.

Abe's the vandal, the voice said. *You know he is.*

Jen did not know that. School, therapies, Colin; things were more hopeful than ever.

Only because you're in denial.

Jen felt the world lurch.

Was she in denial? Maybe her brain was spending all of its energy obscuring unsavory facts about Abe, which was why she couldn't focus on anything of substance?

Or maybe the Scofield voice had piped up because Jen had developed a warped kind of Münchhausen syndrome, where her identity had gotten so wrapped up in Abe's conditions—

Jen stood up abruptly and marched herself to the long table with coffee urns and metal trays of cookies.

Another woman perused what was left of the picked-over treats. With that bushy gray hair and the long floral scarf overwhelming her tiny frame, she reminded Jen of Nan Smalls.

It was Nan Smalls, which made no sense at all unless Jen was now hearing voices and hallucinating. She slipped her right hand inside the left sleeve of her cardigan and pinched her forearm.

The woman, still there, turned and smiled. "Hello, Jen. So nice to see you here."

"Nan?" Jen said hesitantly.

"My son got me into elephants," Nan said. "He found them fascinating."

Jen felt an ache deep in her heart. Sweet chubby-cheeked Danny Smalls had toddled around, stuffed elephant in hand. Years later, his mother was at Maxine's talk, maintaining the connection.

Nature was brutal.

"Have you ever seen gummy elephants before?" Nan was regarding the tray of mini cupcakes, which were white-frosted with pink elephant gummies on top.

"No. Just gummy bears," Jen said. "Well, everyone's seen gummy bears, right?"

"Mmm." Nan selected a cupcake, plucked the gummy elephant off the top, and popped it in her mouth. "I always feel a little thrill eating sticky candy. My ex-husband hated it."

Jen managed a sympathetic cluck.

"It's the ritualized bonding that amazes me," Nan continued.

"With gummy candy?"

"With the elephants."

"Yes." Jen nodded vigorously. "Yes." *Speaking of bonding* . . . "I've been meaning to check in with you."

"Oh?"

"About Abe."

"What about him?"

"Just, you know, how's he doing?"

Do you think he might be destroying private property in his spare time and lying about it for kicks?

Nan beamed. "Colin's wonderful, isn't he?"

The nonresponse said it all.

Danny Smalls. Flower the elephant. The worry about Abe. The moment—this world—was gray and hopeless and suddenly all too much. Jen felt the prick of tears in her eyes.

Nan reached out her hand, paper-thin skin, knobby blue veins, to Jen's shoulder. She spoke in a soft, quiet voice that made Jen's eyelashes flutter. "Please draw strength from this."

Jen felt herself lean forward, into Nan's space. She held her breath.

"'He will cover you with his feathers and under his wings you will find refuge. His faithfulness will be'—"

Without warning, Jen was yanked backward into a patchouli-scented embrace. Her cheek was crushed against Maxine's beaded necklace.

"I'm free," Maxine said. She released Jen from the clutch. "Shall we?"

Jen looked cautiously around the hotel conference room. "There was a woman here when you came up, right? Quoting a psalm?"

Maxine nodded, lowered her voice. "Oy. Sorry. Some of the fans are a bit . . . Well, let's just say that this tour has been confirmation that it takes all kinds to make the world go 'round. Are you *crying*?" Maxine tilted her head and squinted at Jen.

"Your talk was so great," Jen said, in broken voice. "Flower got me, and I know, I know. Preservation of resources."

"Flower is just fine," Maxine said, "very happy at the preserve, I promise. Listen, Laurence, my manager, wants to join us for dinner. He's hoping you don't already have one."

"A manager?" Jen said. "For what?"

"You know, things like this." Maxine gestured to the ballroom, now empty, and its rows and rows of chairs.

"Why on earth would he want to meet *me*?"

"Your book." Maxine overenunciated the words like Jen was being dim. "Your grant."

"I'm just in the research stages."

"Fair warning: he's pretty aggressive. Actually." Maxine snorted. "You'll be an excellent match."

"*Me?*"

"Please. I was there when you hid those books in the library so no one else could find them for that paper on—was it novice management?" Maxine clasped her hands together gleefully. "I can't believe I remember the topic."

"It didn't happen like that," Jen said.

"It did. You hid the whole stack in the lower archives, you little rat."

Jen recalled hazily the jostle of books in arms, a rushed walk, a charged feeling of battle-readiness. The memory should be embarrassing, but Jen only felt a dull melancholy for her loss of ambition.

It had been electric to feel such purpose, to have that fiction of control over her life.

"I was a total asshole."

"No." Maxine wagged a finger. "You were a tigress."

"I've become a soft-boiled egg. I sit in the audience and weep for Flower the elephant."

"Not buying it." Maxine regarded Jen with an annoyingly superior grin. "People don't change that much."

"Hello?" Jen called. She walked into the kitchen. "I'm home." She stepped out of her shoes, rubbed her heels.

The boys had left a half-full pot of congealing ramen noodles on the stove. And a pile of dirty bowls in the sink, but she didn't care.

Dinner had been delightful. Laurence the manager had handed Jen his card, with a sincere-enough *call me whenever you're ready* and a double-cheek kiss. She felt inspired to sit down at her computer and finish that leatherback-turtle study, maybe even take a peek at the one involving monarch butterflies.

Upstairs, a door slammed. There was the thunder of footsteps.

"Hello?" she shouted again. Above her head was the screech of something being dragged across the wood floor. She heard Colin's footsteps on the stairs.

"You won't believe who I saw tonight," she said in a half shout. "I won't make you guess, it was Nan, who said you're wonderful, and then I got a personalized psalm, something about feathers, do you know that one? It made me think of Emily Dickinson, 'hope is the thing with feathers,' which is ironic, because I think it was about worry, which is the opposite of hope. She smelled it on me, but it wasn't entirely my fault because—"

Jen glanced up.

Colin was still in the doorway. He shifted his weight from one foot to the other.

"We have," he said, "a bit of a situation."

CHAPTER TWENTY-SIX

"Holla123 unfriended Abe," Colin said in a rush.

Jen felt an all-too-familiar tsunami of hatred toward Holla123. "That little bastard," she said.

She clipped up the staircase to Abe's room and Colin rushed to keep up. "The thing is," he stammered, "Holla123 is apparently only nine years old."

"What?" Jen stopped midway up the stairs. "Did we know that?"

"No. Apparently his parents didn't realize it was a war game, and saw some of Abe's online communications and were horrified by the violence."

"What did those idiots think? The game is called *Foxhole*."

Colin laughed nervously as Jen knocked on Abe's door.

"Wait. Before you go in—"

Jen opened the door.

"Abe had a strong reaction."

The desk chair had been overturned and the video monitor was upside down and unplugged. A red beanbag chair had been eviscerated. Its white-bead filling covered the entire floor of his room like a fresh blanket of snow.

Abe was hunched like a turtle in the middle of the room, head tucked into knees; a pair of scissors were clutched in his fist.

"I have a new enemy," he said. His voice was muffled.

Jen tiptoed through the beanbag filling and sat beside him, placed a hand on his spine, which felt damp and knobby.

"Holla123 is not the only game in town," Colin said. "We'll find another Foxhole mate."

"The same thing will keep happening," Abe said quietly. "The same exact thing."

This is what the experts didn't get: Abe was vulnerable, not some sophisticated villain.

Yes, said the Scofield voice, *but every villain starts out vulnerable. In superhero movies and life.*

"Why are we moping about a nine-year-old?" Colin said. "What happened to the power of positive thinking?"

Jen and Abe watched him curiously. Given the choice, their family would always hunker down to mope. She had been about to suggest they open the Oreos.

"Let's go do something," Colin said. "Let's play hoops."

"Now?" Jen said. "It's ten o'clock on a school night."

"I don't feel like it," Abe muttered.

"I'm sure your mom will let you earn points for it, right Jen?"

"It might be fun," Jen offered.

"Come on, Abe," Colin said. "A change of scene."

"I really don't want to," Abe said, more firmly.

"For points," Jen said. She felt a little guilty backing the idea when Abe was against it, but Colin was probably right. Doing something was better than wallowing.

"I have to go if it's for points," he said bitterly. As they left the room, he shot an exaggerated angry look in Jen's direction.

She started to shovel the tiny white balls into a pile, an impossible task, given how they clung to her clothes. Abe's look had unsettled her, and Jen wondered if it had been wrong to force him outside. But it was only basketball, she reasoned, and he was with Colin.

She peeked out the window, caught the two of them as they rounded the corner.

Abe followed after Colin in quick steps, like he was trying to keep up, but if Jen didn't know, if she were one of her neighbors glancing out the kitchen window, she'd assume they were two friends around the same age, meeting up for a casual night game.

Jen did not like the way her heart lifted. Ordinariness should not be aspirational, and she did not want to care what her neighbors thought.

Her eyes caught on a flash of light farther up the road. A runner's reflective vest. The figure was slight, their pace even.

A child, Jen guessed, all alone, late at night. That familiar rising tide of disapproval: *What parent would allow this?*

Jen was aware of the irony. She should be more compassionate toward other parents and their choices, but could judgment ever truly be suppressed? It was always there in the wings, certain and outraged.

And it felt so much better than doubt.

CHAPTER TWENTY-SEVEN

I t was a chilly dark morning. As Annie waited on Lena's doorstep, she balled her fingers inside the sleeves of her thin sweatshirt.

Maybe Lena hadn't heard the knock? Annie shook out her hands and pressed the doorbell. Its ring echoed through the house.

She peeked into the dark front window. Lena was probably sleeping in. Or out running an errand.

There was probably an excellent reason why she hadn't returned any of Annie's texts from earlier this morning, but Annie sensed it was a reaction to seeing those photos of Bryce Neary last night. When she'd turned around, Lena's eyes had been cold and hard, her mouth had been a straight line.

Annie had never seen Lena look so—

Mean. Lena had looked *mean.*

After the kids and Mike had gone to sleep, Annie had tiptoed to the den and lifted the photo from the wall. She'd sat with it on the couch, remembered the last time she'd seen Bryce alive, on the night of the Meekers' last party.

She'd been a few feet away from where she was now, on the other side of Lena's house, when she'd felt a hand on her shoulder, and then a rise of hope.

Please be happy, she thought. *Please, please, please.*

When Annie turned around, she looked straight into Bryce's

green eyes. His summer cut made him look a bit like a shorn lamb, innocent and exposed.

Years before, Mike had tried to persuade Annie to position the photo less prominently, but she refused. It was the only way she could think to express how much Bryce Neary mattered. And how sorry she was.

On Lena's steps, Annie was subsumed by a wave of despondency so strong that she could hardly breathe for the thick of it, washed up her nose and down her throat.

It would pass.

And then—who knew when—it would return. No matter how hard you fought for one, there was no such thing as a completely fresh start. Even without the photo of them together, Annie would carry Bryce with her forever.

With trembling hands, Annie grasped in her bag for a pen, scribbled a note on the outside of the envelope, tucked it under the cake carrier's handle, and hurried back to her car.

CHAPTER TWENTY-EIGHT

Lena woke up sweaty, to the sound of her doorbell's chimes.

She had dreamed she was at Bryce Neary's funeral, standing next to Rachel in the back of the hot room with cramping calves, listening to the organ drone. Her eyelids had been so heavy, but whenever she shut them, she could only see one thing: blood seeping onto pale skin.

Lena sat up in her bed, reached for the insulated cup by her bedside, took an icy gulp.

The dream had felt too realistic. The air in the nave had been so thick with overapplied perfume and now, almost fifteen years later, Lena could taste it, heavy and floral, in the back of her throat.

Do not stand at my grave and weep.

It happened when Bryce's college friend stood to recite that beautiful sad poem.

I am in the birds that sing—

Rachel's wails drowned out his young voice. *This is wrong,* she cried. *It's wrong, what you did is so wrong.*

The speaker stopped, uncertain.

Lena caught, a few rows ahead, strangers exchange a pointed look. *That's the daughter of the man who—* A ripple of miscomprehension waved through the crowd.

They assumed Rachel was talking to Tim, but Lena had known that Rachel's judgment was meant for her.

Lena leaned back against her pillow and took another sip of

water. She closed her eyes and slowed down her breaths. Simple as they were, deep breaths helped.

You've gotten away with it, she reminded herself. You're safe now.

Lena thought she functioned well, given the weight on her conscience. She did not abuse substances. She paid her bills on time. She was capable of making small talk, discerning the ghosts from reality. When life required it, she could drag herself onto a plane.

If she had a slight problem with online shopping, so what? She could afford it. Generosity was hardly a crime.

But in the beginning, in those empty days after Rachel left, Lena would wake up from similar dreams just like this—empty and parched—and not leave her bed for the entire day.

She couldn't go back to that.

The doorbell rang again, its chime like an electric shock. Another wave of heat crashed through Lena. Little beads of sweat slickened the skin on her nose, upper arms, neck.

She bolted out of bed and to the window.

Annie's car was parked in Lena's driveway. Lena watched her hop inside it and zip back down the hill like she didn't have a care in the world.

She had left something on the doorstep. Lena opened the front door and pulled her cleaned cake carrier inside, read the note on the envelope.

Thank you for coming last night! We loved having you! Hugs!
She ripped open the envelope.

Dear Lena,
Here is the invitation to my graduation. I really hope you can come.

Love,
Laurel

P.S. Thank you for being so nice to me last night.

Lena's eyes filled with fat tears of relief. Their kindness felt like absolution.

It's not. Rachel's voice in her head was sharp as a tack. *They have no idea what you are.*

We all misjudged the deceased.

I think back to the November book club. I saw someone vulnerable and gentle.

A wolf in sheep's clothing.

Criminals are masters of deception, but to have been so easily manipulated?

Everyone feels duped. Everyone.

CHAPTER TWENTY-NINE

"Your car mirror's gone," Abe said.

It was a brisk morning, and Jen had forgotten her jacket in their rush out the door. They had both slept too late and had fumbled through the before-school routine, but as the leatherback-turtle study had cleansed Jen's system, the basketball game had appeared to cleanse Abe's. He seemed much calmer.

"What?" Jen said.

"Your car mirror is gone."

She looked up from searching for keys in her bag. He was right. The driver's side-view mirror was completely gone—two wires reached futilely into the air.

Jen was momentarily breathless. "Who would do this?" she said.

"The vandal." Abe's tone was matter-of-fact.

"But the vandal's never done anything this severe," Jen objected.

All of these months, Jen had been the one talking down the women of the book club. *It's not personal. It's property damage.*

(Because you thought it might be your son.)

It felt very personal now, though, like she was being punished for something specific.

"Maybe the vandal was mad at you," Abe said. He took a casual bite of peanut butter toast.

Jen peeled her gaze from her poor car, naked and violated, and fixed it on Abe.

"You think the vandal targeted me?"

"How would I know?" Abe shrugged and took another bite.

"Abe, did you do it?" She'd breathed out the question. "It's okay if you did. Just tell me."

"You think I'd smash your car?" His eyes had widened, betrayed.

"No," Jen said quickly. "But I'm sorry for making you go last night. I shouldn't have pushed."

"That's true," Abe agreed. "But it was actually okay. We talked to a girl who was out running."

"Who was that?"

"The one who puked all over Colin at Fall Fest."

"Laurel Perley?"

"We all played this game, horse. Is your car okay to drive?" He looked at Jen's car. "You really should have parked in the garage."

There was a tiny white ball in the part of Abe's hair. Jen plucked it out. They would be finding them forever.

"It's not okay to ruin things," she said. "We have to tell Dr. Shapiro about last night."

Abe shrugged, checked his watch. "Did Dad leave his car here or at the airport?"

"Here. Does Laurel Perley run alone at night a lot?"

"I don't know. Can we take Dad's car? I don't want to be late."

"Sure," Jen said.

She thought of Laurel's messy performance at Fall Fest. She had a rebellious streak. How late was she out running every night?

Not too much of a stretch, Jen speculated, from that to vandalism.

Hey, wake up, Scofield, she thought, *it looks like we have another suspect.*

CHAPTER THIRTY

"The police don't care at all," Janine said. "They really don't."

"It's all been pretty minor." Deb cast a regretful look at Jen. "With the exception of what happened to your car."

"I just read an article about how hate crimes are on the rise," Janine said worriedly. "Is anyone else connecting the dots between this month's book and what's happening here?"

"Janine, you can't compare a popped snowman to genocide."

"Violence is violence. It starts with broken store windows and curfews and escalates rapidly to something much worse. We need to *do* something."

"Like what?"

"I'm aware, ladies, that book club has been a strictly politics-free zone since 2016—"

"For good reason. Anissa Dunne was traumatized. She's never come back."

"I think it's time to reassess."

"Are you kidding me? *Now?* Not for the school shootings or border crisis, or the Black Lives Matter movement—"

"Those aren't *political issues,* those are human-rights issues."

"And we just stay in our safe little Karen bubble."

"Can we please not debate that nickname *again?*"

"If you have a problem with the term 'Karen' you need to ask yourself *why.* Why are you getting so defensive, are you trying to uphold a system—"

"The *system* created the nickname because where is the male equivalent! God forbid women express anger or entitlement, without the world needing to slap them back down—"

"*Ladies,* this is happening here. *Here.*" Janine's shout broke through the discussion. "The vandal is hurting us *in our homes.*"

Around the circle was a cluster of small, worried nods.

"We need to make a unified statement," Janine said. "A celebration of diversity."

Jen, who'd been lazily sipping her drink, choked on it. She felt the sting of alcohol up her noise and struck her chest twice with her fist.

"You alright there?" said Priya, with a small smile.

"Let's turn the last book club into a multi-culti party," Janine was saying, "and instead of food related to the book, we'll bring food reflecting our different heritages."

"That doesn't even make sense."

"Unless you think the vandal is railing against our diversity, which—um." Deb looked around the room with skepticism.

"This isn't about what the vandal thinks, it's about a statement we make to ourselves. We are a melting pot, ladies."

"It's salad bowl."

A furrow appeared on the narrow bridge of Janine's nose.

"Salad bowl, not melting pot, because 'melting pot' implies a disintegration of individual culture."

"Well, whatever, then." Janine threw her hands up. "Salad bowl. I'll bring my mother's cassoulet, and Priya, you can bring those amazing samosas you brought to my Christmas crafting party. Athena, I'm sure there's some wonderful Kenyan dish you can bring, maybe a nice peanut stew, unless that's from some other part of Africa? And Deb can bring a special beverage, and Jen will obviously bring something Chinese, so that's at least five nationalities represented."

"I'm not Chinese."

"Are you sure?" Janine squinted at Jen. "I thought you were part Chinese."

After a moment of openmouthed disbelief, Jen swallowed. "Unless you know something I don't, Janine, my dad is Filipino."

"What a shame." Janine frowned. "I was going to ask you for help with Katie's project on the Han dynasty. Oh well. Why are you all looking at me like that? You'll bring something *Filipino* then—"

"But growing up we didn't really—"

"Filipino food," Janine said firmly, "will be a real treat for the rest of us!"

Jen caught Priya's eye roll, her angry frown.

"Ja*nine*," Priya said.

"What? I'm sorry, I'm sorry. Anyway, Lena I'm assuming your mother was Mexican? Because of the salsa—anyway, is that a bad thing for me to say? Seriously. Why is everyone still looking at me like that?"

"My mom was born in Mexico City," Lena said.

"Perfect. Six different nationalities! Seven, if Carol can bring something Jamaican, yum, yum! We'll need a sign-up sheet."

"My grandma made this amazing dolma."

"Where's dolma from?"

"Turkey."

"Well how about that, we've got Turkey represented too! See? Salad bowl! What else do we have in our glorious family trees, ladies?"

The room erupted with talk of childhood meals and whether it was okay to bring something outside of your heritage, because Harriet wasn't Ethiopian but she knew how to make *doro wot* and would be happy to bring that. Would it be homage or appropriation? No one could decide.

"Or we could just skip the cooking and invest in a neighborhood security camera," Annie said.

Jen held her breath as she waited for the group to jump on the suggestion, but instead the conversation turned to a showy and pointless debate about who should be the creator of a Multi-Culti Night assignment sheet.

(Spoiler alert: it was going to be Janine.)

If the security camera idea resurfaced, Jen was prepared to give a pretty little speech about how Orwellian panic could erode the warm neighborly trust that was the essence of Cottonwood. She'd work to get Harriet on board first and then sell it to the rest.

But why did Jen even care? Laurel Perley, not Abe, was the one who went out late at night, got into who knew what kind of mischief.

Because Jen didn't like thought of the entire neighborhood gunning for a child, any child. It was a matter of principle!

"Jen," Janine said. She twirled her pen like a baton. "Do you have a specific dish in mind, or should I just write down Something Filipino. Yes?"

Jen managed to keep a straight face. "Something Filipino. Thanks for your cultural sensitivity."

Deb snorted loudly, but Janine flashed a distracted smile. "You're welcome, sweetie."

Annie Perley was on the sofa, her hand pressed against her mouth to stifle laughter, her shoulders shaking in mirth. She did not look in the least concerned about an Orwellian panic over-taking the neighborhood, or about video cameras capturing her daughter in the act.

Laurel Perley had come over last week for ice cream and video games after a game of basketball with Abe and Colin. She seemed polite and sweet and not at all like someone who would destroy property.

And then there was Abe.

If Jen had to bet, who did she think the video cameras would capture?

Sure, Jen. Scofield winked. *It's just a matter of principle.*

To: "The Best Book Club in the World"
From: proudmamabooklover3@hmail.com

Hello Ladies!!!!

The book: This month, we will go dark and searing with a true crime read, THE MONSTER NEXT DOOR.

"How well do you know your neighbors?"

A husband, a wife living in a quiet town. No one suspected her tragic death could have been a murder until . . .

Five years later and two states over, the same man is widower-ed (if that wasn't a word before, ladies, it is now!!!)

Horrible luck or has the monster next door left a trail of bodies?

We're definitely going in like a LION with this MARCH pick, hahahahaha!

The place: Deb Gallegos's House, 7:30.

PS. Speaking of local monsters, I'm conducting a poll about whether to move our neighborhood St. Paddy's Day Four Leaf Clover display inside this year . . . FOR PROTECTION.

Please weigh in!! United we stand. . . .

CHAPTER THIRTY-ONE

Annie was on her bed, folding laundry, when Lena called to ask about the dress code for Laurel's graduation.

"Is a sundress appropriate?" Lena asked.

Annie glanced out her window. The sky and ground were the same dove white, and in between them were giant drifting snowflakes.

"How can you even think about sundresses in this weather?" she said. "It's casual. I guarantee that whatever you put on, you'll be the best-dressed there."

"Does Laurel have a dress yet?"

Annie plucked Hank's T-shirt from the laundry basket and shook out the wrinkles. "Laurel does not." She folded the shirt, reached for another.

"Laurel does not what?" Laurel said. Her head poked in Annie's doorway. She had on her snow jacket and hiking boots.

"Lena asked if you had a graduation dress."

"Tell her I'm wearing sweats under my gown," Laurel said, but she was smiling.

"Are you going up to Sierra's?"

"Abe's."

"Again?" This was the second time in a week. "Is your phone charged?"

"Yep. I'll be home for dinner, byeeeee."

"She sounds happy," Lena said. "Lighter."

"She does." Annie paused.

"But?"

"Have you met Abe?"

"He's very handsome."

"I think he's on the spectrum."

"Ah," Lena said. "I can see that."

"I mean, the kid has an aide. They pretend he's a babysitter, but what seventh grader do you know who has a babysitter? I'm not trying to be judgey, it's great if Laurel has neurodiverse friends, but . . . what do they have in common? Abe is really into video games and Laurel has been fighting all year to be treated like a grown-up." Annie paused. "I just don't get it."

"For one," Lena said, "he looks like a teen idol. And she wasn't into running before this year either. She's exploring new interests."

"True."

"How does she seem, in general?"

"Happier."

"I would focus on that then. Maybe Abe's company is just what she needs."

Lena could have stayed on the phone with Annie all morning, but Annie had to dash off to the ice rink to drop off Hank at a skating party.

Lena half wished Annie had invited her to tag along. On this quiet Saturday, her house felt suffocating.

She switched on the news for some noise, opened her laptop.

Melanie had for years teased Lena about her shopping problem, and Lena always countered that clothing wasn't inherently frivolous. Clothing announced who you *were,* Alma had taught Lena. Lena had even, for a millisecond in her youth, considered a career in fashion.

In another life, maybe she'd be behind a desk, barking orders at scurrying assistants.

It was the quiet, Lena presumed, that kept her mind perpetually tangled in all of these alternate paths: What if there had never been an accident, or what if she and Rachel had left Cottonwood together?

We can't stay here.

The first time Lena thought it had been during Bryce's funeral. Two middle-aged men in navy suits had materialized like FBI agents. Lena got a flare of adrenaline before realizing how silly she was being. Only on television did they arrest people at funerals.

Lena still had no idea if the men had been mourners or staff, but they'd helped Lena remove a hysterical Rachel from St. Mary's and put her into the backseat of Lena's car.

We can't stay here.

Lena had reached into her bag, bit a Xanax in half, and held it out to Rachel in the backseat. Rachel had leaned forward to accept it in her open mouth like a baby bird.

That night, Rachel had slept on the sofa, hands flung defensively over her face. The directive returned, tapped Lena on the shoulder.

We can't stay here.

But Lena's mind felt scrambled and frantic. Where would they go? How could she take that first step? She'd watched the sun dip behind the mountains. The realization advanced cold and slow as a glacier.

Lena was an infection that must be quarantined. What Rachel needed most of all was to be free.

She can't stay here.

Melanie's cousin was a trustee at a New Hampshire boarding school with a decent reputation. The next morning, Lena called him and recited an early version of The Story, that she needed to put miles between Rachel and the gossip about her father. A sizable donation helped secure a spot.

Out of all the possible paths forward for Lena, she had chosen the one that gave her nothing but space and time to think, a self-imposed house arrest.

It might not be state-mandated punishment, but she had suffered. At heart, Lena was drawn to festivity, was a lover of parties and noise—and she had not allowed herself to enjoy any of it. (It was slightly pathetic, how she was treating Laurel Perley's graduation like a coronation.)

Now, Lena forced herself to focus on the thumbnail images of clothes on her computer screen. Her mouse hovered over a magnificent Pucci caftan, its print an echo of a minidress Lena had worn to one of her parties a billion years before.

It was a shame she'd donated that dress, which would have looked great on Annie, who dressed too sensibly in fleece pullovers and yoga pants. She'd probably wear overalls to Laurel's graduation.

Annie would look great in the caftan, too, though. Lena's blood warmed as she pictured it: Annie, hair straightened, with a dramatic cat eye.

Annie didn't mind Lena's fussing the way Rachel would have. She would tilt her smiling face upward, sit patiently and wait for Lena to apply that cat eye.

Better to focus on the caftan than that unanswerable question: *Have I suffered enough?*

Two swift clicks, and Lena had bought the dress.

I noticed the outfit right away. It was old-fashioned, and I heard
some people fussing over it, but to me that type of thing always
comes off costumey.

I remember specifically thinking the choice in footwear very
impractical, given that the ground was still wet from the spring
snow.

After the body was found, the detective said as much, that
the shoes may as well have been banana peels. Anyone foolish
enough to hike in them on wet rocks, he said, was basically asking to slip.

CHAPTER THIRTY-TWO

"Why haven't they caught him yet?" Jen's mother whispered into the phone. "I don't understand."

"Because there are bigger crimes than a busted side mirror, Mom."

Jen had accidentally told her mother about the vandalism last week, and it had been their primary topic of discussion since.

"I worry. And Paul won't be there to help. He's never there."

"Because he's working, Mom."

Jen's mother probably couldn't stop her unhelpful worrying any more than Jen could stop her skin itching in response to it, any more than Abe could help his outbursts or the vandal his—or her—midnight destruction.

And if everything was chemistry and genes and drive, should people even be punished for their malfeasance?

(Dear Senator: Attached please find my thoughts on a Criminal Justice Reform bill. Xoxo, Jen.)

"Mom, the doorbell just rang."

"Maybe it's the police," her mother said excitedly, "with news that they caught him."

"Abe met a friend at the basketball court. I'm pretty sure it's her."

"A friend." Her mother's voice had become sugary. "Well, good for him."

"He's had friends before." Jen felt immediately defensive.

"Of course he has, honey." Her mother's voice was an unctuous syrup. Jen was grateful to hang up and answer the door.

"There's good news and bad news," Jen said to Laurel Perley.

"I can take it," Laurel said. She smiled, mouth full of braces.

"Colin won't be here with the pizza until later, but we have some of those amazing cookies from Breadman's? Or I could run out for something?"

"Oh gosh, no," Laurel said. She followed Jen into the kitchen. "Any kind of fruit would be great. But only if you have it already."

Jen regarded Laurel. Whenever she thought about the morass of disordered eating, she was relieved to not have a girl. Not that boys were immune, but they didn't seem as targeted by a barrage of objectifying and confusing images: to be strong and sexy and muscled and waiflike and body-positive, a stance that was communicated by wearing crop tops.

"I'm not, like, scared of calories or anything," Laurel said quickly. "I'm just mindful about how I fuel."

"You're really committed to running, huh?" Jen said.

"My dad ran"—Laurel shrugged—"so . . ."

"That's so sweet," Jen said. "I bet he loves training with you."

"Does Abe's school go up to high school?" Laurel had blurted this, shifted her weight against the kitchen counter.

"Yep. There's a tenth grader there now."

"It sounds amazing. The head teacher—"

"Nan Smalls?"

"Is she, like, a visionary?"

"She's kind," Jen said. "She cares a lot about the kids and the school." *And is very generous with psalms, if that happens to be your thing.*

"I'd love to see it. Maybe I could go with you, and just, like, pick up Abe one day."

"Definitely," Jen said. "It's very small though, certainly not for everyone. I'd be happy to talk to your mom."

"She won't go for it," Laurel said sourly. "She thinks our school district is like the best in the country. Which it's obviously not."

"It's very highly regarded," Jen said, because it was true and because neighborhood mom code required her to Never Denigrate Another Parent's Opinion. "Go on up to Abe's room," she said quickly, to stave off further discussion. "I'll bring some fruit and popcorn."

As she collected the snacks on a tray and climbed the stairs, Jen felt slightly guilty for ever suspecting Laurel Perley of being the vandal. Laurel was a complete improvement over Harper French, who had not only never offered to help Jen in the kitchen, but had once sent her on a wild-goose chase to three different markets for dill-pickle-flavored potato chips.

"Laurel." Jen heard Abe's yell down the hall. "You can't duck the whole time. You have to aim at something."

Jen bristled. If you didn't know Abe, that might sound rude and bossy. But Laurel must know Abe, because she laughed.

"I suck at this," she said amiably.

"You're not that bad," Abe offered. "Do you feel ready? We have one goal: defeating Holla123."

"Who's that?"

Jen held her breath. She burst into the room before he could explain it was a nine-year-old. "Snacks!"

Laurel and Abe sat side by side in front of the monitor. Abe was being a graceful host and had given Laurel the remaining beanbag chair and his favorite headphones.

Would a sociopath share like that, Scofield? No, he would not.

Jen put the popcorn down on the floor between them.

"Thanks, Mrs. Chun-Pagano." Jen was relieved to see Laurel grab a handful of popcorn. "Who's Holla123?"

"*Our* mortal enemy," Abe said, mercifully stopping before providing a colorful explanation of why Holla123, homeschooled third grader, needed to be vanquished. "We will rain down terrors on him."

"Okay then," Laurel said.

"All right?" Jen said. "I guess I'll go get some work done." Since Laurel Perley had been coming over, Jen had finished the leatherback-turtle study and was halfway through the monarch butterflies. Her notes were organized, and all felt right with the world.

"Thank you, Mrs. Chun-Pagano," Laurel said. "Abe, thank your mother."

"Thanks, Mom."

The vandal had been quiet, and as a consequence, so was the Scofield voice in Jen's head. She shut the door behind them.

Walking back down the hall, Jen heard laughter. She smiled to herself, and the simplicity of it struck her: all it really took was a new friend.

People talked, before the body was found, about their friendship. Intense, was the consensus. Mercifully brief.

If anyone knows the exact nature of what happened between the two of them, no one's talking about that.

We only know that it was unhealthy. A toxic combination that shouldn't have been allowed.

Where were the parents? people whispered. How did they miss the red flags?

Obviously, they've forgotten how sneaky teenagers can be.

CHAPTER THIRTY-THREE

They cornered Annie at book club. She was alone at the food table, had just sliced off a gooey hunk of Brie and was trying to slide it from the knife to her plate.

"We're having a friend-tervention," Deb Gallegos said. Priya gave Annie a small sympathetic smile.

"Now?" Annie said. Across the room, people were starting to settle in their seats for the discussion.

"You're out of control. You dragged Sierra from third period?"

"Oh," Annie said. "That was months ago."

"Well I only just learned about it," Deb said, "so humor me, Annie, by explaining why you yanked my daughter from class to pump her for information about her best friend. You're the school counselor. Aren't you there to, you know, to support all of the kids?"

"Only part-time," Annie joked weakly. "There's a reason I'm second-in-command."

Deb's mouth tightened.

"I'm so sorry," Annie said. "I was way out of line. Did I freak out Sierra?"

"Only about your mental state."

"It's not that we don't understand your worry," Priya said. "Fall Fest was very disturbing. But it was also forever ago."

"When does this end?" Deb pressed. "You'll get a job at the

high school? You'll go to every party, wait to jump in and body-block Laurel from drinking too much or making out with some-one?"

"I'm over Fall Fest," Annie said. She caught the skeptical glance between the two of them. "Really."

Deb folded her arms across her chest. "Can I offer some advice? From a mom with a little more, you know, crow's-feet?"

Annie managed a nod.

"If you're a safe harbor, your kids will volunteer things. But if you insist on being supercop, they'll run in the other direction."

Priya nodded. "That's so, so true."

"Since Fall Fest, we're watching them so carefully," Deb contin-ued. "We'd have seen any signs of monkey biz."

"We got you, Annie," Priya said. With a sweep of her hand, she gestured to the other women. "We all do."

Annie nodded. "I know."

Deb's face softened. "Okay, friend?" She reached out a hand and squeezed Annie's arm.

"He's getting away with it!" Janine's voice was a shriek from across the room.

"Okay," Annie said.

"He's getting away with it," Janine shouted. Her short blond curls were frizzed with outrage. "It kills me."

Lena agreed that the Monster Next Door didn't look innocent. One of his wives had vanished without a trace. Another had died after a fall in the kitchen.

Throughout the book, the obsessed retired detective explained how suspicious it all was: the life-insurance policies bought be-forehand, the power-washer rental, the internet searches for dis-solving acid, and so on. (There was always an obsessed retired detective in these stories. Thankfully, Lena's local police force seemed to have a much healthier work/life balance.)

"He's probably eating spaghetti and meatballs right now," Janine continued, "watching *Jeopardy!*"

"That's an oddly specific picture, Janine."

"I mean he's just living his life. People like that don't have a conscience."

"What do you mean, people like that?" Harriet said.

Lena realized her hands had gripped onto her kneecaps. She relaxed them, folded them neatly in her lap.

"People who think laws don't apply to them," Janine said. "Criminals."

"Some people snap in the moment," Jen said.

"Not buying it," Janine said. "There's a line that decent people don't cross."

"Hard disagree," Jen said. "People are complicated. Morality is relative."

"I'm not convinced he did it," Harriet said. "Based on the chart."

"What chart?"

Harriet held up her legal pad, on which she'd drawn a complex series of boxes. "His actions on the night of the first would-be murder." With her pen, she pointed between two boxes. "With seven minutes between his convenience-store run and the time of death, I don't think he could have done it."

"You made a chart, Harriet?"

"There were so many facts, and I needed to keep them straight. I mapped out the second would-be murder as well."

Deb balled a fist and held it in front of her mouth, pretended to cough the word *obsessive*.

"You don't need that to know whether he did it," Janine said. "He did. And he got off scot-free."

Lena had been in her forties—a baby—when the accident happened, but she had acted like her life was over. What second acts might have been possible if she'd had a different mindset? If she hadn't entombed herself in the silence?

Suddenly breathless and itchy, she walked away from the discussion and over to Deb's kitchen window. She switched the latch, cranked it open, inhaled the cool air.

"Move over."

Lena shifted over to make room for Annie, who settled next to her.

"Deb and Priya just told me I'm an awful parent," she said. "And bad at my job. And they're one hundred percent right."

"They don't really believe that," Lena said loyally.

"I used to feel balanced," Annie said. "All I do is worry now, search through Laurel's pockets. I never find anything, yet I can't stop. What's the cure for constant worry?"

"Having fun?"

"Right," Annie said. "We're not dead yet. Let's do something frivolous. Like . . . we could go to that new wine bar everyone's talking about?"

"We can do better than that," Lena said.

"Yeah, that's lame. We could—I don't know, there's that spa in the mountains that everyone talks about? River Rock something?" Annie's voice was skeptical. "I hate strangers touching me, though."

"Think bigger," Lena said.

If you looked at it one way, she was as much of a victim as anyone else. Starting with that last party, Lena's whole life had been stolen from her, due to events beyond her control.

"Bigger than the spa?" Annie turned to face Lena, one eyebrow arched. "You don't seem like the Vegas type, Lena."

Lena could see it as if it were already happening right there on her patio: Candles lining the stone wall. A table piled with food. The jangle of pop music. Kids running and laughing and dancing in the purple dusk, Laurel in the center, twirling around on the dance floor.

"What then?" Annie said. "I can tell you have something specific in mind."

Lena breathed in the cool night air. Her pulse sped up like something illegal had hit her bloodstream. The Perleys needed fun.

Don't pretend this is for them, Rachel scoffed.

Damn the guilt. Lena had sacrificed enough.

"I'm throwing Laurel a graduation party," Lena said.

To: "The Best Book Club in the World"
From: proudmamabooklover3@hmail.com

Bonjour! Bring a smock and your creativity to this month's meeting, ladies!

The book: THE ARTIST'S LOVER

Suzanne Valadon. Her face may be recognizable, but her story has remained largely untold. The subject of Toulouse-Lautrec's THE HANGOVER and, for a time, his lover, Suzanne was ahead of her time, a single mother, an artist in her own right, a rule breaker to rival them all.*

THE ARTIST'S LOVER, a "meticulously researched," "lyrical" "tour through artist colony France," tells Suzanne's story, through her eyes.

April in Paris, ladies! Who can resist? Be there (MY house again, hooray!) or be square!!!

*She painted male nudes, y'all!

CHAPTER THIRTY-FOUR

ny interest?

Jen's former colleague from the Bay Area had emailed her a link to a registration form for an academic conference in Atlanta. Five days in June. International Ethology and Animal Aggression.

She *was* interested.

Jen from Before would've been on the conference's faculty, putting final touches on her paper. Jen from Now could barely picture how to pack for five days, but was still grateful to feel that new-school-supply rush of excitement while reading about the various panels.

Someone was making a ruckus in the kitchen. Drawers and cabinets opened and slammed shut. "Everything okay in there?" she shouted.

"Just me," Colin said. "Looking for popcorn." He leaned in the doorway to the dining room.

"In the garage," Jen said. "Nice shirt."

She'd offered him first dibs on a bag of Paul's clothes heading to donation. In true hipster fashion, he'd swooned over everything— the stained pink seersucker suit and the ugly bold-print shirts. He wore the worst one now—a spectacularly loud red button-down stamped with fish and pineapples, which Jen remembered from a costume party years ago.

But there was something off with Colin. He smiled with effort and his shoulders hunched forward.

"Are you okay?"

"Just a little pain here." Colin tried to straighten himself up, winced, pressed a hand into his side. "Dr. Internet says it might be an ulcer."

"You need to see a real doctor."

"It's the end of the semester. Too much work."

"Take some days off. We'll manage, and I'll ask people here for the name of someone good."

"Thank you." He eased himself down in the chair. "I've been meaning to ask you: Who is Harper?"

Jen felt a precipitous drop in her stomach. "Harper was a girl in Abe's class at Foothills." Her voice sounded too prim.

"Okay." His fingers worried the top button of Paul's old shirt. "They didn't get in a knife fight, did they? Abe said something to that effect the other day."

"What did he say?"

"It was strong language. 'Cross me and I'll cut you like Harper,' something like that? With anyone else, I would be worried, but I know Abe has that dry sense of humor. He was joking, right?"

It would be impossible for Jen to adequately communicate what Foothills had been like—the months of terror and bullying that had resulted in the Harper French stabbing. If she told Colin now, the story would be about Abe Pagano's irrepressible violent streak.

More than Dr. Shapiro or even Paul, Colin had become a touchstone for Jen. He talked about Abe in a way that made the challenges seem manageable, a mere part of Abe, rather than what defined him.

He was the necessary counterpoint to the Scofield voice. And he was real. There was no point in even telling Colin, Jen decided. It was ancient history and irrelevant.

"He was joking," Jen said.

"Right." Colin chuckled, then winced. "I figured a stabbing would have come up." He braced himself against the table and hoisted himself up.

"We're getting you a doctor's appointment," Jen called after him as he hobbled away. The thought of doing so made her feel slightly better about the lie.

CHAPTER THIRTY-FIVE

t was a gorgeous April morning and Annie was reclined on a chaise in Lena's backyard with a breeze ruffling her hair. The grass glittered in the sunlight. An insistent chickadee sounded its two-note chirp.

Across from her, Lena and Laurel leaned toward each other, passed binders back and forth, talked about party decorations and food and the cake. Annie closed her eyes, lifted her face to the sun, saw a sepia-toned image dance across her eyelids.

A lawn full of people in pashminas and linen suits.

"Mom."

Annie opened her eyes.

Lena and Laurel were both looking at her.

"Your dresses arrive tomorrow," Lena said, and from her tone it was clear she was repeating the information. With her dark-framed glasses and white button-down shirt, Lena looked very professional. "We'll find a time for you to try it on?"

"Can't wait."

"You were saying something about the dance floor," Laurel said.

"I always put it there," Lena said in a brisk voice. Party planning had infused her with a formidable energy that both impressed Annie and made her want to hide in the bushes.

Watching the lawn from the cisterna plum, branches tickling her arms.

The party planning was making memories come back to Annie in pieces, bits of fuselage washed to shore. She busied herself with rolling up her pants legs, exposing her pale shins to the sun.

Lena's floaty green dress. Rachel leaned over the bar, her giant eyes watching Bryce.

She'd been just a few years older than Laurel. What was Rachel like now? The more Annie tried to look past the question, the bigger it became.

If Annie saw for herself that Rachel was okay, maybe the tide could do its job, sweep up the beached wreckage and wash it back out to sea.

"The DJ will be under a tree." Lena sighed. "If Laurel still insists on a DJ and not a live band."

"Laurel insists on a DJ," Laurel said, grinning. "It's going to look awesome. Can you imagine, Mom?"

"Yep," Annie said. Could she ever.

FIFTEEN YEARS EARLIER

Bryce was being Bryce.

It was taking him forever to get Annie's orange juice from the bar because he was working overtime to charm the sour-faced girl behind it.

He still looked the high school track star. When he flung his lean arms sloppily to emphasize a point, his short sleeve slipped to expose a long tendon, the slight bulge of his biceps.

Annie clocked the girl responding to his goofy chuckle, how her obsidian eyes glinted and she swallowed quickly. Her smile lingered for a minute after Bryce bounded back to Annie, two glasses in hand.

"You made a new friend," Annie said.

"Who?" He handed Annie the juice. "Rachel?"

Rachel Meeker? Annie stole a longer glance.

Rachel's features were thick bold lines. They overpowered the planes of her face, and while she'd probably grow into them, right now she looked too severe. Or maybe she was mad, somehow knew that Annie was about to break her heart.

"What are we looking at?" Bryce said in a stage whisper.

"Rachel Meeker," Annie whispered back. "I think she has a thing for you."

"Not age-appropriate," Bryce said. He shook his head clumsily and held a finger in the air. "But I was telling her, as I will tell you, Annie, that after this, there's a party down the hill. At Dan's. No. Dave's." He closed his eyes, bit his lip, swayed very slightly. "I forgot the kid's name. The kid with the rabbits, you know? Chris's cousin. He's got a hutch for them, an actual rabbit hutch."

"You're drunk." Annie felt annoyed at his sloppiness, left behind by it, which was hardly fair. She ignored her phone, which was trembling in her bag.

"Not as drunk as I will be," Bryce said with indignation. "I've got the whole night planned. Should we ask Rachel for a bottle?"

Annie didn't understand why she suddenly felt so guilty watching Rachel Meeker behind the bar. With her doting mother and ornate braids and perfect princess bedroom, she did not need any sympathy.

Shaken, Annie took a delicate sip of orange juice, returned her attention to Bryce, who hiccupped, pointed clumsily at her chiming bag.

His brow furrowed. "You gonna get that?"

CHAPTER THIRTY-SIX

For the book club meeting, Janine had transformed her living room into an art studio where the women could create their own still-life paintings. Their subject was a vase of flowers and a glass half filled with Deb Gallegos's themed drink (Untitled— Pernod and champagne and lemon juice).

Later, the group would agree that while the experience had been lovely, they wouldn't re-create it. Everyone had been too contemplative, a bit in their own orbit.

Deb pushed her chair closer to Annie. "This isn't book club," she muttered, "it's study hall. We should've gotten a live model." She glanced at Annie's painting. "You're a terrible artist."

Annie had to agree. Her canvas looked like blueberries on toast. "I know," she said. "Wasn't this supposed to be empowering?"

"Speaking of nudes," Deb whispered, "have you heard of the hot untouchable?"

Annie shook her head. It was difficult sometimes to keep up with Deb.

"I overhead Sierra on the phone asking 'is the hot untouchable coming to the party.' She won't tell me who she was talking to. Is Laurel seeing anyone?"

Annie frowned. "Laurel's been spending time at Abe Pagano's house. But I don't think—"

Deb's brows lowered to indicate that no, she couldn't picture the pairing either. "Haley seemed the likely candidate anyway. But I had to ask."

"Definitely Haley."

"But it was strange. Sierra usually has a compulsion to tell me things, so I'm a little proud of her—maybe she's finally learned to keep a secret—but I'm also dying to know. What qualities would make a teenager *untouchable*? I really hope it's not something *class-based*. Are we raising elitist snobs or—"

"What are we whispering about?" Janine popped her head over the easel.

"Laurel's party," Deb said.

"Oh yes," Janine sighed. "Poor Katie has a bit of the green-eyed grouchies. How's the planning going? Anything I can do to help?"

Janine's forlorn look indicated that perhaps *Katie* wasn't the jealous one after all.

"Lena's a powerhouse," Annie marveled. "She's got it more than covered."

All three of them looked ahead to Lena, who gracefully dabbed at her canvas.

"The party is way bigger than Laurel," Annie said. "It's not even about her anymore. Tell Katie that it's really for everyone at this point."

To: "The Best Book Club in the World"
From: proudmamabooklover3@hmail.com

Ladies . . . drumroll please! . . . it's (SOB) our Final Book Club Meeting of the Year!!!!

    The book: IPHIGENIA, based on the Greek Myth of the daughter of Agamemnon, sacrificed by her own Father so that he could start the Trojan War, avenged by her Mother, who was then murdered by Iphigenia's siblings—her own children. (And I thought Christmas at my in-law's was awkward!)

    The place: Priya's house at 7:30.

    The food: It is our much-anticipated MULTI-CULTI NIGHT, when we celebrate the ~~Melting Pot~~, oops I mean SALAD BOWL, that is Cottonwood Estates! Bring your appetite and sense of adventure and of course: a dish from your heritage!

    LET'S CELEBRATE OUR DIFFERENCES, LADIES, AND OUR UNITY!

    Thank you everyone for making this the BEST. YEAR. EVER!!! Words cannot express how much I treasure this incredible community of ours! I better stop—I'm starting to tear up right here at the computer! Mwah, mwah!

CHAPTER THIRTY-SEVEN

There were only two days left until the party.

"Final countdown," Annie chirped as she handed Lena the caftan she'd just tried on. The arms and shoulders had fit her perfectly, just like Lena had pictured when she had bought it.

"Not a surprise that it needs to be hemmed," Annie said with a nervous giggle as Lena looped the thread onto her sewing machine. "Everything needs to be hemmed on me!"

She paced back and forth along the perimeter of Lena's crafting room. Lena wanted to send her on a made-up errand, clear the room of her jittery energy.

"I'll have Laurel try her dress on too when she gets home from Abe's, where she is *again*," Annie said.

Lena looked up. There had been a sharp note in Annie's voice. "Is everything still okay?"

"Great." Annie was still pacing. "She's talking to us again. I don't know why I feel so . . . bottled up this week. Do you think it's the party?"

Lena pressed the sewing machine's pedal. "Maybe."

"Why are you so calm?"

"Hilde the party planner," Lena said. "She's a dynamo. You'll see when you meet her."

Lena remembered how she used to wake up with a jolt the morning of a party with a weird stage fright, task lists multiplying in her head.

You seem more plugged in, Melanie had said a few weeks ago. I think it's because you've given yourself permission to live.

Melanie was almost right. Lena had given herself permission to forget.

All of these years, Lena had confused grief and guilt, but the grief was not Lena's, it never had been, and the guilt was self-generated. It could be ditched by the side of the road, it turned out, to become smaller and smaller in the rearview, until it was practically indistinguishable from the rest of the landscape.

Annie had stopped her pacing to stand uncomfortably close to Lena's shoulder. The way she peered at the hemming process made it impossible for Lena to concentrate.

Lena pointed to the stitch in the caftan. "I don't think the thread matches."

Annie sucked in her lips noisily. The smack reverberated in Lena's ear. "Looks fine to me."

"If you don't mind," Lena said, "could you grab some extra thread from the closet? Top of the stairs, third door on the right, middle shelf, in a wicker basket."

Annie repeated the instructions, flashed a thumbs-up, left the room.

"Take your time," Lena called after her. "Just grab all the pinks."

Relieved, she returned to the hemming.

Upon closer examination, Lena saw the thread color *was* a little off. She leaned over the dress, carefully ripped out the stitches.

"I'm leaning toward going to that academic conference I told you about," Jen said. "The one in June."

She and Paul were in the car, driving home from an impromptu date night at a downtown sushi spot. Through the windshield, the moon was large and full, and the sky around it an electric blue.

"You should go," Paul said.

Jen glanced over to the passenger seat. "I'd be away for five days."

"So?"

"Is it that easy?"

"Sure."

Jen did have a light optimistic feeling that it might be that easy, that the Paganos might be approaching something close to balance.

Since March—right around the time Abe had become friends with Laurel—there had been nary a square of toilet paper hung from a tree in all of Cottonwood Estates. Her worry that Abe was the vandal seemed a million years behind them, just like that horrible meeting at Foothills with Dutton.

In retrospect, she was almost grateful for it—and even for that uncomfortable call with Scofield—because they were now in a better place, with a small but legitimate circle of support.

Abe had *two* friends, if you counted Colin. He had Dr. Shapiro and Nan and the Kingdom School, which had its faults but was a good fit.

And Jen had the women of book club, not the Hitchcockian murder of crows she had imagined in darker moments, but more a circle of clucking mother hens.

As she turned into their driveway, Jen realized that the spot between her scapulae, usually rock-hard, was relaxed. Her entire body felt warm and content.

There were less complicated children out there, but there were also parents who might have handled it all better. In the name of protecting Abe, Jen had lost nuance, self-awareness, her career: everything that had made Jen *Jen*.

Almost everything. When Maxine Das had recalled Jen as the tigress from graduate school, Jen hadn't initially recognized herself because all of that fire and drive wasn't channeled toward the pursuit of tenure anymore.

It had all been repurposed, focused on Abe.

Jen had been stuck in tigress mode for years. But there were reinforcements now. Maybe the beast could finally loosen her hold.

CHAPTER THIRTY-EIGHT

Annie found the spools of thread exactly where Lena had directed her, in a large wicker basket, lined neatly and color-coordinated in rainbow order. She scooped up all of the ones that might be construed as pink.

The upstairs hallway smelled like Lena's perfume and fresh paint. Annie remembered more on the walls, which now seemed stark. Rachel's room was only a few feet down the hall. Annie walked toward it, keeping her footsteps soft and slow. She pressed her weight against the doorknob, and twisted it open.

It was still a teenaged girl's bedroom. Mint-green duvet and oversized pink fluffy pillow shams. The same giant giraffe in the corner. On the bedside table was Rachel's eleventh-grade summer reading: *The Great Gatsby, The Taming of the Shrew.* A gray sweatshirt was folded over the back of the desk chair, like Rachel was about to shrug into it, plop down on the bed.

Over the desk was a giant posterboard collage. Images of Olympic medals, swimmers diving into pools and standing on winner's podiums. *Excellence,* Rachel had cut-and-pasted. *Champion. Winner. 100 Fly.*

Annie had had no idea that Rachel was so obsessed with swimming. What else didn't she know?

She wanted to rifle through the desk drawers, spread everything out on Rachel's bed and spend the rest of the evening poring through it, but she forced herself to leave before Lena would notice she'd been gone too long.

"Could these work?" Annie said.

She had returned from upstairs mellowed, and she carefully lined up the pink spools, and inexplicably a red and two purple ones, next to the sewing machine, for Lena's examination.

When Lena heard the ascending scales of her ringtone, she looked around the sewing-machine table for her phone.

"It's over here." Annie darted to the shelves across the room, picked up the phone. "Oh my god. Oh my *god*."

"What?" Lena said.

"Oh. My. God. It's Rachel!" Annie's face flushed pink and she hopped in place like a sweepstakes winner. "Rachel would like to video chat!"

In a clumsy rush, Lena rose from her stool. Her knees jostled the sewing machine, and the caftan slipped to the floor along with the seven unraveling spools of thread.

Lena had the sensation that she, too, was falling, head over heels over head. Her feet tangled in the caftan's silk and she watched helplessly as Annie reached out a fingertip to press Accept.

"Well, hello, Rachel Meeker," Annie said into the phone. "How are you?"

CHAPTER THIRTY-NINE

Jen found Abe alone in his room, stretched out on his bed with his computer on his lap. He was so absorbed in his programming that he didn't notice her in the doorway.

She smiled, watching him type, chuckle at the screen. "What's so funny?"

He slammed shut the top of the computer. "Nothing."

"Where's your Foxhole buddy?" Jen pointed to the beanbag chair.

"Do you mean Laurel Perley?" Abe said. "She's not my Foxhole buddy."

"Oh? What's her title then?"

"Either a nullity"—Abe tilted his head—"or an enemy."

"But, but, but," Jen sputtered, "she was just here, debating which takeout place to order from."

"Everyone needs fuel," he said flatly. "Sharing a physical location does not confirm friendship."

"What happened this time?"

"You saw what you wanted to see."

"Laurel's a sweet kid, Abe. She's not Harper French, and if you can't maintain a friendship with her, then—"

"Laurel is more like Harper French than you think. Remember how Harper used to smile and feign kindness only to lure me into the group so they could be really mean to me?"

"You're saying that Laurel lures you into a group to be mean?" Jen looked around the empty room. "What group?"

"Laurel has ulterior motives. She is false pretense personified."

"I don't even know what that means."

"I'm happy to stop talking about it."

"What happened?"

"I told her to leave."

"But why? Was there a disagreement? Did you ask Colin to help mediate whatever it was?"

"Colin." Abe snorted. "I've started to doubt his intelligence."

"Abe, you get stuck in patterns with people, and if you don't learn how to change them—"

"Then I won't have a pretend friend like Laurel, who excels at acting all phony-nice."

"After his appointment, I'm sure Colin will help smooth things over, whatever this is."

"What appointment?"

"Remember, for his ulcer? Mrs. Gallegos got him an appointment with that doctor and he's taking the next couple of days off."

"What ulcer?"

"Abe! He's been walking around like this." Jen hunched over in pain. "How did you miss it?"

"I don't need him to smooth things over. I have a plan."

Jen felt light-headed. She gripped the molding around his doorway for support.

"It's legal," Abe clarified. "On a literal level, no one will be harmed."

"They better not be, if you have any desire to get your hands on that monitor."

Abe scowled at her. "You always side with everyone else. It's a bit unmaternal. And no matter what you think, I have the right to express my anger."

"Anger about what?"

"Using people is not okay, and Laurel needs to understand that."

"Using you? But for what?"

"This conversation is going nowhere," he said.

Jen couldn't really argue with that.

CHAPTER FORTY

"I'm sorry," Rachel Meeker said. Her face filled the phone screen. Her heavy eyebrows were lifted in confusion. "I'm trying to reach my mom?"

"She's right here." Annie swung the phone around so Rachel could see Lena. "I'm her friend Annie."

"Okay?" Rachel's lips bent in a small polite smile.

She looked fine, Annie decided. Her hair had been chopped very short, which required confidence, didn't it? Her eyes were big and dark and worried, but that was probably because Annie was gawking at her.

"Has your mom told you about this party she's throwing for Laurel? Oops, you probably don't know who Laurel is, she's my daughter. You haven't met her yet, why would you have, that'd be silly, what a silly thing for me to say."

"Yes," Rachel said slowly.

Yes *what*?

Annie was aware she was talking too much, but Rachel wasn't saying enough. "If I look familiar," Annie said, "we were on swim team together a million years ago. You were like, seven or something."

"I don't remember," Rachel said. Her chin had receded into her neck. "I'm sorry, I just don't remember."

.   .   .

When Lena snatched back her phone, there was mild surprise in Annie's eyes.

"I'll call you when we're done," Lena said to Rachel. She smiled reassuringly—*you did just fine.*

"Okay," Rachel said in a meek voice.

"She seems great," Annie said hesitantly, after Lena hung up. "Was it . . . okay that I picked up?"

"Fine," Lena said. "She's always been a little shy."

Annie seemed to accept the fabrication, but Lena recognized Rachel's behavior and it wasn't shyness.

After the funeral, during Rachel's final weeks at their house, she'd run upstairs when cars pulled into their driveway, freeze at the doorbell rings of people dropping off their casseroles.

She'd been so petrified of exposing Lena. *I'm worried the truth will spill out of me,* she'd said.

After all of this time and distance, Rachel was still scarred by how Lena forced her to lie. And obedient enough to continue to do it.

It was heartbreaking, but more than a little reassuring, too.

FIFTEEN YEARS EARLIER, 1:42 A.M.

Gary meant for Lena to show up just as she was, but Lena was vain enough to take the time to change into her silk pajamas, blot off her night cream, swipe on some mascara, pinch her cheeks.

On her way downstairs, she paused before Rachel's door for a moment, decided against leaving a note.

There was no point. Lena would be back before Rachel woke up, and no one ever needed to see her parent like this, so free and elated.

When Lena walked into the kitchen for her car keys, the oven clock said 1:52. They were by the fridge, right where she'd tossed them after a last-minute errand to buy extra white rum for the party.

She scooped them up, slid on her flip-flops, and opened the door to the garage.

CHAPTER FORTY-ONE

Jen couldn't get comfortable. She kicked off the covers, pulled them back on. Paul, snoring lightly next to her, turned onto his side.

She had texted Colin to ask what happened between Abe and Laurel. Abe hadn't been in the best mood, he replied, but he didn't think anything too dramatic had occurred. Did Jen want him to cancel his doctor's appointment? No, Jen replied. Nothing is more important than that.

Tomorrow morning, she'd call Dr. Shapiro, who might have some ideas of how to proceed: apology notes, or group therapy sessions, or an amendment to the point system.

This time will be different.

Jen repeated it until she started to drift off. A door slammed. She opened her eyes. Had it been real, or part of a dream?

What popped into her head was that quote everyone misattributed to Einstein, about how the definition of insanity was doing the same thing over and over and expecting different results.

This time will be different.

But her brain stuck on something that didn't lie flat:

Laurel Perley is a lying little brat.

The thought was a dissonant chord. Embarrassed by her indecency, she stared at the dark ceiling.

CHAPTER FORTY-TWO

Janine's texts started at seven fifteen on Monday morning.

Jen, making the coffee, recognized their rhythm: the single chime, then a trickle, finally a deluge of overlapping alarms, like blue jays sounding their frantic warnings.

The vandal has struck again!

Out of the kitchen window, Jen could see her neighbors' rooftops. She imagined the breakfast scenes beneath them—worried clucks over coffee mugs. Lined brows, can-do brainstorming about security gates and cameras. They all thought they were invested, but no one felt the news as deeply as Jen did.

Paul had already left for the airport, which meant that Jen was alone with Abe in the kitchen. He sat behind his laptop at the banquette, cereal bowl untouched. There were circles underneath his eyes as he typed. He wore the same dark T-shirt and ankle-baring track pants that he had worn last night.

Jen hadn't asked him whether he'd done it. If he said no, could she believe him? If he said yes—

"Abe, I thought I heard a door slam last night?"

He continued typing.

"Abe."

"Huh?"

"Did you slam the front door last night?"

"What?" He blinked.

"The door. Did you go out late?"

"Yeah." He nodded. "I took out the trash."

Was that a metaphor?

"When?"

"Midnight. I dunno. Why? You're always saying that we can't wait until morning because the trucks come super early."

She was always saying that. The trucks did come early.

"But that's all you did?"

"Yep."

With effort, Jen kept her voice steady. "Because the vandal broke one of the windows at Laurel Perley's house last night. Was that your plan for justice, Abe?"

"My plan's more sophisticated," he said with a shrug. "But it does sound kind of like justice."

"They think it's a disgruntled student," Annie said with an eye roll. She swigged the latte Jen had bought her from the espresso cart, the fancy one on Main Street. "Oh, this is delicious."

"A student?" Jen said.

There was something going on with Jen's hair, which was normally glossy and pin-straight but this morning clumped in irregular waves. She wore stained striped pajama pants and a holey T-shirt and—although Annie was trying not to examine too closely—didn't seem to have bothered with a bra.

"Or a former student. They saw something similar a few years back," Annie said, "and when the police realized I work at the school, they kind of seized on it. Don't worry, though, I told them alllll about how Multi-Culti Night will stop anything like this from ever happening again. Although now I'll have to miss it because tonight is the only time the window guy can come."

Annie paused for Jen's laughter.

She'd been pretty pleased with her joke about Multi-Culti Night, which seemed the type of dry snark Jen would appreciate, but it hadn't even registered with Jen.

"Do you have any disgruntled former students?" Jen said.

"It's not a student," Annie said. "It's the vandal, obviously, and it sucks but I suppose it was our turn. Between you and me, we've had so much drama this year, with, you know, Fall Fest and Laurel, that this doesn't seem like such a big deal." Annie shrugged. "Maybe I should be more worried."

"Do they know anything?"

"Not really." Annie took another gulp of the latte. The taste was so complex, rich and layered. "Is it the beans or the machine?"

Jen stared at her blankly.

Everyone seemed almost disappointed that Annie wasn't in hysterics about the window, and maybe if the kids had been in the den when the rock sailed through, she would have been.

The impact hadn't even been loud enough to wake any of them, or even Yellow, who apparently lacked basic watchdog skills. They had woken up to the peaceful but surreal scene of a wren hopping around their living room, and a neat pile of glass on the floor.

"The coffee," Annie said. "What makes it so good? I can't thank you enough. It's a toss-up whether I'm more grateful for this or for Deb's window guy. He's doing the job for free, you know, because he owed Deb a favor. She's a little vague on why, though."

Jen didn't even smile. Her gaze drifted over Annie's shoulder to the broken bay window.

"Are you okay?" Annie said.

"Did Laurel say anything about last night?"

"No, but she had an early graduation rehearsal this morning and then a bunch of her classmates are having a goodbye-to-Sandstone picnic."

"Apparently Abe asked her to leave last night, and I think they had a bit of a fight? I know he can be rude, unintentionally, he doesn't intend to be—"

"Was she mean to him?" Annie asked. "She was so moody this year, and although it's gotten better, you know what I think it's been this whole time?"

Jen shook her head.

"Perfectionism. Yesterday I saw one of those vision boards, do you remember those? I had sort of an epiphany and I think because Laurel's driven and quite intense, she can take it out on the rest of us, so for a kid who . . ." Annie trailed off because Jen had never opened up about Abe's being on the spectrum. ". . . who's a little younger, like Abe? Maybe it gets confusing?"

"Oh, well"—Jen's smile was wan—"I wasn't there."

Annie wondered if it would be inappropriate to hug Jen. The way her thin cotton T-shirt exposed the undercurve of her breast made Annie want to bundle her in a sweatshirt.

Jen's eyes blinked full of tears. "Maybe we should sit out the party."

Annie reached out and placed her palms against Jen's goose-bumped upper arms. "Laurel will be heartbroken if Abe's not there and Lena and I will both be heartbroken if *you're* not."

"Do you mean that?" Jen said quietly. The tears had spilled over her lower eyelids. She didn't even bother to swipe them away.

"Yes." Annie squeezed Jen's shoulders reassuringly. "Promise me you'll be there."

"Okay." Jen gave a small, grateful smile. "I promise."

CHAPTER FORTY-THREE

"I *know* Annie Perley."

Rachel had called Lena from her future in-laws' house on the Cape. She wore sunglasses and a big floppy sun hat. Behind her was a brilliantly blue sky. "And she acted like she knew me too."

"She was just surprised." Lena's hands were sticky with fondant for Laurel's cake, so she wiped back her bangs with her forearm. "Because you seemed so surprised."

"Mom," Rachel whispered urgently.

"I get paranoid sometimes too, Rachel, but Annie was just being friendly."

Rachel looked over her shoulder warily. "What if she knows something?"

"Annie trusts me with her children. She doesn't know anything."

"Shh," Rachel said.

"Babe." Lena heard Evan's voice. "My mom wants to know which bike you want to go into town?"

"I usually use the one with the flower basket," Rachel said brightly. "Babe, I'm videoing my mom."

"Oh, hello dear!" Evan pushed his face into the frame next to Rachel's, straw hat against straw hat. "You look very blue over there. Is it an art project?"

"It's cake fondant," Rachel said.

"Wonderful!" Evan said. His fedora was a size too small. It sat atop his head like a fez.

"Does it look like the color of the ocean to you?" Lena held up the fondant. "Baja blue?"

"What will Laurel Perley know about Baja blue anyway?" Rachel said. "She's in a landlocked state."

"She wanted a beach theme." Lena had kept things restrained, though: beach themes could so easily veer tacky.

"Awesome!" Evan said. "Who's Laurel Perley?"

"A neighborhood kid," Rachel said. "For some reason my mother is throwing her a massive party."

Lena watched Evan's face for a flinch or a protective glance. She often wondered what, if anything, Rachel had told him.

Not the truth: Evan wouldn't be able to muster so many "dear"s for Lena if he knew that.

"Remember," Evan said. "The whole point of a party is fun! So have fun!"

"Smart boy," Lena said.

CHAPTER FORTY-FOUR

Jen, wobbling on her tiptoes on the stepstool, reached a hand into the top cabinet, blindly felt for the edges of the large serving platter.

Janine had banned takeout containers. She wanted the food to appear, she had instructed the group, as though it had been homemade with love.

The restaurant that Jen had ordered from, on the other side of the city, didn't even have the roast pig that Jen barely remembered from childhood barbecues at her uncle's house.

In a panic, she had rattled off a few unfamiliar names from the menu in front of her—*lumpio, sure, and one of the bulalo and throw in a sisig, please.* The women would stuff their faces on these dishes that meant nothing to Jen, to—what—prove how accepting they were?

It was a total farce.

They wouldn't really be accepting once they found out Abe was the vandal.

If.

If Abe were the vandal.

Maybe they would be accepting. Not every parent was like Jen, a Canada goose, ready to attack.

Although she was certainly passive enough when it came to challenging Abe. This morning, on the drive to school, she'd kept the questions raging in her head, hidden behind her regular cheery *Have a good day.*

She had just set down the platter on the counter when her phone rang with a call from an unfamiliar number.

Jen answered it with a curt "Yep."

"Jen, it's Nan Smalls. I want to schedule a chat. About Abe."

Jen saw right through her gentle tone: this was how it started, how it always all started, with Dutton and the entire parade of others before him.

"Now?"

"I'm in Eagle County for a faith-based educators' conference this weekend, but I'm back tonight. Maybe first thing tomorrow?"

"Paul's out of town until tomorrow afternoon."

Pause.

"That's unfortunate, but this won't wait. The cleaners are doing their year-end sweep at the school, and I'd like us to not be interrupted by vacuuming. Would you consider meeting at the Village Bean on Main Street? Around nine?"

There was probably an underground network on which the principals could warn each other: *When you expel Abe Pagano, do it in a public place. The mother is batshit.*

"Of course."

"See you then," Nan said, and hung up.

Where was her psalm? Was Jen so beyond hope she didn't even get a psalm?

How many of these school principals pretended to love kids but in truth, only had time for the ones who were cookie-cutter perfect, a neat fit into whatever box—

Stop it, Jen.

Who understood the painful impossibility of protecting your child more than Nan? If Nan couldn't handle Abe—

Jen lifted the platter above her head and let it go. A million sharp slivers all over the kitchen floor.

For a second things felt better, but soon after came the exhausted realization that no one else was going to clean it up.

· · ·

The late-spring night was so lovely that Annie decided to wait for the window guy outside on the front steps. To the west, the setting sun streaked an electric orange-pink across the sky, and while it was a beautiful sunset, Annie's mind was on that video call with Rachel Meeker.

Next to her, Yellow barked and ran to meet Laurel, who was skipping down the hill. *Skipping!* No more hunched shoulders— she was back to her old self. It had all been a phase, something to get through, like when three-year-old Hank had refused to wear pants.

Annie decided that Rachel Meeker was probably doing just fine now. She might have caught Rachel at a bad time, or maybe she was rough around the edges. Either way, the woman on the phone didn't seem too far a stretch from the awkward girl behind the bar fifteen years before.

People were who they were, after all.

But that vision board! That silly Proustian vision board had transported Annie back to her early twenties.

Years ago, Annie would have made one just like it. Not the sports part: what resonated with her was the naked dissatisfaction. Happy people didn't make things like that.

Given a stack of magazines and some glue, what would Laurel create?

Deb and Priya spoke about their youth as a golden time of self-ishness and possibility. If Annie tried to commiserate, they'd wag their heads. *Talk to us after you turn forty.*

But looking at Rachel's dang vision board had confirmed what Annie had momentarily forgotten: youth sucked.

You were powerless. And maybe, yes, you had options ahead of you, especially if you grew up in a place like Cottonwood, but they *overwhelmed.* So many possible futures, and no idea how to use your brain or body to get there. Fuckups were un-avoidable.

Annie should have recognized what everyone had been try-ing to tell her: Laurel's behavior at Fall Fest had not been about alcoholism or DNA time bombs, but about youth and all of its frus-trated want.

It had been an epic parenting fail, how Annie had rushed in all scorched-earth, assumed it was about *her* and her own demons. Luckily, Laurel seemed to have largely worked things out for her-self in the simplest of ways: a new friend, a new hobby.

"I'm coming from up there because Haley's mom dropped me at Sierra's," Laurel said quickly as she plopped down on the step next to Annie. "And before graduation, I'm going for a long run. I've been slacking on my training."

Annie chose not to point out that Laurel's training schedule was entirely self-imposed. "Did you hear it's supposed to snow?"

"Yes, and fear not, Mrs. Meeker is prepared. They're putting a giant tent in her yard." Laurel tugged at her shoelace. "Thank you for keeping it just us tomorrow."

"There'll be a couple of hundred people at Lena's."

"I meant the graduation lunch. I really didn't want any big soppy Perley family thing."

"I get it."

Haley was excellent with hairstyling, so it must have been she who created the elaborate braid in Laurel's hair, heads of dande-lions woven through. Absentmindedly, Annie reached out and patted it. That Laurel didn't even flinch felt like a gift.

Laurel checked her watch. "Don't you have book club tonight?"

"This is the only time the window guy can come and Dad is working so he can be free tomorrow."

Laurel glanced back, at the cardboard.

"People have been so supportive," Annie said. "Abe's mom stopped by this morning with coffee. Did you guys have a fight?"

"I wouldn't call it a *fight*."

"I told his mom they should still come to the party."

Laurel sighed. "I wish you hadn't done that. He's just . . . it's always all about him, you know?"

"Interpersonal relationships don't come naturally to people like him."

"What do you mean?"

"His autism."

"No." Laurel scrunched up her face. "He's got something different. He gets violent."

There was a tight coil in Annie's chest. "What do you mean, violent?"

"I don't know. He lashes out. What's the word for someone who doesn't care about other people's feelings? You know, the kid that probably tortures kittens for fun?"

Annie blinked. "A sociopath?"

"Some other thing. A disorder. Colin told me once after Abe had a big meltdown."

"Has he ever hurt you?"

Laurel shrugged. "He's yelled a few times, and thrown things. He's big into punishments. When people wrong him."

"That's not okay," Annie said. The casual way Laurel said it made Annie's stomach turn. "That's abusive behavior, Laurel. You shouldn't be anywhere near that." She turned around to look at the jagged glass that remained in the window frame. "Did he do that?"

Laurel shrugged again. "I wouldn't put it past him."

The motive is the easy part. It's the same reason for murder as in ninety-nine percent of mystery novels:

Revenge.

CHAPTER FORTY-FIVE

"The tamales are here, and they're beautiful!" Janine trilled. "*Bienvenidos*, Lena! Guys, she rendered her own lard, just like her mother Alma used to do, even with all the work of Laurel's party."

"It was nothing," Lena said. "I have a party planner."

"The chickpea curry is exquisite," Harriet said. She dipped a spoon into the bowl on her lap.

"Thank you," Priya said. "I was worried there was too much ginger."

"Deb, did your family really make this eighty-proof moonshine?"

"Probably?" Deb shrugged. "But the recipe is from online."

"So," Harriet said. "On to the book?"

No one responded.

"*Iphigenia*?" Harriet repeated. "Anyone?"

"True confession," Janine said with a guilty glance around the room. "I didn't finish it. I'm sorry, the end of the year is crazy."

The rest of them paused for whatever brag was coming next—Katie's lacrosse or mock trial or even the twins' basketball—but none came.

"I didn't read it either," Lena said.

"You're excused," Deb said. "You rendered your own lard. I didn't read it either."

"I didn't even start it," Jen said. This was a surprise to the women, but given that Jen seemed to have not taken the time to brush her hair, people decided to believe her.

"Did *anyone* read it?" Priya said. "It was incredible."

"The best book of the year, I think," Harriet said.

"Absolutely. The writing was gorgeous."

"Fill us in," Deb said.

Priya and Harriet looked at each other helplessly.

"'Query,'" Harriet read from her notes, "'whether this Greek Chorus crafts the narrative or just reports it? As a reader, what authority did you give its voice?'"

Blank looks all around.

"Okay, here's another: 'What is the difference between vengeance and protection?' No one? Okay—we could discuss the role of prophecies."

"Prophecies?"

"You know how the Greek gods hand down prophecies to characters, outlining how they're going to suffer and die and then the characters turn themselves into all sorts of pretzels to thwart the prophecy but never can. The prophecies just create blind spots?"

"Such interesting discussion topics!" Janine said.

"Yes," Harriet said with a sigh of disappointment, "it could have been great."

"Jen," Deb said, "can't you give us one of your mini-lectures so we feel less stupid?"

"Are you okay, Jen?" Priya said. "You seem not yourself."

"Abe's not doing so well, guys. His school wants to meet tomorrow. I think to kick him out."

"Nan wouldn't do that," Priya said quickly. There were some tiny uncertain nods around the room. "I'm sure it will be fine."

"I don't know," Jen said. "We always seem to find ourselves here."

"In second grade," Priya said, "Taylor tripped one of her friends, stuck out her foot because they were in a fight, and the way the girl landed on the pavement, she bit through her lip and needed stitches. I thought Taylor was going to get expelled."

"Katie got a bad grade on her Latin test," Janine blurted. "Last week, and she told the teacher that she wanted to die. They're making her meet with a counselor."

"A counselor is never a bad idea," Priya said gently.

"She's been so angry, too, *so* resentful all of a sudden," Janine said. "I don't even know where it's coming from, what did I even do, and sometimes I think—"

With an awkward squeak of her chair, she jumped up and hurried out of the room.

"Excuse me," Deb said, and followed her.

"Way to bring the party, Jen."

Jen started to laugh; everyone did. "I'm sorry," she said helplessly.

"Don't be," Priya said. "It's good to discuss this stuff."

"How did the Taylor situation resolve?"

"Wade golfs with someone on the school board and he called before our meeting, which is kind of unfair, I know, but the point is Taylor didn't mean to even draw blood. It was bad luck, and a total overreaction on the school's part. Kids make mistakes."

"Does anyone by any chance golf with Nan Smalls?" Jen asked. "Or have dirt on her, skeletons from her past?"

She had expected sympathetic laughter but Harriet suddenly became very interested in the state of her cuticles and Lena abruptly got out of her chair, tripped on Harriet Nessel's bag, and, for a few tortured silent seconds, worked to untangle her feet from its straps. She hurried out of the room, which was silent but for the sound of her footsteps echoing down the hall.

"Another one bites the dust," Jen said, but no one laughed.

"What?" Jen looked around helplessly. "What did I say?"

CHAPTER FORTY-SIX

Lena had last seen Nan Smalls fifteen years ago, back when she was still Nan Neary.

She and her ex-husband Gary sat together at their son's funeral, in the front pew of St. Mary's, so close that Lena could see Nan's curly hair cascade down Gary's sleeve.

Lena had read in the local paper about Nan's wedding to Wesley Smalls six years after that, how the two had met in a grief support group Wes had formed after his own son Danny had drowned at a summer camp, years before Bryce's death.

The article made their happiness sound like a reward after years of suffering, and it was clear from the quotes of the wedding guests that the couple's bond was deep and faith-based. Since the accident, Nan had apparently become quite religious.

Gary Neary had moved to Phoenix the year after Bryce was killed. He had established a dental practice in Scottsdale and had remarried—a woman named Margot. A cycling club website had posted a photo of their group, and Gary and Margot were top left, second row, grinning after a metric century.

He looked like a stranger.

They were all different people now.

Nan had cut off all her hair, let it gray completely. Lena guessed that she wouldn't have recognized her if they had bumped into each other on the street, although Lena had taken care through the years to avoid that very scenario.

Lena had sat down several times to write sympathy notes to the Nearys, but all her drafts were stale with platitudes.

Your tragedy, our tragedy, thinking of you, every parent's worst nightmare.

The Nearys probably preferred to not hear from Lena anyway, because while there might have been the spark of something between Lena and Gary, in the end it came down to what was between Lena and Bryce, how she had knelt over his lifeless body in the blood-soaked grama grass, with one urgent thought that drowned out all else:

Quick, Lena, hide the body so no one finds out. There's still time.

Please join us in a Neighborhood Celebration
for Laurel Perley's graduation.

June 1st at 6 p.m.
5112 Cottonwood Lane

Festive attire
No presents please

CHAPTER FORTY-SEVEN

The meteorologists were falling over themselves in excitement about last night's freak snowstorm. An inch had fallen between midnight and sunrise, the most in June since 1963, and no one could believe it.

When they started to play that song about snow in June for the third time, Jen switched off the car radio and sat in silence. Main Street was dark and gray and sloshy and as deserted as she'd ever seen it. The leaves of the Tatarian maples that lined the sidewalks drooped under the frost.

She might be excited about the snow, too, Jen supposed, if she weren't waiting for Nan.

Poor Nan.

Jen hadn't been able to apologize enough for bringing up Nan at book club. She hadn't known; she had thought Nan's son drowned.

Danny Smalls was Wes's son from his first marriage, Priya explained. Wes and Nan had met afterward, in a grief support meeting.

The other women had told Jen the whole story—how Nan's first husband, the one who hated gummy candy, was a man named Gary Neary, a local dentist who had moved into Cottonwood after the divorce, how Nan had, before Bryce died, been a bit of a hippie.

When Lena finally emerged from the bathroom, her mascara wilted, Jen apologized some more. And then Lena apologized for making a scene. And Jen apologized again for turning the final book club meeting into apology poker.

Nan Neary seemed like a lovely person, Lena said, and she was sure that Nan would be fair to Abe. When she wished Jen luck for tomorrow, Jen stammered that it really wasn't important and again, she was sorry.

For a few awkward minutes, no one really knew what to say, until finally Deb Gallegos checked her watch and said, "Can we wrap this up, guys, because the stripper will be here in five minutes."

It didn't really make sense, and was more exploitative than funny, if Jen thought about it too hard, but it was an excuse to laugh. When they all filed out, exhausted, they felt a little closer for having burrowed through.

Long live Multi-Culti Night.

As tragic as Nan's story was, Jen needed to focus on Abe, and whatever he had done, *what had he done*?

Colin didn't know, although Jen had not been able to stop asking him. She could feel him getting annoyed at the frequency of her texts. His responses were further apart and increasingly terse. I didn't see anything. I don't know. IDK.

Nan probably hadn't even told Colin anyway because she knew how close he was with the Paganos.

But, no, the Kingdom School was so tiny, Colin had to know if Abe had done something bad enough for Nan to take notice.

Jen felt a flash of anger at Abe. Everything had been going so well, and he'd ruined it. She'd done everything she could think of, and it still wasn't enough.

Maybe he was beyond help.

Whenever she sat still for a minute, Jen could feel deep in the marrow of her bones one terrifying cell of hatred toward him. Small but powerful, it could probably spread like a cancer.

CHAPTER FORTY-EIGHT

Annie left the house on graduation day for her early-morning walk in snow boots, down jacket zipped up to her chin.

She was almost at her mailbox when she saw the small blue sedan idled on the side of the road. Annie crossed the street and rapped on the window.

Colin looked up from typing on his phone, smiled, rolled down the window.

"Hi Mrs. Perley." He shivered. "I'm just on my way to the Paganos'. Everyone's so excited for the party, but can you believe this weather? Snow in June?"

Annie glanced back at her house, still and dark. "Laurel mentioned that Abe has some sort of diagnosis."

"I can't say anything," Colin said. He pushed his hair over his ears. "I really can't."

"I disagree, Colin." Annie employed her strictest teacher voice.

Colin looked at her with pleading eyes. He lifted his shirtsleeve to his mouth and started chewing on the cuff.

"You may feel that you have an obligation to the Paganos," Annie pressed, "but you also have one to Laurel. I'm an educator, Colin. Same as you."

Colin's struggle was so transparent that Annie could see the exact moment when decency won. His shoulders sagged and the words tumbled out in a mumble.

"Abe has conduct disorder."

"What?"

"He's doing really well, though, so much better than at his last school and he hasn't hurt anyone. Objects, but not people—"

"He hurt someone?"

"He was friends with this girl Harper, and he stabbed her."

"He *stabbed* a child?"

"In art class. She wasn't seriously hurt."

"The way Laurel was talking about him last night, it sounded like an abusive relationship."

"No," Colin said. "Absolutely not. He's never hurt Laurel and he never would. I'm there with them all the time."

"*All* the time?"

He shifted again. No. Not always.

"But this is unreal. Jen has known this the entire time, and she hired you, presumably to monitor him, and she hasn't said one word?"

"You're getting the wrong idea, Mrs. Perley. Abe's not a bad kid. He's just a little more sensitive than the rest of us, and has very high standards—"

"I don't give a crap about his high standards," Annie said in a spit. "Might he have, for example, gotten mad at Laurel and thrown a rock through our window as punishment? Is that the type of thing someone with conduct disorder might do?"

Colin was silent for a such a long, tortured minute that his slight nod felt redundant.

CHAPTER FORTY-NINE

"I still can't believe it. An inch of snow," Lena said to Rachel. "Should I put you on video, so you can see? I'm in the yard now, and listen to it crunch under my feet."

"Wow."

"Thankfully, the party planner insisted on a tent."

"Smart," Rachel agreed.

"She's been worth every penny. Oops, I found more trash."

Lena bent down toward the glint of silver. Another protein-bar wrapper, the fourth one this month. Someone on Rudy's staff. Lena suspected the new guy with all the muscles. He went shirtless at every possible opportunity, no matter the weather.

"What do you think would have happened?" Rachel said.

"If we didn't have the tent?" Lena straightened up. "It probably would have been fine. The roads are clear and the sun will melt everything."

"Not the tent." Rachel spoke in a whisper. "Seeing Annie Perley has dragged it all up. I couldn't sleep last night. We should've told the truth. Like I wanted to."

Lena crumpled the wrapper in her fist. A bitter taste rose in the back of her throat. "Nothing good would have happened."

"What about what's *right*?"

"Honey, Tim Meeker was a crappy father and a horrible husband," Lena whispered. "In his final moments, your father helped us. That's what's right."

Lena swallowed, hard, and stared out over the neighborhood. A jogger bobbed up the road, stopped at Lena's driveway, put her hands on her knees.

"I'll call you back," Lena said, her voice dry. "Laurel's here."

Laurel hadn't seen Lena's wave. She reached into the pocket of her running tights and slipped out her phone.

"*Laurel!*" Lena shouted, and Laurel spun around quickly and dropped the phone on the road. She bent to pick it up.

"Is it broken?" Lena said.

"No." Laurel held up the phone. "It's all right."

"Well." Lena turned in a slow circle, arms extended. "What do you think? Do you want to come inside the tent to see? Oh dear." Another wrapper lay on the ground by the gate. This was getting ridiculous. She was going to have to say something to Rudy.

She straightened up and turned all the way around again, but Laurel was gone, vanished so quickly it was like she'd never been there.

"That was odd," Lena said aloud to the empty yard.

She'd check in with Annie after graduation. Lena considered herself an expert on dirty secrets, and Laurel Perley sure looked like a girl who was keeping one.

CHAPTER FIFTY

Jen watched Nan walk slowly down Main Street in a puffy black parka that emphasized the stoop of her shoulders.

Jen pushed her own shoulders down and back against the driver's seat. She couldn't stop trying to picture Nan at her age, Indian print top, long flowing hair, saying goodbye to her son, taking for granted that she would see him tomorrow.

Then that middle-of-the-night phone call, blowing up Nan's whole life.

Jen was already tearing up. She should go inside, hands raised in surrender. *Don't worry, I completely understand. Not a good fit.*

What if I start to cry during the meeting, she had asked Paul in a panicked phone call.

You won't, he said, you're a fighter.

There was a lot wrong with his statement, but she was too over-whelmed to pick it apart. Because she was *not* a fighter, or at least she did not want to be one anymore.

Nan walked gingerly up the steps to the coffee shop, hand gripped onto the railing. Jen waited until she was inside before stepping out of the car.

It was warm and steamy inside and she and Nan greeted each other pleasantly enough, ordered their coffee, and settled in the back corner, as far as possible from the people at the other two other tables: a couple in flamboyant biking jerseys, a woman breast-feeding a baby under one of those gauzy wraps and watching something on her phone.

Jen claimed the command seat facing the door. She pictured Paul nodding with approval.

Nan shrugged out of her coat. "Let's get to it," she said. "I don't want to waste your time." As Nan reached into her bag, Jen felt the conversation careen out of her control.

Across the room, the baby shifted underneath the wrap. The mom had dark circles under her eyes, clutched her coffee double-handed, like it was salvation.

Pal, Jen thought, *you have no idea what's ahead.*

Nan pulled out her phone and slid it on the table. She didn't have a passcode, Jen noted, and her fingers were shaky and too-deliberate. They hovered over the mail app and after some consideration tapped into the saved-emails folder.

"Ah, here it is," Nan said.

The message was from Colin. Subject line: *As discussed.*

There were no contents, just an attached file that Nan frowned at over her glasses.

"I don't believe you've seen this?" she said. She turned the phone so it was facing Jen, and she pressed play.

CHAPTER FIFTY-ONE

All of the parents were grumbling about the eighth-grade graduation having been moved inside. They had all been robbed of that beautiful mountain backdrop, plus the auditorium had a musty smell and horrible acoustics.

But when the PA system crackled with the low resonance of the opening bars of *Pomp and Circumstance,* and Laurel and her classmates walked down the aisle in their Kelly-green robes, a satisfied hush settled over the room.

Principal Hamoush approached the podium, and repeated, as she did every year, that *this* class held a special place in her heart.

It's only eighth grade, Annie's brain reasoned. But it felt *big,* seeing Laurel up there.

Almost big enough to eclipse the fact that Laurel had befriended a psychopath. Annie should have been more alert, asked more questions. And yesterday morning, she'd practically begged Jen Chun-Pagano to come to the party.

If Jen dared to show up, Annie was prepared to have a Difficult Conversation about her abusive son, no matter how uncomfortable things got.

Principal Hamoush started reading the names of the graduates for their walks across the stage, and Mike elbowed Annie in the ribs.

Fifteen years ago, they'd had no clue what they were getting into and it flew by, just like people said, so fast, *too* fast, and tissue, where was a tissue?

Annie's hands fumbled fruitlessly in the front pocket of her bag until Lena handed her two, folded and fresh.

"One for you, and one for the proud papa," Lena whispered. She smiled and pointed her chin in Mike's direction.

FIFTEEN YEARS EARLIER

Annie felt Bryce watch her face as she flipped open her cell phone and read the text.

Meet me inside.

He had been there, right by the house, watching her for who knew how long. He cocked his head slightly toward the door, which was propped open for the caterers and their heavy trays.

Not like this, she wanted to object. She watched helplessly as he slipped inside.

"Excuse me," she said to Bryce.

CHAPTER FIFTY-TWO

"What a beautiful family," Lena said.

After the graduation ceremony, it had taken forever to get the Perleys lined up for a family photo because people kept stopping for hugs and high fives and gleeful "see you tonight!"s.

Lena took a step backward to better frame them within her phone screen. She forced herself to smile even though a cold lingering pressure remained in her chest from the morning's conversation with Rachel.

The Perleys looked lovely, at least, and the photo's composition would be good. Mike and Annie perched behind Laurel, and Hank kneeled in front, his arms flung wide. Whether by accident or design, they were color-coordinated in shades of blue that cooled the shiny vibrance of Laurel's green gown.

"Say cheese," Lena said.

"Not cheese." Mike grinned. "Say *time for high school.*"

"*Time for high school!*" they sang out-of-sync as Lena snapped away.

"Hey Perleys," said a tall balding man in a sports coat. "Want me to take one with Grandma in it?"

"Oh," Lena demurred, "I'm just the photographer."

"Lena"—Mike reached out his arm toward her—"get in the photo."

"Come on, Lena!"

With a sweaty, sticky hand, Hank reached out to Lena, pulled her next to him. She allowed his warmth to melt the doubt.

Lena wouldn't have done anything differently that night: there was no point in looking back.

evel five of Abe's game noisily played out on Nan's phone. So far, Jen hadn't seen anything out of the ordinary.

Nan just wasn't used to this generation's exposure to violence. The Kingdom School didn't even do lockdowns. It existed in some innocent alternate universe.

Jen glanced at Nan. She must be at least a little impressed by the graphics, which were clear and crisp and as professionally done as any game they'd ever bought. Abe had structured level five so that the player's point of view was from behind a giant machine gun. When it expelled bullets, the entire screen shook.

Part of Nan's concern was probably that the target appeared to be a human girl. When she was cornered in the otherwise empty room of the haunted house, the hero's gun ripped holes into her flesh and she collapsed dead on the floor, gushing blood.

It wasn't ideal, Jen could admit, but nor was it Abe's fault that Corporate America had decided teenaged boys should maim things for recreation.

When the video ended, Nan focused on stirring her cappuccino with the tiny metal spoon, like she was giving Jen space to process the images.

"This is what video games are like these days," Jen said.

She hoped her twist of a smile communicated that she agreed they were awful, but such was life.

"Yes." Nan stirred the spoon faster. *Clink, clink, clink.* "But Colin was worried that the girl looks like a friend of Abe. That it's cyberbullying."

Clumsily, Nan rewound the video to the scene where the girl was first trapped in the gun's graticule and paused the frame.

Lanky. Curly brown hair down past her shoulders. Dressed in jeans and hiking boots. Arms raised defensively, her mouth open in a scream, two dimples appearing in her cheeks.

Jen's throat went completely dry. Laurel.

Nan was back to stirring the damn spoon.

Arguments ran through Jen's head in Paul's voice: *You can't kick out someone for a picture! Freedom of expression is a fundamental right! How can you be sure that's even Laurel?*

Jen felt her hands start to shake. To settle them, she wrapped them around the coffee cup. "What do *you* make of it?"

"I'm worried," Nan said. "I may have dropped the ball here."

Wait. What?

The new mother across the coffee shop swapped the gauze cocoon baby to the other breast and watched Jen with a beatific smile. She was not exhausted, Jen realized, but blissed out.

"I've been distracted," Nan continued, "and Abe and Colin seemed to get along so well and—not that I'm trying to excuse myself, I obviously need to make amends—but I haven't gotten to know him the way I usually do my students.

"I'm aware he's more of a gamer than a reader, but I was thinking Abe and I could maybe read one of his vampire books together over the summer. Initially it might be a way for us to connect."

"You're not kicking him out?"

"No." Nan appeared startled at the suggestion. "For the moment I'm more interested in figuring out why he created this. Is Abe just expressing pain? Does he have a plan to hurt people? We just need to get to the bottom of this, but I am not abandoning him."

Nan handed her neatly folded paper napkin to Jen. She paused as Jen swiped it under her eyes.

"I would like your honest input on how we proceed in the short term." Nan's voice was gentle as it pinned her to the wall. "Do you think Abe has plans to hurt his friend?"

CHAPTER FIFTY-FOUR

As soon as the Perleys got home from graduation, Mike grabbed Laurel's shoulders and steered her to the couch in the den.

"Wait right here," he said.

"Aren't we supposed to go up to Lena's?"

"Dad has a surprise first," Annie said. "A good one."

They hovered over Laurel, watched as she slid off the silver wrapping paper, creaked open the velvet box, and looked up at them uncertainly.

"What's this?"

"A family heirloom," Mike said. He sat next to her on the couch. "It was your great-great-grandfather's and he passed it down to his oldest son, and so on and so on. Grandma and Grandpa wanted to give it to you in person so badly, but they told us we could. That's Saint Nicholas, the patron saint of children."

"And sailors and brewers," Annie said with a laugh, but Laurel didn't even crack a smile.

"As far as heirlooms go, it's a little underwhelming I guess," Mike said, his voice tinged with hurt. "But generations of Perleys believe it's good luck. It's been through three wars and everyone who wore it came back alive, so . . . put it on and we can send a photo to Grandma and Grandpa."

"For fuck's sake." Laurel snapped shut the velvet jewelry box. "Don't give it to *me*."

"Why not?" Hank said.

"I'm not a Perley," Laurel said. "You are, Hank, but I'm something else."

Annie felt the room tilt to the left.

"What do you mean something else?" Hank said.

"Mike's not my dad," Laurel said. She looked at Annie, who felt a rushing in her ears. "Tell him."

"He is," Hank said. "Yes he is your dad." He looked from Mike to Annie. Back to Mike. His voice rose with a squeak. "Right?"

"He's *your* dad," Laurel corrected. "My father's name was Bryce Neary and I'll never meet him because he's dead." Her laugh was sharp. "We're all supposed to forget about him, apparently."

Across the room Mike's face had drained of color. When his eyes met Annie's, she felt a pinprick of pain drill through the shock.

"Say something," Laurel said. Her hands rose in frustration. "I'm right. Say I'm right."

"No," Annie said. Her voice came out high, strangled. "Not exactly."

CHAPTER FIFTY-FIVE

Lena stood inside the party tent, next to Hilde the event planner.

Around them was the symphony of preparation. Caterers placed down balloon centerpieces. On the southern edge of the lawn, two men rolled the luxury porta-potties down a ramp from a truck bed. By the cottonwood tree, DJ Lightning set up his booth.

"You did a wonderful job," Lena said.

Hilde allowed a brisk nod. With red-apple cheeks and short ponytail, she reminded Lena of the captain of a field hockey team.

But Lena didn't know if she'd even played field hockey, or whether she was single or attached, gay or straight, a dog or cat owner. Over the past few weeks, Hilde had been a pleasant efficient hum in the background of Lena's life, not a new paid best friend.

This felt like progress.

"The caterers will start warming things at five," Hilde said. She checked her watch, which made Lena check hers, too. The Perleys were running late.

"I need to change," Lena said.

"Go," Hilde said. "I'll talk party pacing with DJ Lightning."

Lena was on the stairs when Rachel called. She picked up, started speaking immediately. "Rachel, I was thinking about what you said and—"

"I remember Annie." Rachel spoke in a rush.

"I know, and I want to apologize for what I said about your father. I understand how complicated—"

"I remember her."

Lena suppressed a sigh. There's a difference between grief and guilt, Rachel, and you have to let it go. I wasn't a perfect parent, but you have to let it go.

"Okay," Lena said soothingly. "I can hear that you're upset."

"*You're not listening.*" Rachel's yell exploded through the phone. "She was at our party. I noticed her at the bar, and then later I was getting extra napkins and I saw her sneaking up the back stairway. She looked different then, she had this really long hair, and this short low-cut dress. She looked like, well, she looked like she was going to—"

"She looked like she was going to what?" Lena's throat tightened around a hard lump.

"Please don't make me say it," Rachel said.

CHAPTER FIFTY-SIX

The problem was that Abe didn't see the problem with his video game. He was proud.

"Dr. Shapiro thinks it's okay," he said.

His laptop was open in front of them on the kitchen table, frozen on that last horrific screen. Jen reached out to shut it.

"Dr. Shapiro said *go kill Laurel Perley in your video game?*"

"No, but she's always telling me to channel my feelings into something harmless."

"This isn't what she meant. How would you feel if Laurel killed *you* in a video game?"

A small smile. "She's not really smart enough to do that."

Jen sighed with frustration. "The game is so disturbing that Colin—*Colin*—forwarded it to her."

"Colin is not as loyal as you think."

"What does that even mean?" Jen did not understand why Colin hadn't come to her first.

Yes you do. You know exactly why. Jen was so in denial, so incapable of seeing Abe clearly that even Colin believed telling her would be pointless.

"I'm trying really hard," Abe said. "But everything I do is wrong."

Do you think Abe has plans to hurt his friend?

Jen had looked Nan squarely in the eye and said, *Of course not.*

"Like the vandalism?" Jen said.

"I didn't do that."

"I spend a lot of time defending you." Jen's voice was cool. "But I don't know that I believe you."

Abe's neck flushed an angry red. "I'm. Not. The. Vandal." His scream ripped his voice raw. "Stop *doubting* me."

He snatched the pepper shaker from the table, hurled it across the room. Jen watched dispassionately as it crashed into the surface of the island and bounced to the floor, where it broke open, bleeding peppercorns.

She couldn't do it anymore. Her heart was a husk and all she wanted to do was sleep.

The door from the garage slammed open and shut. "It's me," Paul yelled. "Back from the mines."

"Hello, gang!" Paul was slightly breathless as he arrived in the kitchen, suitcase behind him. He looked back and forth between them and the broken glass and the peppercorns spilled across the floor. "What'd I miss?"

No one is writing any condolence notes to the deceased's parents. People blame them for creating a monster and setting him loose on the world.

I think that life tends to be more complicated that.

He did awful things, yes, but he was so, so young. He had his entire life ahead of him.

I seem to be alone in wanting to believe there was hope for his redemption.

CHAPTER FIFTY-SEVEN

CONGRATULATIONS LAUREL!
A hand-painted sign had been posted on the gate to greet party guests. Above it was a giant rainbow balloon archway.

The dull throbbing in Annie's head intensified as she walked through. Lena was across the lawn, in a canary-yellow party dress that seemed to glow in the late-afternoon light.

She waved excitedly, speed-walked over to Annie, looped her arm through.

"You look wonderful, but you'll still let me do some makeup, yes? The cat eye, as discussed, but first, a tour," she said. "Most of the food will be in that tent, except for the butler-passed. Chicken nuggets and mac and cheese for the kids is over there, and on the other side will be the sushi chef, who isn't here yet, but Hilde says he's en route. Hilde!" Lena shouted at a woman in a dark suit, who had one finger pressed to her ear and talked into a headset. "This is Annie, mother of the guest of honor."

Hilde nodded distractedly at Annie.

"Here is the promised adults-only area," Lena continued, chipper and mile-a-minute. "Hilde persuaded me to do the Moroccan Fantasy theme with the rugs and throw pillows. I didn't go for the belly dancer or the hookah, I thought that would be a little *too* too—but this is as far away from the speakers as possible, ha, ha, and there'll be a little bar here, but I don't want you to worry, the bartenders will card anyone and everyone they're not sure of, and the DJ will be fabulous, I think, he's got all sorts of goodies for the kids, but loud, you know. He'll be loud."

After the briefest of eye contact, Lena looked away.

"That caftan looks fantastic on you," she said. "I knew it would, the blue brings out your eyes. How does Laurel look in the lavender dress? Where *is* Laurel?"

"I came up first," Annie said. "To talk."

Lena's shoulders sagged. She gestured to the couch closest to them. "Shall we sit?" She spoke in a high pitch. "Let's sit."

Annie nodded. They sat down shoulder-to-shoulder.

"Laurel is not Mike's biological child," Annie said.

Next to her, Lena went entirely still.

"We weren't going to ever tell her. But in science, they did a lab that tested their blood types, and she'd remembered Mike's from the school blood drive." Annie gave a dry laugh. "She's known since October, apparently. We've been trying to talk it through for hours, Mike and I, trying to explain why we didn't tell her, and Hank is so upset, and Laurel's just. She's just—"

Lena stood up, then sat back down. She pressed her lips together hard enough that they seemed to disappear and nodded several times to herself, as if coming to terms with a new reality.

"Should we cancel tonight?" she asked finally.

"Laurel insists on having the party. For her *real* friends, she says, and she claims to be over it, that she's already dealt with it, which is obviously bullshit."

For the first time since Annie had arrived, Lena looked directly at her. Her brown eyes seared. It was Annie's turn to look away.

"Did you know my late husband Tim?" Lena said.

Annie's palms felt hot and itchy. She flattened them against the skirt of her silk caftan, which she didn't deserve, should have never accepted. She was a parasite.

"I worked for him," she said. "He hired me right after college."

"How was he," Lena said evenly, "as a boss?"

Annie kept her eyes on the giant cottonwood tree. There was fluff trapped in its boughs, trembling in the wind, itching to snow down on the neighborhood.

"Not the best," she said.

CHAPTER FIFTY-EIGHT

By design, Annie did not remember much about her affair with Tim Meeker.

They met in the interview. Annie had a little crush from the start.

First, there was that voice, so gravelly and sexy, and he wanted to make her comfortable. He didn't seem concerned about her proficiency in PowerPoint. He cared about her taste in music and books, where she wanted to travel.

"I've been at your house before," she admitted, and told him about the swim-team party. "Please tell your wife how lovely it was."

"She and I are basically separated," he said. "Same house, different lives."

Tim's habit was to go to the hotel bar next to their office after work. Annie didn't remember when or why she started tagging along, sharing a scotch, but soon there were also steak dinners, nights at the hotel, outdoor concerts, weekends in the mountains.

Lately, despite her best efforts, she'd been recalling more: the hazy thrill of secrecy from keeping things quiet at work, waking up in a hotel room, sun too bright and a splitting headache, walking the snowy streets of a mountain town arm in arm and laughing.

He bought her a car, which seemed like proof of his generosity, or in hindsight, of the transactional nature to their relationship. They drank a lot.

She could not remember anything about their time together without feeling a stifling heat of regret and shame and she didn't want Laurel anywhere near that feeling.

Tim Meeker had ultimately been as disposable as he'd wanted to make her.

"I'm sorry," Annie said to Lena now. "I'm so sorry."

"I'm sorry for you, Annie," Lena said. "I wish I'd been there to protect you from him."

"He wrote me a check to go away." Annie's eyes welled. It still, after all this time, shocked a little, how stupidly hopeful she'd been when she slipped inside this house.

"He wasn't a good person."

"I need you to listen, Lena," Annie said. "Please. What happened later that night was my fault. All of it."

FIFTEEN YEARS EARLIER

Tim wanted Annie to know that she would not walk away empty-handed. He made her sit next to him, in that stupid desk chair, while he left a voicemail for HR: His assistant Annie would be leaving for greener pastures. He was authorizing a generous departure bonus to be issued to her immediately.

"If you want a work reference," Tim said to her, "just write one up and get it to Maureen. I'll sign anything."

He leaned forward, pressed a cold hand to Annie's bare knee. He forgot himself for a moment, and his index finger traced her patella. When a mocking peal of laughter slipped through the open window from outside, he stopped himself, turned the gesture into a brusque pat.

Annie's hand was on the doorknob when he said her name.

"You should leave through the garage," he said. "Take the back staircase down, then a left through the mudroom."

She stopped in the hall, balanced herself against the wall. The band returned from their break, and she staggered downstairs to the grind of guitar chords, the lead singer's shouted count: *One two three four—*

It was after she stepped into the garage, cold and fluorescently lit, and saw Tim Meeker's little hunter-green two-seater that her numbness splintered, gave way to the warmth of rage.

Annie tasted metal as she looked around the room at all the toys—the kayak, the skis, the bag of golf clubs with that stupid knit tassel hanging from it.

She was just seventeen, you know what I mean

She hoisted a club, cool and heavy, out of the bag. It took several swings to break the front headlights.

Annie was half aware of the beat shifting underneath her. She paused to catch her breath.

'Cause you're fine and you're mine and you look so divine

And then she walked around to the back of the car and smashed the brake lights, too.

CHAPTER FIFTY-NINE

Lena wanted to press her hand to Annie's mouth.

Stop talking.

But Annie did not. She hugged a throw pillow to her chest and pulled its tassels as the words bled out of her.

She was the reason, Annie said, that Bryce didn't see Tim on the road. Lena must hate her. Lena watched Annie and realized that yes, she did. She hated Annie with a passion too consuming and fiery to be contained. The hatred was going to erupt and spill over both of them like molten lava, preserve them, charred, in this spot forever.

And Annie would never know the real reason.

Maybe if Annie could shut up for a moment, but no, she kept gushing out her truth, and it changed everything Lena knew. The facts that Lena had just now—after fifteen years—started to accept hadn't been facts at all.

Annie claimed she'd give anything to do that night over, she'd been close with Bryce in high school, and he was such a good person, he had deserved the future she had stolen from him.

Aside from the therapist, Mike was the only person who knew. He was Annie's best friend from college, always a little in love with her, always right there with her. They'd never even told Laurel's grandparents.

After Tim's death, all of those stories came out about his DUIs, and Annie remembered the ones Tim had told about his own father. She supposed a part of her had been petrified for Laurel from the beginning.

It was incredibly frustrating that Laurel didn't understand how much better it would have been, to keep believing Mike was her biological father. You lied about the most important thing in my life, she had accused, and Annie couldn't make her see that the lie had been a gift.

Except—

Annie stopped fiddling with the pillow and forced eye contact with Lena.

Around them, suited caterers did the final preparations, lit the tea lights, placed the silver trays on the buffet tables.

Annie had always craved a connection to Lena and Rachel. She'd insisted they live in Cottonwood to be close to them, which Tim's large check had allowed them to afford. She used to walk past the Meekers' house every day, try to catch a glimpse of either of them.

She'd fantasized that they would see Laurel and just *know*.

A year or two after the night of the accident, Annie sat in Deb Gallegos's backyard as their daughters, bare-chested in swim diapers, splashed in an inflatable wading pool.

Out of the corner of her eye, Annie saw Lena's white SUV drive past. She noticed the absence of that familiar pounding in her ears. Her body wasn't twitching to follow.

She *liked* Cottonwood, she realized, she was happy here.

It was beautiful, there were excellent schools and friendly neighbors. Their family could grow here, could pretend to be just another boringly comfortable unit until it felt like the truth.

"Please say something." Annie's voice was plugged and nasal. "Do you want me to tell Rachel? I can tell her that the accident wasn't all her father's fault."

"God, no," Lena said.

"I'm sorry," Annie said. She started to cry again.

Lena allowed herself a moment before she put her hand on the rough pillow, atop Annie's fingers. Annie sniffled, glanced up.

Lena could tell Annie everything. It was an appealing thought: the two of them carrying the burden together.

But in Annie's eyes, Lena saw a hint of something released.

What good would it serve?

From the street came the sound of a car door slamming. "Look at the balloons," a voice said, "the balloons!"

Don't be selfish. Rachel's voice in Lena's head was unyielding: *Give her this.*

"It was an accident," Lena said. "It was all a horrible accident."

Annie's exhale was shaky and relieved. She shut her eyes and pressed the tips of her fingers into them. Her shoulders slouched, then heaved.

"We're going to be fine, dear," Lena said. The phrasing was an echo of something she'd heard before.

Evan. She sounded like Rachel's Evan, reaching through a dark, cold void, trying to manufacture a closeness from nothing.

Lena gripped Annie's hand a little too hard. "It's all going to be fine."

CHAPTER SIXTY

Jen, supine atop her bedspread, cold bathroom towel compress over her eyes, could hear the vacuum in the kitchen.

At the gentle knock on the door, she lifted the compress. Paul hovered by the bed. "Abe is vacuuming up the glass," he said worriedly.

"I don't trust him anymore."

Paul sat down next to her on the bed. "You just need a break."

"Colin has an ulcer and is barely returning my texts, Laurel has a rock through her window, Harper got slashed. The bodies keep piling up. And I just defend him."

"You love him."

It wasn't love. It was ego or pride or something even more animal, gnawing, ugly, selfish. If this was love, Jen didn't understand how the world kept spinning under the weight of it.

"Well," Paul said. "Abe's cleaning up down there at his own insistence. I think he's worried about you."

"He's worried about his getting his computer monitor," Jen said dryly.

"He seems genuinely contrite and concerned."

Jen gave Paul an incredulous look.

"I know, I know: I'm not here and I'm an idiot." Paul's voice was hurt. He was upset, still, about Jen's accusations all of those months before over dinner.

"You're not a *total* idiot." She tried to smile.

"We talked for a long time. I don't think he's the vandal. Honestly, who even knows whether the conduct disorder label fits."

"Are you kidding?"

"I'm not. He's grown up a lot this year, Jen. He's trying so hard, and if the diagnosis pins on his lack of remorse, well, let me tell you: he has buckets of remorse and self-doubt."

Jen searched Paul's face.

"Yes, it's messed up that that's good news, but welcome to our world. You do see the real him, Jen, that's what I'm saying."

Maybe this was what co-parenting Abe required: together on a seesaw, trading off who was grounded and who held sky-high delusions. This time it was Paul up where the air was too thin.

Jen sniffed. "You smell like airline coffee."

"My seatmate spilled it over me on the plane. I'm going to shower."

When she heard the water from the shower whoosh through the pipes, Jen sat up, scanned her phone for new texts.

The last one she'd received was Colin's lie, from early this morning. His reply to Jen's desperate What's the meeting about, any idea?

IDK

She imagined Colin waiting at the doctor's office, hunched in pain, debating how to reply to the madwoman, and finally concluding that his best bet was to go around her.

At what point had he seen the truth about them?

CHAPTER SIXTY-ONE

"Amazing party!"

Everyone Annie had talked to in the past hour had said some version of this, and she hadn't figured out how to respond.

Thank you didn't feel right: she'd had nothing to do with the planning. *But I had nothing to do with it* had sounded defensive.

"Isn't it?" Annie said now, and the new Cottonwood resident whose name Annie couldn't remember smiled eagerly.

There was another dip of silence between them.

The food tent was crowded and steamy with body heat. People kept jostling past each other, and their voices blended in an angry aggressive hum that bounced off the canvas walls.

Annie's head felt like it had been split open with the effort of the conversation with Laurel, with coming clean to Lena. She could barely think, let alone manage small talk.

But Lena had said it was all going to be fine, and Laurel was on the dance floor having what appeared to be the time of her life.

So. It was probably all going to be fine?

"Have you tried the ribs?" Annie said finally.

The last person Annie had talked to, or maybe the person before that, had been going on and on about the ribs and their tamarind glaze.

"Well no," the woman said slowly, "because of the whole vegan thing that we just discussed."

"Right." Annie smacked her forehead. "Of course."

No one else in her family seemed to have had trouble clicking into party mode.

Mike was parked by the bar, laughing with Wade Jensen. Hank was on the sushi line for the fourth time, and Laurel was on the dance floor, in the middle of a crush of her smiling and laughing and shrieking girlfriends.

Why did you think it was Bryce, Annie had asked.

You have a giant photo of him with the family pictures, Laurel had said. She'd found out through an old yearbook that he'd been a runner. She'd stalked Nan Neary at the Kingdom School, too, although she'd been too shy to approach.

Annie and Mike's attempted explanations—that they had tried to give Laurel the best possible truth—were insufficient.

Laurel would never forgive them, their relationship had been permanently damaged, probably. Perhaps, though, based on the dancing and the shrieking, Annie could hope there hadn't been too much damage to *Laurel*? Could a truly traumatized person act so happy?

But Laurel had been faking so much for months now, Annie realized with a shiver, and all alone.

First thing tomorrow, Annie was calling a therapist.

"I bet the ribs are great, though," the new Cottonwood resident said helpfully. "All the food is amazing."

"Me too," Annie said quickly, and while she had meant she also bet the ribs were amazing, she'd ruined the poor woman's generous attempt to salvage the conversation.

Through another awkward moment of silence, Annie labored to think of an appropriate question. Where was Janine?

This woman deserved Janine.

Second thing tomorrow, after the therapist call, Annie would ask Janine to track down this new resident, send along one of her *welcome to the neighborhood* emails with all the restaurants and hot spots.

Janine probably had one just for vegans.

Across the room, one of the Sandstone dads grabbed two mini

lamb chops from a caterer's tray. He caught Annie watching and raised one as if to say *Cheers*.

She turned to the new resident, was about to ask whether she'd met Janine, but the woman was gone. Annie stood alone in the center of the crowded tent, unsure where to go.

"Annie!"

It was Priya, fresh and summery in a blue floral maxidress, her dark hair pulled into a high ponytail. With the hand that wasn't holding a drink, she grabbed Annie's arm.

"This is insanity," she said. "Follow me."

Holding the drink aloft like a beacon, Priya led them through the tent to the Moroccan Fantasy lounge area where Deb Gallegos sat on a couch, an entire tray of appetizers on her lap. She waved cheerfully.

"Have you been here the whole time?"

"The trick," Deb said, "is to catch the caterers as they come out the side door." She handed a glass to Annie, who took it, sat down on the sofa, stretched out her legs.

"You're wearing flip-flops with your dress?" Priya sounded impressed.

"I have gossip," Deb sang. She rubbed her hands together with devilish glee. "Apparently, someone and the hot untouchable have been making out up here all spring."

"Up *here*?" Annie said.

"They have a key to the gate somehow," Deb said, "and they pass it around, because there's apparently a clearing back there that's very romantic. Annie, don't look so uptight. They're fourteen. They make out. That's what they do."

"Lena gave Laurel a key," Annie said wryly. "So that's the how."

"Really?" Deb sounded almost impressed. "Laurel's had quite a year of oat-sowing, hasn't she? The question is—where is the hot untouchable? Is he here? Or—" Deb gripped Annie's arm. "You don't think it's a *she*?"

Priya frowned. "I doubt they'd be so dramatic about a same-sex relationship. This generation is so much less homophobic than we were."

"You never know, though. Annie, could you imagine: We could be in-laws! Think of the Thanksgiving dinners!"

If Annie told Deb and Priya the truth right now, their heads would explode. They'd find out at some point and, after their shocked gossip, they'd be there for her. But she couldn't handle that tonight.

"Oooh," Priya said. "Glow sticks."

It was getting dark and the DJ had thrown a box of them onto the dance floor. The kids scrambled to loop the flashes of neon around their necks and heads and wrists.

"Mrs. Perley?"

Annie turned her head toward the polite young voice. Colin hulked behind her sofa.

She should be welcoming, but she only felt annoyed seeing him standing there in his ill-fitting seersucker suit with a stain on the lapel, pants tucked in those silly cowboy boots.

"Did you just arrive, Colin?" Annie said. "There's lots of great food under the tent—"

"Do you mind if I sit down?" Colin said. "There's something I need to show you."

"Me?" Annie said. How could there be more *anything* tonight?

"I went back and forth about whether to say something," Colin said, "but really you need to know."

As the dread pooled in Annie's stomach, he crouched down between all three of them.

"Here," he said. "It's on my phone."

Lena pressed her back against the side of the house. There were so many damn people at this party.

All of these years of shouldering a burden for which someone else—Annie—had been partially to blame.

She wanted to call Rachel, or was the news too bittersweet to share?

A man in a Hawaiian print shirt approached, shouted something at her. Lena put on her hostess smile.

"What's that?" she said.

"Can you believe these people?" he shouted. His breath smelled of garlic.

"Which people?"

"*These* people." He hiked his IPA bottle over his head, used it to draw a sloshy circle. "They have a five-car garage that's almost empty. Five cars!"

"For you." Harriet Nessel appeared next to the man. She pushed a small white box at Lena. "My daughter-in-law gave them to me for Mother's Day."

Lena peeled open the top. Tiny little soaps in the shape of birds in cardboard nests. Only one was empty. The moment was hazy with déjà vu—they'd had this exact exchange before, Lena and Harriet.

But then the man pushed between them.

"Their garage," he said, "is basically an airplane hangar!"

"Find some coffee," Harriet suggested in a curt tone, and with a surprisingly strong arm, propelled Lena out of the tent.

"It's a wonderful party, dear," Harriet said conspiratorially, "but next time maybe don't invite so many *strangers*." She pointed a finger toward the Moroccan Fantasy area. "I wonder what they're talking about?"

A handful of women from book club stood in a tight cluster. Deb Gallegos clutched her heavy silver choker. Priya had her arms around Annie's shoulders.

"Something juicy," Harriet said. "Should we go see?"

When Lena and Harriet came closer, Annie pushed a phone into Lena's palm.

"I'm going to kill Abe Pagano," she said.

Miss Marple would report it without hesitation. Same with Inspector Gamache, but justice looks a little different off the page.

I've gotten as far as tracing the numbers on my phone. 9-1-1.

Hello? I'd like to report a murder.

When I imagine the flash of police lights reflecting against darkened houses, my stomach twists in objection.

But when I think about letting the foothills absorb the secret, that doesn't sit right either.

I don't know what to do.

CHAPTER SIXTY-TWO

"Why aren't you dressed for the party yet?"

Abe stood in the doorway to Jen's bedroom. He'd changed into khaki pants and a polo shirt and had slicked back his hair, pulled it into a tiny ponytail. His unworn loafers, bought early last year in anticipation of bar mitzvah invitations that had never materialized, reflected the overhead light. They were at least a size too small.

"Because we're not going."

"You need to get out of bed." Abe walked stiff-legged—the shoes must be killing him, but he did not complain—into Jen's closet. She could hear the hangers squeaking over the rod.

"This is pretty." He emerged with a bloodred, in-your-face silk sundress with a voluminous flounce around her feet. She'd had it for years but never worn it because every time she tried it on, she thought *nope*.

"Totally inappropriate," Jen said. "Why do you even want to go?"

Nan's gentle, concerned voice. *Do you think Abe has plans to hurt his friend?*

"The points," Abe said matter-of-factly. "I wrote my apology note to Laurel, and Dad said that's fifty points. I get another fifty when I hand it to her. I don't have to be her friend, but he explained to me that I can't get stuck in the usual cycle. I have to break free."

Jen searched his face. *Feel free to chime in, gut.*

He held up the dress, gave the hanger a shake. Neutral it was not. At the thought of showing up in that dress, Jen started to laugh the hyenic laugh of a madwoman.

Abe smiled. "What?"

Jen's phone chimed with an incoming text.

She reached into her pocket and glanced at the screen.

"Deb Gallegos," she said aloud.

"What does she say?"

Jen was sure it was nothing good.

CHAPTER SIXTY-THREE

Deb returned to the Moroccan Fantasy area with three champagne flutes balanced in her hands. She carefully handed one to Priya and the other to Annie.

"Cheers," she said.

"Cheers!" Priya sang.

DJ Lightning was playing something wordless and beat-driven. Most of the party guests had moved from the food tent to the dance floor, which was now aglow with the neon sticks.

"I want to dance," Deb said. "Would Sierra be mortified? She never used to be embarrassed by me, but I sense it coming."

Annie ignored her. "Jen should have said something to us about Abe's diagnosis, right?"

"Yes." Deb nodded.

"Poor Jen," Priya said.

"Not poor Jen. Jen is asleep at the wheel."

Annie caught them exchange a look.

"What," she said.

"Try and have fun," Deb said gently. "You've been obsessing about this for hours. What can you do about it tonight?"

It wasn't *their* children who'd been animated and riddled with bullet holes, Annie supposed.

"I'd like to dance," Priya said tentatively.

Where was Janine? Janine would be right next to Annie, spitting bullets.

"Abe's the vandal, right?" Annie said. "We can agree?"

"Lena." Deb reached her arms overhead to flag down Lena. "Annie needs you." She and Priya linked arms and ran to the dance floor with the speed of escaping convicts.

"Laurel's made such bad choices," Annie said when Lena sat down. "Giving your garden key to Haley, becoming friends with a sociopath. I've watched her so closely, and I had no idea."

"It's nothing incurable," Lena said. "Nothing permanent."

"What does that mean?"

"Lena." Mike rushed over. "There's a starry-night situation with the glow sticks in the flower garden."

"A what?"

He grimaced. "You better come with me."

"I'll be right back," Lena said apologetically. Annie watched in frustration as they left her alone in the tent. She needed to harness someone else into this feeling.

Where on earth was Janine?

"Starry, starry *night*," the group of boys chanted in unison.

Lena watched as one of them broke open the glow stick he was holding and spattered its fluorescence all over her hyacinths.

The group cheered and began the chant anew.

"Starry, starry *night*! Starry starry *night*! Starry starry *night*."

More glow sticks were broken open and spattered on the lawn, Mike Perley's pants, the low-hanging tree branches.

Lena reached, grabbed a child by the collar. A round face turned toward her. She recognized the impish grin and spiky eyelashes of one of Janine's twins.

"Where is your mother?"

He tried to wiggle away, but she caught him by the arm, repeated the question through gritted teeth.

"Where is your mother?"

He shrugged and pointed to the patio.

Janine wore ripped jeans and a Mickey Mouse T-shirt and her hair had been stuffed into a baseball cap.

Lena wasn't trying to be fussy, but everyone else, even the stranger in the Hawaiian shirt, had made a little effort to look nice.

Janine's hand was gripped around her daughter's arm, and she was pulling the girl roughly through the path between the tables.

Lena frowned.

They were grim-faced and hunched, like they were walking through a storm.

"I updated my apology note to Laurel," Abe said. "To include making the video."

"It doesn't matter," Jen said from her bed. It was dark outside now, and she was never, ever leaving.

Deb's text said Annie had seen Abe's video and was pretty upset. She'd ended it with a frowny-face emoji.

How did they even see it, Jen kept asking Abe and Paul. The thought of them all up there, gossiping about her son. Jen rested a pillow over her face and decided she could stay here forever.

"Here," Abe said. She heard the heavy paper of his note hit her bedside table. She lifted the pillow.

The Laurel Apology, Take Two, "I'm Sorry I Murdered You in a Video Game" Edition. Abe had selected very tasteful stationery: an ivory notecard with a gold border, the most expensive in the Paganos' collection.

"We're like hours late now," he said. "I can hear the party."

"You can?"

"Listen," Abe commanded.

Jen tilted her head. There was the hint of a thrumming bass in the background.

"I made the note more honest," Abe said. "It might be *too* honest, you tell me."

Oh boy.

"Read my note. I'll accept feedback."

"Fine." She folded open the paper.

Sorry for not understanding, yes, strong start.

. . . *The video was unkind* . . . True enough, if a bit mildly put.

. . . *When you hurt me* . . .

Nothing after that made any sense.

Jen backtracked to the beginning, tried to read it more slowly. In her hands, the note card shook.

"Abe," she said, "are you sure this is what happened?"

"Yes."

She regarded him, from crooked part to those skinny shoulders, which jerked in anticipation. *Did I do okay?*

What cold comfort that she could read his face after all.

She had to go find Annie.

CHAPTER SIXTY-FOUR

"There you are!" Annie had never been so happy to see Janine, even if she was dressed for a field trip to the recycling plant. "I didn't know you even owned ripped jeans. I have news, Janine. Big news."

Annie leaned down to Katie. "Sweetie, go join the twins and everyone else on the dance floor."

But Katie didn't move. Janine flattened her palms around the girl's shoulders, gave them an authoritative squeeze.

Katie reached into her pocket and took out a note, which she unfolded. It reminded Annie of an awards show: *I'd like to thank the Academy.*

But Katie's speech didn't start that way.

"I'm sorry, Mrs. Perley," she began, and her voice was noticeably gruff for a thirteen-year-old, "for breaking your front window."

"Did you hear?" Harriet Nessel grabbed Lena's shoulder rather harshly.

"Did I hear what?" Lena wondered whether Harriet was aware that the back of her floral shift had been splashed with the contents of a glow stick. It was as splotchy and phosphorescent as Lena's flower beds.

Even unflappable Hilde was ruffled. She was at the DJ booth, her shirt untucked and her arms gesturing wildly, imploring DJ

Lightning to do something, anything to compel the kids to the dance floor.

"The vandal," Harriet said, "is Katie Neff."

"Janine's Katie?"

"She did all of it! She just cornered Tabitha Donaldson to apologize for the snowman."

"Oh my, but why—"

"Everyone, back on the floor. Back on the floor!" DJ Lightning chanted. "It's time to do the Hose!"

"The Hose?" Harriet said. "Is that an actual dance?"

She did not stick around for an answer but beelined to the table closest to them. "Did you hear," Lena heard her announce, "the vandal is Katie Neff! Janine's girl."

The Hose was an actual dance, Lena decided, and a popular one, based on the way the kids streamed to the dance floor. Laurel Perley walked toward the DJ booth, perhaps to request something else?

It occurred to Lena that she'd barely seen Laurel all night.

Rachel's sister.

It was impossible now not to see Rachel in Laurel's long strides across the lawn. When they hurried, their torsos tilted forward in the exact same way.

Where was Laurel off to? Not the DJ booth. With a furtive glance over her shoulder, she passed it, headed straight toward the back gate.

Had it just been this morning that Lena had seen Laurel jog up the hill and slink away?

A girl with a secret.

Jen walked quickly up the dark street to Lena's house. The flounce of her dress kept catching in her slippery kitten heels, tripping her. Impatiently, she yanked up the front.

"Clap your hands," shouted a DJ's amplified voice over the music. "Wiggle like a hose. Now slide back. Do the hose."

When she reached the path to the party, Jen hesitated. It really did look lovely.

The dance floor was full, and illuminated by rows of twinkly lights. There was a giant tent with tables of food and an insanely over-the-top lounge area with stuffed couches and poufs and Moroccan rugs and Jen was about to barrel into all of it like a grenade.

There was Annie, in the lounge area with Janine. Jen took a breath and stepped onto the lawn. A caterer immediately shoved a cake plate in Jen's hand and chirped, "Homemade caramel filling."

"No thank you."

Harriet appeared to her right, linked an elbow through Jen's arm. "Did you hear? Katie Neff is the vandal."

"Really?" Jen stopped.

"Janine found photos, selfies of Katie in the vandalism act, can you believe it, like trophies? I really did not see this coming and I hope she gets help. That's quite the dress, dear. Va-voom! Oh! Excuse me, Athena doesn't know yet."

So the vandal wasn't Abe.

Jen's knees buckled. She steadied herself against the back of a chair, and then straightened up.

It had never been Abe.

She wished she had never asked him. How must that feel, to have your own mother doubting you, assuming the worst?

Still, she felt lighter as she walked toward Annie's table, until she got there and everyone stopped talking.

(Because there was still the matter of Abe's video.)

(And worse than that, the note.)

Annie turned toward Jen. She was dressed in full-on glamour, in a floor-length flowy silk thing with a geometric pattern. Her face was pale and unmade.

It was awful, the dismissive look Annie flicked at Jen.

"Jen," Janine said. "Katie has an apology for you too after she finishes Mrs. Perley's."

Katie looked down at the paper in front of her.

"It was my problem," she read. "It had nothing to do with you." She glanced up at Annie. "It did a little. I was jealous of Laurel. Why does she get a party? She's not even related to Mrs. Meeker."

"Stick to the script," Janine said.

"But I know now," Katie read, "that it was an unhealthy way to express my anger. Although—"

Katie put down the note again, blinked behind her glasses. "It felt great to break things."

"It did not," Janine said with a sense of outrage.

"You didn't hurt anyone, Katie," Annie said with a resigned shrug. Pointedly, she said, "It's not like you stabbed anyone."

"Who stabbed someone?" Katie said, and from her tone, it was clear the idea intrigued her.

"Annie." Jen held out the note card. "This is from Abe."

"An apology note?" Annie said. She clasped her hands to her chest. "What a well-mannered community we all are. What wonderfully raised children. My daughter was going through something this year, and your son saw that and took advantage and you gave no warning, Jen. No warning that he might hurt our children, just for sport."

"Please, just read it." Jen placed it on the table in front of Annie.

"Should Katie and I leave you two?" Janine asked.

"Please." Jen nodded.

"Stay," Annie said. Her voice was commanding enough that no one dared to move as she opened Abe's note card.

"'Dear Laurel,'" she read in a hauntingly mocking voice. "'I am so sorry about the video game. It was unkind'"—eyebrow raise—"'and I would never really hurt you. I know it was wrong, though, and you're not worth it anyway.'

"This is great stuff, Jen," Annie said. "You must be so proud."

"Don't read it aloud," Jen said.

"Are you worried, Jen, that people will find out your big secret? That your son is a sociopath?" Annie said. She lifted the note and cleared her throat. "'You guys hurt me by going off together, even if Colin's your boyfriend'—"

Annie stopped and frowned.

"This can't be true."

Jen shifted nervously.

"Katie," Janine said in a chirp. "Let's go find Mrs. Meeker and apologize to her."

Jen watched Annie's face turn ashen as she read the rest.

> . . . *even if Colin's your boyfriend.*
>
> *I thought we were all friends together, which is why I yelled when you two started locking me out of the room and why I was hurt when you guys went places on the weekends and didn't invite me.*
>
> *What I'm supposed to do is not focus on that but on the good parts, like how Colin helped me with the music for my video game.*
>
> *I regret calling you both bad people and throwing your special keychain. I'm sorry it broke.*
>
> *Congratulations on graduating eighth grade and thank you for inviting me to your party.*
>
> *From, Abe Pagano*

"Laurel." Lena had sprinted to the fence to catch up with her. "You're hard to catch up with."

"Hi, Mrs. Meeker."

There was a glow band around Laurel's neck and several around her wrist, but even with a pink light cast over her face, how had Lena missed it?

The dimples, the brow. It was breathtaking how, from some angles, the girl was all Tim. The hair was Tim's mom Angela's—a weak-willed, spoiled woman—but Laurel didn't need to hear about Angela just now.

"Thanks again for the party," Laurel said.

"Are you having fun?"

"Yes." And then she hesitated and inhaled, just like Rachel. "Did you know?"

"No."

"Aren't you mad?"

"Actually, I'm thrilled. We need to tell my daughter Rachel."

"Will she hate me?" Laurel asked in a flat, low voice.

"She'll be overjoyed. She used to ask for a sister all the time."

Laurel smiled. Her dimples deepened.

The protein-bar wrappers, the keys. Lena was fairly certain what had been happening in the woods over the past month and Laurel was not going through that gate.

"You'll be like peas in a pod. You know what?" Lena held out her hand, made her voice as firm as possible. "Let's go and call her right now."

Annie's pupils were dilated as she looked rapidly between the note and Jen. When she spoke, her voice was strangled. "How old is he? She's only *fourteen*."

"Twenty-five," Jen said.

"Where is he?" she said. "Right now. Where? Find him."

Jen looked around the party. "There, by the edge of the lawn."

With her caftan billowing behind her, Annie marched across the lawn.

"Last song," the DJ shouted. "Get your dance on, people."

Jen stood still and watched Annie disappear through the open gate and into the woods. Afterward, she thought of the many other things she might have done, but she supposed she wasn't the type of person who took action when Abe wasn't involved.

CHAPTER SIXTY-FIVE

Annie was going to kill him.

She hurried along the forest trail, barely aware of the uneven rocks beneath her flip-flops. All she could feel was this nuclear rage, capable of stripping the entire damn forest down to pebbles and sticks.

But when she saw him in the moonlight, sitting cross-legged on Waterfall Rock, the power drained away. She was aware of the thin fabric of her dress, the flimsy rubber soles of her shoes.

Colin jumped to his feet. "Mrs. Perley," he said.

He'd always been in the background.

Even earlier today, when she'd leaned into his car window, Annie had never bothered to observe him. That gentle, little boy's face, wide plane of pale cheek. He was deceptively kind-looking.

"Are you enjoying the party?" Colin tried again.

"Hardly," Annie said. It came out weak. She cleared her throat. "You were expecting my daughter."

"No," he said. He balled up his hands in the sleeves of his seersucker jacket, hiked up his shoulders. "I just needed fresh air. Sometimes parties get too much."

"She's fourteen."

He started smoothing his hair behind his ears quickly. "I really don't know what you heard, Mrs. Perley."

"Abe wrote a letter about you."

"Abe Pagano?" Colin said. "You know that he's a pathological liar, right?"

A leap of hope in her throat. Annie should have considered that.

"Maybe Laurel has a crush, but nothing has happened between us. Like we discussed, I'm an educator, Mrs. Perley. I respect boundaries."

The darkness cast shadows over Colin's face, but his voice was soft and earnest and she wanted so badly to believe him.

In her mind, facts shifted like images in a kaleidoscope: Jen's face, Abe's boxy scrawl. Their betrayal of Laurel.

She'd felt shut out all year, had been desperate to connect with anyone, and Annie knew how *that* could be exploited.

"Seriously, Mrs. Perley. You've got it completely wrong." It was the light way Colin said it, like he was close to laughter.

The truth clamped on to Annie like shackles. "How long," she whispered. "How long were you—"

For what felt like a minute, he didn't speak. Finally, he shrugged and looked around as if in acknowledgment that no one else could hear.

"Long enough." There was the hint of a drawl in his voice.

The rage returned in a lightning bolt. It ripped through Annie's skin and shocked her bones, propelled her forward, arms extended in attack. He captured her right wrist with a rough grab and pulled her toward him.

His elbow hooked around her neck and his forearm pressed against her windpipe. They were alone out here, Annie realized. No one would even know where to look for her.

His breath dampened her ear. "I can't let you tell."

She couldn't breathe. He was squeezing too tight. A gush of liquid cascaded down her nostril; she felt her body being jerked backward across the rock. Desperately, she scratched at the slippery fabric of his jacket.

I can't breathe.

He loosened the headlock to allow Annie a desperate raggedy gasp of air before he spoke, matter-of-fact.

"It needs to look like an accident," he said. "You're going to have to fall."

CHAPTER SIXTY-SIX

Lena scanned the lawn for the flames of still-burning tea lights.

There was mud on the dance floor, trash around the lawn. A raccoon feasted on a kabob by the porta-potties, completely undeterred by Lena's presence.

There was a giant hole in the yard that might make Rudy the landscaper cry, and Lena could not even begin to mourn the hyacinths.

As Alma would say, it was all the mark of a good party.

Lena had turned to go inside when she saw it in her peripheral vision—a ruffling of movement over by the woods.

Annie Perley hurried across the muddy lawn, passed the raccoon without seeing him. Lena had to reach out her arms to physically stop her.

"Annie?" Lena said. "Mike thought you went home. He must be worried."

There was something wrong with Annie. Her mouth hung slack. Her right nostril was caked with blood. The caftan's shoulder seam had been torn open.

"Annie?"

"We need to call the police," she said. "I killed him."

CHAPTER SIXTY-SEVEN

After hearing Annie's story, Lena felt a tempest within her. "Are you sure he's dead?"

"I stared at him for a while," Annie said. "He was face down in the water. Aren't you going to call the police?"

Lena understood the need to stop and think first, to coax Annie inside to her usual spot on the sofa, dab a wet washcloth to her face, fold a chenille throw over her lap and boil the water for a mug of tea, text Mike that, as it turned out, Annie had been here all along, helping clean, and might be a little while still.

"What do I tell the police?" Annie wondered aloud. "Do you think they'll arrest me right away?"

"It sounds like self-defense," Lena said. "But if they're involved, Annie, the news of it will be everywhere, and out of your control, regardless of whether you're around to protect Laurel from it."

Annie considered that. Her fingers stroked the throw tucked around her lap.

"I'm sure no one was on the trails," Lena said, "but did anyone see you leave the party?"

"Maybe Jen?"

"She wouldn't say anything," Lena said.

"How do you know? I was awful to her."

"Just a feeling."

Annie made a sound between a gasp and a laugh. "Oh my god, how will I explain it to Laurel?"

"You won't," Lena said. "What is there to explain?"

Neither one of them verbalized the thought that passed between them: *Who would ever know?*

It was all so clean, Lena marveled. Annie didn't even know to be grateful for how clean it was.

Lena moved right next to Annie on the sofa, faced her, took Annie's hands—slightly thawed—in her own.

"It can be surprisingly easy," Lena lied, "if you let it."

FIFTEEN YEARS EARLIER, 1:45 A.M.

Lena palmed her keys, opened the door.

Tim's car had been parked at an awkward angle in the darkened garage. The windshield was cracked and torn in two spots. Its edges peeled up like it was made of a flimsy plastic. Rachel sat upright in the driver's seat.

Lena ran through the shards of glass that covered the garage floor, flung open the car's front door, and touched Rachel's arm, which was cold and clammy. "What happened?"

Lena moved Rachel's heavy limbs, tried to assess damage. The splotches of blood on the skirt of Rachel's dress seemed to be from a wound on her palm. The cut didn't appear deep.

"What happened?" Lena pressed both of her hands against Rachel's cheeks, forced eye contact.

Rachel's lids squeezed shut. Lena pinched her bare upper arm, and they flew back open.

"I don't know." Rachel sounded genuinely perplexed. Her breath was sour and hot. "I feel really sick."

"But the windshield . . . " Lena's voice screeched out of her. "What hit it?"

"Don't know."

"Tell me where you went, Rachel. At least tell me that."

. . . .

Lena's headlights were the only illumination on Canyon Road. Her grip on the wheel was tight and dry and she drove slowly, scanned the blue grama grass on the roadside.

She got out of the car after she felt the bump underneath her car, bent down to look at a blue sneaker planted upright in the middle of the road.

The wind died down, diminished to a gentle rustle that waved through the tall grass as if beckoning Lena closer.

He'd landed mostly on his back, the leg with the shoeless foot stretched toward the road, the other tucked under him at an awful angle.

His face was unblemished but for a golf-ball-sized crater collapsed in the middle of his forehead. The hair on the side of his head was soaked with blood and matted with tiny seed heads. There was a spread of darkness under him. Lena couldn't tell where he ended and the earth began.

She kneeled, pressed two fingers lightly against his exposed wrist, and averted her eyes from his, which were open and vacant. His skin was soft and a bit warm, but she felt no pulse other than a beat deep within her.

You could hide him, Lena.

Quickly, hide the body so no one finds out.

But her legs were running to the Nessels' house and she was knocking and ringing the bell.

When Harriet came stumbling to the door in her nightshirt, Lena's voice was an unfamiliar shriek. *You need to call 911.*

"What happened," Harriet demanded.

It wasn't a decision. It wasn't thought-out. It was something essential that clicked together within Lena.

It was Tim. The lie felt true as it spilled out of her mouth. *It was Tim.*

She waited for questions, a challenge, but Harriet nodded gravely, wrapped her arms around her chest.

. . .

At home, she had to assume that there wasn't much time.

Lena moved the car's seat and mirrors back to Tim's setting. She wiped its interior with hand towels, which she threw in the washing machine along with dirty napkins from the party.

She coaxed Rachel upstairs, stepped her out of the rest of the bloody dress and forced her into the shower. She bandaged the cut on her hand, used pillows to prop her in her bed.

She threw the dress on the logs with the gauze and the blood and the wrappers, lit the outdoor fireplace, watched the fire jump as it consumed it all.

There were so many mistakes, too many.

But when the police knocked, they didn't focus on them.

Lena led them to Tim's study, let her shock unspool as she told them how she had woken up, seen his car, and raced down the hill. Seen that poor boy, that poor boy, that poor innocent child—

The tall officer had tears in his eyes. He jerked his gaze away from Lena's; she saw the clench of his jaw.

Lena's last memory of her husband was him propped between the officers' shoulders, messily objecting to being escorted out of the house, his eyes justifiably confused.

On her way upstairs to check on Rachel, Lena caught her reflection in the dark window.

What had she just done, with barely a thought, by the strength of something deep and ancient?

There were a million things that could go wrong, but Lena decided to stay focused on the details, not the big picture, no thoughts about the boy—oh god, the boy—or his parents, his *parents,* how she'd been on her way to Gary's—

Stay focused.

When she received the early-morning call about Tim's death, Lena's first reaction was that this removed an entire set of complications.

Rachel presented a problem: she was hysterical, insistent on confessing. The girl could hardly sit still long enough for Lena to make her understand that coming clean would be an empty gesture.

It would be a pointless sacrifice, Lena scolded, completely self-indulgent. What made sense was to piece together the evening, determine who might know something, and then consider their options.

Bryce had invited Rachel to the party, Rachel said, and after Lena shut the door to her room, Rachel had slipped to the dark garage, driven herself down the hill in Tim's car. It dawned on Rachel too late that she didn't belong there.

It was older kids and they ignored her. She'd hung on the side, watched them play beer pong, gathered the courage to play two rounds, said goodbye to no one, walked to her car alone.

No one saw me, Rachel insisted. No one ever sees me.

Thank your lucky stars if that's true, Lena snapped.

After months of nervous silence, Lena began to finally understand that those four hours were hers alone.

But in Lena's mind, the two names will forever be fused: Bryce Neary and Rachel Meeker.

How many times will she be overcome at the thought of their young lives intersecting: passing each other at a playground, on the riverbank searching for clams, the invisible line connecting them: *she will kill you, she will kill you, she will kill you.*

And I will cover it up.

August 5

The body of a Juniper County man was found in a creek by hikers at 3 P.M. on Sunday, August 8th.

According to County Coroner Gomez, David Ratzen, 25, a.k.a. Colin Williams, was discovered in a creek below the Lynx Hollow hiking trail. Mr. Ratzen had been reported missing on June 11th, after he failed to pick up a paycheck from the Kingdom School, where he was an employee. He was also a first-year graduate student in the master's program at The Seminary of the Foothills, focusing on religious musical studies and education.

He was last seen on June 1, when he was a guest at a party in Cottonwood Estates, the subdivision that abuts Lynx Hollow trail. His car was later found on a deserted side road at the southeastern border of the neighborhood.

Since his disappearance, Ratzen has been the subject of an ongoing police investigation. The sheriff had been in communication with at least two Texas district attorneys in regards to outstanding warrants for Ratzen on charges of indecency with a child by contact and exposure, stemming from Ratzen's employment at Music Beats Academy and Harker County Middle School's theater department. "It's a complex situation, to say the least," a spokesperson said. "This guy was clearly on the run."

Ratzen was declared dead at 3:30 P.M. on Sunday. His body was sent to the medical examiner for an autopsy to determine the exact cause of death. No foul play is suspected.

"I think it's a sad but necessary reminder," the spokesperson said. "We tend to get casual with nature, to think of the trails as our backyards, but precaution—proper footwear, knowledge of the weather— can be the difference between life and death."

Jen Chun-Pagano knocked on my door today. She was selling raffle tickets for the Kingdom School. Before I could invite her in for tea, she launched right into her sales spiel—they were hiring a consultant and writing a charter school petition and putting together a board of trustees. From now on, everything would be by the book.

I bought twenty dollars' worth of tickets, and Jen handed me the receipt with a big smile that faded when I asked how she and Abe were doing, in light of the article in last week's paper.

I'll never forgive myself, she told me, for bringing him into our neighborhood. I was totally fooled.

Don't be silly, I said. No one blames you.

Jen's eyes flashed with gratefulness, and I suppose I took that as an invitation to further connect on the issue.

Have you seen Annie? I gestured across the street toward their house, which was as quiet as it had been all summer. I'm a little worried.

I saw her walking with Lena once or twice, Jen said, but I was rushing somewhere and didn't stop to chat.

I leaned closer to her, wondered if she could sense the way my heartbeat had accelerated. "I think they were together at the party, Annie and Colin. I saw them—"

"Harriet," Jen said. "Stop."

I stopped.

Her face went through a range of emotions, and I saw, even in the afternoon shadows, that her eyes were pink and puffy.

"I'm sorry to be abrupt," she said. "And I understand the desire to speculate, but you must have imagined seeing them together." Her voice was ragged. "Everyone needs to move on."

I looked behind Jen, to our neighborhood, bathed in sunshine. Just uphill on Red Fox Lane, a group of children took turns jumping a skateboard over a ramp they'd set up.

I hadn't seen many kids out since the accident, and their laughter, the hiss and scrape of wheels on pavement, seemed a harbinger. People were starting to feel safe again.

I chose to see the value of Jen's point.

Everyone needed to move on.

AUGUST

To: "The Best Book Club in the World"
From: proudmamabooklover3@hmail.com

To my dearest book club sisters:

It is with heavy heart that I resign my post as book club president. In the best interests of the group, I wanted to excuse myself ASAP so a new, more suitable leadership can take over. If I haven't yet apologized to you individually, I will.

Acting as your president has been one of my life's great honors. I know the book club will continue to thrive. I will miss it more than you can imagine.

Your Former President,
Janine

P.S. If I can make one last recommendation, it would be that, in light of recent events, we should switch the Tolstoy for something upbeat and positive. I have humbly attached a list of more suitable titles.

SEPTEMBER
To: "The Best Book Club in the World"
From: proudmamabooklover3@hmail.com

Hello ladies! What a deluge of love I've received! The letters, the visits, the baked goods (thank you, Lena!!!! Yum! Yum!)!

What choice do I have but to heed your passionate demands and return as president? So: there will be no changing of the guard. In fact, my first order of business will be to AMEND the BYLAWS to allow for LIFETIME APPOINTMENTS! MONARCHY, ANYONE????

(Kidding, kidding, hahahahahahaha ☺☺☺)

The book: THE LITTLE MAGIC BOOKSTORE by Wendy Nolan

I personally found this charming escapist tale about the power of stories to be JUST what the doctor ordered. (And it's not like Anna Karenina is going anywhere but SPOILER ALERT: the ending would be a little too much right now.)

The place: Harriet Nessel's house, 8854 Dakota Way.
The time: 7:00 p.m.
To bring: Anything, nothing. Let's get through this one, ladies.
Onward and upward!!!

Your Devoted Book Club ~~President~~ EMPRESS,
Janine

CHAPTER SIXTY-EIGHT

The women were already circled around Harriet Nessel's living room when Jen creaked open the screen door like it was a portal to one year before.

The nonregulars crowding the room, Janine's frantic welcome speech, Harriet's impatient glance down to her yellow legal pad, the empty space next to Annie Perley on the couch where Jen squeezed in.

Annie spoke first. *How's Abe?*

Good. How're Laurel and Hank? Jen made a point to keep her voice smooth and easy.

Fine, Annie said, her voice a pitch too high. *Everyone's good.*

Jen was relieved. Book club was not the time or place to lay it all bare. The ritual of this—the superficial hum of conversation—was making her feel safer than she had in a while.

Maybe Annie felt the same, although her smile looked pasted on. Lena sat on the other side of Annie, and although she was leaned into a conversation with Priya, Jen could sense her listening to them, ready to swoop in if Jen said the wrong thing.

Lena *had* to know what Annie had done, right?

Did Mike?

Because Jen hadn't told Paul—a burr between them, admittedly—but telling him would mean giving it oxygen, examining everything that had happened in a more thorough way.

Jen had allowed it all to happen; she'd *made* it happen.

Colin had seen her desperation. He'd used the weakest, worst parts of her—her Abe-blindness, her fatigue—as a way in. All year he'd been her yes man, agreeing with her complaints and soothing her worry.

Or maybe that part hadn't been a lie; Jen didn't know anymore. She could not tell fact from fiction.

Why didn't you say something sooner, she'd asked Abe. Didn't you know it was wrong?

Colin said I misunderstood, Abe said, *and he threatened to take away points if I said anything. But I didn't misunderstand, did I?*

Colin had never even gone to the doctor's appointment that Deb had set up for him, and there had probably been no ulcer either.

All of those nervous tics, the bleeding vulnerability?

He didn't deserve the absolution, but wasn't it likely that someone had once hurt Colin, too?

When Jen thought about how for a few hours she'd sided with Colin, doubted her own son, she became shaky with anger, understood in a flash what trespass against your child could incite.

It wasn't the worst thing, Jen had concluded, to have Colin disappear. Maxine Das could reason that nature required it.

As the introductions traveled around Harriet's living room (*"most fun thing you did this summer"?*—lordy, Janine), Jen swore she could feel, in the space between her shoulder and Annie's, an electric charge able to sear through all of the ways they fooled themselves, the rules and layers and clubs and community traditions, their good intentions to raise good people and make the world a better place.

Once, two years later, when they were both slightly tipsy and waiting for Priya to drive them home after a particularly giddy book club, Jen came close to saying something to Annie, but by then, the space between them had become less charged and she allowed the moment to pass.

If she had asked, though, this is what she would have learned:

Even two years after that night, Annie was uncertain how, exactly, she survived it.

He must have slipped on the rock. It was the only thing that could explain how he loosened his grip for just long enough to allow Annie to scramble away. There was a scuffle, and for a split second, Annie had been stronger or at least better positioned.

She had pushed him right then. Hard.

He was there, and then gone. It seemed almost supernatural until she heard it, over the rush of water.

"Please."

She felt herself walk to the edge. Just below her, Colin was suspended on the rocks. He grasped an exposed root on the cliffside and was trying to hoist himself back up.

"Mrs. Perley. Please." He reached out a hand for a brief second. "Please?"

The effort and shock had caught up to her, and Annie's body had begun to shake in jerky tremors. She managed her limbs into a crouch, gauged the distance between them. Five feet, maybe six.

He looked up at her with pleading eyes.

Had she found a branch, had she slipped off her caftan to use as a tether, she believed she might have reached him.

But she didn't. She didn't extend a hand or search for a branch. She didn't do anything except wait for him to lose his grip, watch him fall down into the rocks below.

She had the clarity of mind to think that he had been right, it would probably look like an accident.

Two years later, she might have even admitted to Jen that she'd felt satisfied watching Colin fall, that she hadn't felt one ounce of regret as it happened.

So maybe it's for the best Jen didn't ask.

When Paul's company is sold a few years later, he retires with the security of vested stock options, and Jen, who has two books under her belt, gets the opportunity to resume teaching again on the West Coast.

Abe, done with the Kingdom School, moves with them.

It's ten years after Laurel Perley's graduation party that Jen will scroll idly through social media and see Laurel, grown and gorgeous, again a graduate, this time with a blue mortarboard cap on her head.

Jen has followed the other kids, too—knows that one of Priya's sons plays major-league baseball and her daughter manages the family car dealerships, that Katie Neff, who does something political in Washington, D.C., writes strident lengthy posts about how the government wants to take all of our liberties that Janine always forwards with a "PLEASE SHARE ☺!"

In the graduation photo up on Jen's screen, Laurel's arms reach to loop around Hank (so tall now, pink bow tie, crisp white shirt) and Annie (hair gone white, two heads shorter than her children). To Annie's left is Mike, beaming, crow's feet deepened, and then Lena Meeker, her long caramel hair and smooth skin suspiciously unaged. (She's definitely had work done, she must have, but it's subtle and natural enough that Jen can't pinpoint exactly what.)

Next to Lena is a woman who Jen assumes is Lena's prodigal daughter Rachel, with thick curly hair cut short, gray at the temples, dimples similar to Laurel's.

Peering closer, Jen thinks that *they* look more like siblings than Laurel and Hank do, or maybe it's just how closely their faces are positioned together and their matching dimples and smiles.

Family! boasts the caption.

Jen, who is not in a book club now that she's teaching, thinks that she ought to join one; a part of her misses the camaraderie. She comments on the photo, something generically supportive and enthusiastic and forgettable.

She can't help but wonder about the real story behind the picture—is Laurel okay? Does she have daily ups and downs like

Abe, who is about to start work as a programmer (fingers crossed it sticks), but with no plans or desire to ever date or leave home (a relief, Jen feels, as well as something to mourn).

Abe isn't as volatile now—at least, Jen doesn't think so—but he's still Abe, and the three of them remain their own little island. She tries not to think about what happens when they die, because the worry leaves her breathless, and because that's the rub of being a parent: there are some things you just can't control.

Which doesn't mean you don't try.

Is Laurel's off-track college graduation (two years late by Jen's calculation) traceable to the way Jen ushered Colin into her life like a Trojan horse? Or has he managed to fade into the background?

When Paul asks *what are you gawking at,* Jen will show him the photo and he'll shrug. Who's that?

Really, Paul?

From Cottonwood? Remember Laurel's awful party where we thought Abe might be the vandal and that terrible video game he made? The night that Colin . . .

Sweet Jesus, Paul will say. I blocked that out.

Jen will fervently wish that she were capable of doing the same.

She'd be so much more productive without all of this noise in her head, but she feels less alone when she imagines Annie tuned to the same frequency.

We'd do anything for our children, you and I, Jen imagines saying. She likes to think that Annie would tilt her white head in agreement.

Not that it's anything to brag about.

Back to the fever of that September:

On the couch before the book club discussion started, Jen felt desperate to diffuse the electricity between herself and Annie. She gently nudged Annie's shoulder and pointed to Harriet Nessel, pitched slightly forward in her big striped chair, watching them intensely.

Annie's face relaxed for a minute.

"Are we in trouble, Harriet?" she said, a teasing smile in her voice.

Harriet frowned. With a click of her pen against the legal pad, she leaned back against her chair.

"Enough chitchat," she said. "It's time to discuss the book."

ACKNOWLEDGMENTS

I have felt my agent Allison Hunter's belief in this book, and me, at every step of the journey (which is truly saying something, as we took the scenic route). In addition to being smart as a whip, Allison is loyal, patient, supportive, and such excellent company that it is possible to meet her for a lunch that morphs into dinner with no idea of how the time has flown. Thank you, AH, for everything.

My extremely heartfelt thanks to my editor, Christine Kopprasch, who is as fiercely talented as she is kind. I am so very grateful to have been taken under your wing.

Flatiron Books is filled with first-rate professionals at the top of their games. Thank you to Maxine Charles, Samantha Zukergood, Jordan Forney, Nikkia Rivera, Katy Robitzski, Allyson Ryan, Donna Sinisgalli Noetzel, Bob Miller, Megan Lynch, Marlena Bittner, Gillian Redfearn, Lisa Amoroso, Morgan Mitchell, Keith Hayes, and everyone else there who contributed their expertise to *The Neighbor's Secret*. Also, thank you to the incomparable Amy Einhorn.

I'm indebted to the following people for their efforts in championing the book: Kristina Moore at Anonymous Content, and Tanya Farrell and Kelly Cronin at Wunderkind. Thank you also to Natalie Edwards and the rest of the Janklow & Nesbit team, and Clare Mao for your early and insightful notes. An eternal thank-you to the lovely Kerry Donovan.

Thank you also to some of my favorite authors: Chandler Baker, Kimberly Belle, Michele Campbell, and Laura Hankin. Their willingness to read and blurb *The Neighbor's Secret* was no small favor, as they are all busy crafting amazing novels of their own.

Maggie Shapiro's donation to the wonderful Horizons program, which provides opportunities to the underserved students of Denver, earned her the right to lend her name to a character. Thank you, Maggie, for your generosity, and for letting me use your good name.

Thank you to Samantha Heller, who is always my first reader and usually my last, too, for the crash course in blood inheritance and for all your advice—both already given and not yet asked for. Thanks to Raj Bhattacharyya, Kannon Bhattacharyya, and Dashiell Bhattacharyya for valuable input on everything from fancy wines to character names to the layout of a middle-school party to "Starry Starry Night." Thank you to Sue Ann Heller, for your unflagging enthusiasm.

Glen, Zoe, and Georgia, you are everything to me. There is no sufficient thank-you for all of your love and support.

L. Alison Heller is the author of *The Neighbor's Secret*, *The Never Never Sisters*, and *The Love Wars*. She lives in Colorado with her family and two dogs.